TILLIE:
A MENNONITE MAID

*"The girl's fair face looking out from a halo of
tender little brown curls"*

TILLIE:
A MENNONITE MAID

A Story of the Pennsylvania Dutch

HELEN R. MARTIN

WITH ILLUSTRATIONS
BY FLORENCE SCOVEL SHINN

BARNES & NOBLE

NEW YORK

Originally published in 1904

This 2009 edition published by Barnes & Noble, Inc.

Barnes & Noble, Inc.
122 Fifth Avenue
New York, NY 10011

ISBN: 978-1-4351-2052-5

Printed and bound in the United States of America

1 3 5 7 9 10 8 6 4 2

Contents

LIST OF ILLUSTRATIONS

TILLIE:
A MENNONITE MAID

CHAPTER ONE

"OH, I LOVE HER! I LOVE HER!"

TILLIE'S SLENDER LITTLE BODY THRILLED WITH A peculiar ecstasy as she stepped upon the platform and felt her close proximity to the teacher—so close that she could catch the sweet, wonderful fragrance of her clothes and see the heave and fall of her bosom. Once Tillie's head had rested against that motherly bosom. She had fainted in school one morning after a day and evening of hard, hard work in her father's celery beds, followed by a chastisement for being caught with a "storybook"; and she had come out of her faint to find herself in the heaven of sitting on Miss Margaret's lap, her head against her breast and Miss Margaret's soft hand smoothing her cheek and hair. And it was in that blissful moment that Tillie had discovered, for the first time in her young existence, that life could be worthwhile. Not within her memory had anyone ever caressed her before, or spoken to her tenderly, and in that fascinating tone of anxious concern.

Afterward, Tillie often tried to faint again in school; but, such is Nature's perversity, she never could succeed.

School had just been called after the noon recess, and Miss Margaret was standing before her desk with a watchful eye on the troops of children crowding in from the playground to their seats, when the little girl stepped to her side on the platform.

This country schoolhouse was a dingy little building in the heart of Lancaster County, the home of the Pennsylvania Dutch. Miss Margaret had been the teacher only a few months, and having come from Kentucky and not being "a Millersville Normal," she differed quite radically from any teacher they had ever had in New Canaan. Indeed, she was so wholly different from anyone Tillie had ever seen in her life, that to the child's adoring heart she was nothing less than a miracle. Surely no one but Cinderella had ever been so beautiful! And how different, too, were her clothes from those of the other young ladies of New Canaan, and, oh, so much prettier—though not nearly so fancy; and she didn't "speak her words" as other people of Tillie's acquaintance spoke. To Tillie it was celestial music to hear Miss Margaret say, for instance, "buttah" when she meant but-ter-r-r, and "windo" for windah. "It gives her such a nice sound when she talks," thought Tillie.

Sometimes Miss Margaret's ignorance of the dialect of the neighborhood led to complications, as in her conversation just now with Tillie.

"Well?" she inquired, lifting the little girl's chin with her forefinger as Tillie stood at her side and thereby causing that small worshiper to blush with radiant pleasure. "What is it, honey?"

Miss Margaret always made Tillie feel that she *liked* her. Tillie wondered how Miss Margaret could like *her!* What was there to like? No one had ever liked her before.

"It wonders me!" Tillie often whispered to herself with throbbing heart.

"Please, Miss Margaret," said the child, "pop says to ast you will you give me the darst to go home till half-past three this after?"

"If you go home till half-past three, you need not come back, honey—it wouldn't be worthwhile, when school closes at four."

"But I don't mean," said Tillie, in puzzled surprise, "that I want to go home and come back. I sayed whether I have the darst to go home till half-past three. Pop he's went to Lancaster, and he'll be back till half-past three a'ready, and he says then I got to be home to help him in the celery beds."

Miss Margaret held her pretty head on one side, considering, as she looked down into the little girl's upturned face. "Is this a conundrum, Tillie? How can your father be in Lancaster now and yet be home until half-past three? It's uncanny. Unless," she added, a ray of light coming to her—"unless 'till' means *by*. Your father will be home *by* half-past three and wants you then?"

"Yes, ma'am. I can't talk just so right," said Tillie apologetically, "like what you can. Yes, sometimes I say my we's like my w's, yet!"

Miss Margaret laughed. "Bless your little heart!" she said, running her fingers through Tillie's hair. "But you would rather stay in school until four, wouldn't you, than go home to help your father in the celery beds?"

"Oh, yes, ma'am," said Tillie wistfully, "but pop he has to get them beds through till Saturday market a'ready, and so we got to get 'em done behind Thursday or Friday yet."

"If I say you can't go home?"

Tillie colored all over her sensitive little face as, instead of answering, she nervously worked her toe into a crack in the platform.

"But your father can't blame *you*, honey, if I won't let you go home."

"He wouldn't stop to ast me was it my fault, Miss Margaret. If I wasn't there on time, he'd just—"

"All right, dear, you may go at half-past three, then," Miss Margaret gently said, patting the child's shoulder. "As soon as you have written your composition."

"Yes, ma'am, Miss Margaret."

It was hard for Tillie, as she sat at her desk that afternoon, to fix her wandering attention upon the writing of her composition, so fascinating was it just to revel idly in the sense of the touch of that loved hand that had stroked her hair, and the tone of that caressing voice that had called her "honey."

Miss Margaret always said to the composition classes, "Just try to write simply of what you see or feel, and then you will be sure to write a good 'composition.'" Tillie was moved this afternoon to pour out on paper all that she "felt" about her divinity. But she had some misgivings as to the fitness of this.

She dwelt upon the thought of it, however, dreamily gazing out of the window near which she sat, into the blue sky of the October afternoon—until presently her ear was caught by the sound of Miss Margaret's voice speaking to Absalom Puntz, who stood at the foot of the composition class, now before her on the platform.

"You may read your composition, Absalom."

Absalom was one of "the big boys," but though he was sixteen years old and large for his age, his slowness in learning classed him with the children of twelve or thirteen. However, as learning was considered in New Canaan a superfluous and wholly unnecessary adjunct to the means of living, Absalom's want of agility in imbibing erudition never troubled him, nor did it in the least call forth the pity or contempt of his schoolmates.

Three times during the morning session he had raised his hand to announce stolidly to his long-suffering teacher, "I can't think of no subjeck"; and at last Miss Margaret had relaxed her Spartan resolution to make him do his own thinking and had helped him out.

"Write of something that is interesting you just at present. Isn't there some one thing you care more about than other things?" she had asked.

Absalom had stared at her blankly without replying.

"Now, Absalom," she had said desperately, "I think I know one thing you have been interested in lately— write me a composition on Girls."

Of course the school had greeted the advice with a laugh, and Miss Margaret had smiled with them, though she had not meant to be facetious.

Absalom, however, had taken her suggestion seriously.

"Is your composition written, Absalom?" she was asking as Tillie turned from the window, her contemplation of her own composition arrested by the sound of the voice which to her was the sweetest music in the world.

"No'm," sullenly answered Absalom. "I didn't get it through till it was time a'ready."

"But, Absalom, you've been at it this whole blessed day! You've not done another thing!"

"I wrote off some of it."

"Well," sighed Miss Margaret, "let us hear what you have done."

Absalom unfolded a sheet of paper and laboriously read:

GIRLS

The only thing I took particular notice to, about Girls, is that they are always picking lint off each other, still.

He stopped and slowly folded his paper.

"But go on," said Miss Margaret. "Read it all."

"That's all the fu'ther I got."

Miss Margaret looked at him for an instant, then suddenly lifted the lid of her desk, evidently to search for something. When she closed it her face was quite grave.

"We'll have the reading-lesson now," she announced.

Tillie tried to withdraw her attention from the teacher and fix it on her own work, but the gay, glad tone in which Lizzie Harnish was reading the lines,

> When thoughts
> Of the last bitter hour come like a blight
> Over thy spirit—

hopelessly checked the flow of her ideas.

This class was large, and by the time Absalom's turn to read was reached, "Thanatopsis" had been finished, and so the first stanza of "The Bells" fell to him. It had transpired in the reading of "Thanatopsis" that a grave and solemn tone best suited that poem, and the value of this intelligence was made manifest when, in a voice of preternatural solemnity, he read:

> What a world of merriment their melody foretells!

Instantly, when he had finished his "stanza," Lizzie raised her hand to offer a criticism. "Absalom, he didn't put in no gestures."

Miss Margaret's predecessor had painstakingly trained his reading-classes in the Art of Gesticulation in Public Speaking, and Miss Margaret found the results of his labors so entertaining that she had never been able to bring herself to suppress the monstrosity.

"I don't like them gestures," sulkily retorted Absalom.

*"'The only thing I took particular notice to, about
Girls, is that they are always picking lint
off each other, still'"*

"Never mind the gestures," Miss Margaret consoled him—which indifference on her part seemed high treason to the well-trained class.

"I'll hear you read, now, the list of synonyms you found in these two poems," she added. "Lizzie may read first."

While the class rapidly leafed their readers to find their lists of synonyms, Miss Margaret looked up and spoke to Tillie, reminding her gently that that composition would not be written by half-past three if she did not hasten her work.

Tillie blushed with embarrassment at being caught in an idleness that had to be reproved, and resolutely bent all her powers to her task.

She looked about the room for a subject. The walls were adorned with the print portraits of "great men"—former State superintendents of public instruction in Pennsylvania—and with highly colored chromo portraits of Washington, Lincoln, Grant, and Garfield. Then there were a number of framed mottos: *"Education rules in America," "Rely on yourself," "God is our hope," "Dare to say No," "Knowledge is power," "Education is the chief defense of nations."*

But none of these things made Tillie's genius to burn, and again her eyes wandered to the window and gazed out into the blue sky; and after a few moments she suddenly turned to her desk and rapidly wrote down her "subject"—"Evening."

The mountain of the opening sentence being crossed, the rest went smoothly enough, for Tillie wrote it from her heart.

EVENING

I love to take my little sisters and brothers and go out, still, on a hilltop when the sun is setting so red in the West, and the birds are singing around us, and the cows are coming home to be milked, and the men are returning from their day's work.

I would love to play in the evening if I had the dare, when the children are gay and everything around me is happy.

I love to see the flowers closing their buds when the shades of evening are come. The thought has come to me, still, that I hope the closing of my life may come as quiet and peaceful as the closing of the flowers in the evening.

Matilda Maria Getz

Miss Margaret was just calling for Absalom's synonyms when Tillie carried her composition to the desk, and Absalom was replying with his customary half-defiant sullenness.

"My pop he sayed I ain't got need to waste my time gettin' learnt them cinnamons. Pop he says what's the use learnin' *two* words where [which] means the self-same thing—one's enough."

Absalom's father was a school director and Absalom had grown accustomed, under the rule of Miss Margaret's predecessors, to feel the force of the fact in their care not to offend him.

"But your father is not the teacher here—I am," she cheerfully told him. "So you may stay after school and do what I require."

Tillie felt a pang of uneasiness as she went back to her seat. Absalom's father was very influential and, as all the township knew, very spiteful. He could send Miss Margaret away, and he would do it, if she offended his only child, Absalom. Tillie thought she could not bear it at all if Miss Margaret were sent away. Poor Miss Margaret did not seem to realize her own danger. Tillie felt tempted to warn her. It was only this morning that the teacher had laughed at Absalom when he said that the Declaration of Independence was "a treaty between the United States and England"—and had asked him, "Which country, do you think, hurrahed the loudest, Absalom, when that treaty was signed?" And now this afternoon she "as much as said Absalom's father should mind to his own business!" It was growing serious. There had never been before a teacher at William Penn schoolhouse who had not judiciously "showed partiality" to Absalom.

"And he used to be dummer yet [stupider even] than what he is now," thought Tillie, remembering vividly a school entertainment that had been given during her own first year at school, when Absalom, nine years old, had spoken his first piece. His pious Methodist grandmother had endeavored to teach him a little hymn to speak on the great occasion, while his frivolous aunt from the city of Lancaster had tried at the same time to teach him "Bobby Shafto." New Canaan audiences were neither discriminating nor critical, but the assembly before which little Absalom had risen to "speak his piece off," had found themselves confused when he told them that

On Jordan's bank the Baptist stands,
Silver buckles on his knee.

Tillie would never forget her own infantine agony of suspense as she sat, a tiny girl of five, in the audience, listening to Absalom's mistakes. But Eli Darmstetter, the teacher, had not scolded him.

Then there was the time that Absalom had forced a fight at recess and had made little Adam Oberholzer's nose bleed—it was little Adam (whose father was not at that time a school director) that had to stay after school; and though everyone knew it wasn't fair, it had been accepted without criticism, because even the young rising generation of New Canaan understood the impossibility and folly of quarreling with one's means of earning money.

But Miss Margaret appeared to be perfectly blind to the perils of her position. Tillie was deeply troubled about it.

At half-past three, when, at a nod from Miss Margaret the little girl left her desk to go home, a wonderful thing happened—Miss Margaret gave her a storybook.

"You are so fond of reading, Tillie, I brought you this. You may take it home, and when you have read it, bring it back to me, and I'll give you something else to read."

Delighted as Tillie was to have the book for its own sake, it was yet greater happiness to handle something belonging to Miss Margaret and to realize that Miss Margaret had thought so much about her as to bring it to her.

"It's a novel, Tillie. Have you ever read a novel?"

"No'm. Only li-bries."

"What?"

"Sunday school li-bries. Us we're Evangelicals, and us children we go to the Sunday school, and I still bring home li-bry books. Pop he don't uphold to novel-readin'. I have never saw a novel yet."

"Well, this book won't injure you, Tillie. You must tell me all about it when you have read it. You will find it so interesting, I'm afraid you won't be able to study your lessons while you are reading it."

Outside the schoolroom, Tillie looked at the title— *Ivanhoe*—and turned over the pages in an ecstasy of anticipation.

"Oh! I love her! I love her!" throbbed her little hungry heart.

CHAPTER TWO

"I'M GOING TO LEARN YOU ONCE!"

TILLIE WAS OBLIGED, WHEN ABOUT A HALF-MILE FROM her father's farm, to hide her precious book. This she did by pinning her petticoat into a bag and concealing the book in it. It was in this way that she always carried home her "li-bries" from Sunday school, for all storybook reading was prohibited by her father. It was uncomfortable walking along the high road with the book knocking against her legs at every step, but that was not so painful as her father's punishment would be did he discover her bringing home a "novel!" She was not permitted to bring home even a schoolbook, and she had greatly astonished Miss Margaret, one day at the beginning of the term, by asking, "Please, will you leave me let my books in school? Pop says I darsen't bring 'em home."

"What you can't learn in school, you can do without," Tillie's father had said. "When you're home you'll work fur your wittles."

Tillie's father was a frugal, honest, hardworking, and very prosperous Pennsylvania Dutch farmer, who thought he religiously performed his parental duty in bringing up his many children in the fear of his heavy hand, in unceasing labor, and in almost total abstinence from all amusement and self-indulgence. Far from thinking himself cruel, he was convinced that the oftener and the more vigorously he applied "the strap," the more conscientious a parent was he.

His wife, Tillie's stepmother, was as submissive to his authority as were her five children and Tillie. Apathetic, anemic, overworked, she yet never dreamed of considering herself or her children abused, accepting her lot as the natural one of woman, who was created to be a child-bearer, and to keep man well fed and comfortable. The only variation from the deadly monotony of her mechanical and unceasing labor was found in her habit of irritability with her stepchild. She considered Tillie "a dopple" (a stupid, awkward person); for though usually a wonderful little household worker, Tillie, when very much tired out, was apt to drop dishes; and absentmindedly she would put her sunbonnet instead of the bread into the oven, or pour molasses instead of batter on the griddle. Such misdemeanors were always plaintively reported by Mrs. Getz to Tillie's father, who, without fail, conscientiously applied what he considered the undoubted cure.

In practising the strenuous economy prescribed by her husband, Mrs. Getz had to manœuver very skilfully to keep her children decently clothed, and Tillie in this matter was a great help to her; for the little girl possessed a precocious skill in combining a pile of patches

into a passably decent dress or coat for one of her little
brothers or sisters. Nevertheless, it was invariably Tillie
who was slighted in the small expenditures that were
made each year for the family clothing. The child had
always really preferred that the others should have "new
things" rather than herself—until Miss Margaret came;
and now, before Miss Margaret's daintiness, she felt
ashamed of her own shabby appearance and longed
unspeakably for fresh, pretty clothes. Tillie knew perfectly well that her father had plenty of money to buy
them for her if he would. But she never thought of
asking him or her stepmother for anything more than
what they saw fit to give her.

The Getz family was a perfectly familiar type among
the German farming class of southeastern Pennsylvania. Jacob Getz, though spoken of in the neighborhood
as being "wonderful near," which means very penurious,
and considered by the more gentle-minded Amish and
Mennonites of the township to be "overly strict" with his
family and "too ready with the strap still," was nevertheless highly respected as one who worked hard and was
prosperous, lived economically, honestly, and in the
fear of the Lord, and was "laying by."

The Getz farm was typical of the better sort to be
found in that county. A neat walk, bordered by clamshells, led from a wooden gate to the porch of a rather
large, and severely plain frame house, facing the road.
Every shutter on the front and sides of the building was
tightly closed, and there was no sign of life about the
place. A stranger, ignorant of the Pennsylvania Dutch

custom of living in the kitchen and shutting off the "best rooms"—to be used in their mustiness and stiff unhomelikeness on Sunday only—would have thought the house temporarily empty. It was forbiddingly and uncompromisingly spick-and-span.

A grass plot, ornamented with a circular flowerbed, extended a short distance on either side of the house. But not too much land was put to such unproductive use; and the small lawn was closely bordered by a corn-field on the one side and on the other by an apple orchard. Beyond stretched the tobacco- and wheat-fields, and behind the house were the vegetable garden and the barnyard.

Arrived at home by half-past three, Tillie hid her *Ivanhoe* under the pillow of her bed when she went upstairs to change her faded calico school dress for the yet older garment she wore at her work.

If she had not been obliged to change her dress, she would have been puzzled to know how to hide her book, for she could not, without creating suspicion, have gone upstairs in the daytime. In New Canaan one never went upstairs during the day, except at the rare times when obliged to change one's clothes. Every-one washed at the pump and used the one family roller-towel hanging on the porch. Miss Margaret, ever since her arrival in the neighborhood, had been the subject of widespread remark and even suspicion, because she "washed upstairs" and even *sat* upstairs! In her bedroom! It was an unheard-of proceeding in New Canaan.

Tillie helped her father in the celery beds until dark; then, weary, but excited at the prospect of her book, she went in from the fields and upstairs to the little low-roofed bedchamber which she shared with her two half-sisters. They were already in bed and asleep, as was their mother in the room across the hall, for everyone went to bed at sundown in Canaan Township, and got up at sunrise.

Tillie was in bed in a few minutes, rejoicing in the feeling of the book under her pillow. Not yet dared she venture to light a candle and read it—not until she should hear her father's heavy snoring in the room across the hall.

The candles which she used for this surreptitious reading of Sunday school "li-bries" and any other chance literature which fell in her way, were procured with money paid to her by Miss Margaret for helping her to clean the schoolroom on Friday afternoons after school. Tillie would have been happy to help her for the mere joy of being with her, but Miss Margaret insisted upon paying her ten cents for each such service.

The little girl was obliged to resort to a deep-laid plot in order to do this work for the teacher. It had been her father's custom—ever since, at the age of five, she had begun to go to school—to "time" her in coming home at noon and afternoon, and whenever she was not there on the minute, to mete out to her a dose of his ever-present strap.

"I ain't havin' no playin' on the way home, still! When school is done, you come right away home then, to help me or your mom, or I'll learn you once!"

But it happened that Miss Margaret, in her reign at William Penn schoolhouse, had introduced the innovation of closing school on Friday afternoons at half-past three instead of four, and Tillie, with bribes of candy bought with part of her weekly wage of ten cents, secured secrecy as to this innovation from her little sister and brother who went to school with her—making them play in the school-grounds until she was ready to go home with them.

Before Miss Margaret had come to New Canaan, Tillie had done her midnight reading by the light of the kerosene lamp which, after everyone was asleep, she would bring up from the kitchen to her bedside. But this was dangerous, as it often led to awkward inquiries as to the speedy consumption of the oil. Candles were safer. Tillie kept them and a box of matches hidden under the mattress.

It was eleven o'clock when at last the child, trembling with mingled delight and apprehension, rose from her bed, softly closed her bedroom door, and with extremely judicious carefulness lighted her candle, propped up her pillow, and settled down to read as long as she should be able to hold her eyes open. The little sister at her side and the one in the bed at the other side of the room slept too soundly to be disturbed by the faint flickering light of that one candle.

Tonight her stolen pleasure proved more than usually engrossing. At first the book was interesting principally because of the fact, so vividly present with her, that Miss Margaret's eyes and mind had moved over every word and thought which she was now absorbing. But soon her intense interest in the story excluded every other idea—even the fear of discovery. Her young spirit was "out of the body" and following, as in a trance, this tale, the like of which she had never before read.

The clock downstairs in the kitchen struck twelve—one—two, but Tillie never heard it. At half-past two o'clock in the morning, when the tallow candle was beginning to sputter to its end, she still was reading, her eyes bright as stars, her usually pale face flushed with excitement, her sensitive lips parted in breathless interest—when, suddenly, a stinging blow of "the strap" on her shoulders brought from her a cry of pain and fright.

"What you mean, doin' somepin like this yet!" sternly demanded her father. "What fur book's that there?"

He took the book from her hands and Tillie cowered beneath the covers, the wish flashing through her mind that the book could change into a Bible as he looked at it! Which miracle would surely temper the punishment that in a moment she knew would be meted out to her.

"*Iwanhoe*—a novel! A *novel!*" he said in genuine horror. "Tillie, where d'you get this here?"

Tillie knew that if she told lies she would go to hell, but she preferred to burn in torment forever rather than betray Miss Margaret; for her father, like Absalom's, was a school director, and if he knew Miss Margaret read novels and lent them to the children, he would surely force her out of William Penn.

"I lent it off of Elviny Dinkleberger!" she sobbed.

"You know I tole you a'ready you darsen't bring books home! And you know I don't uphold to novel-readin'! I'll have to learn you to mind better'n this! Where d'you get that there candle?"

"I—bought it, pop."

"Bought? Where d'you get the money?"

Tillie did not like the lies she had to tell, but she knew she had already perjured her soul beyond redemption and one lie more or less could not make matters worse.

"I found it in the road."

"How much did you find?"

"Fi' cents."

"You hadn't ought to spent it without astin' me dare you. Now I'm goin' to learn you once! Set up."

Tillie obeyed, and the strap fell across her shoulders. Her outcries awakened the household and started the youngest little sister, in her fright and sympathy with Tillie, to a high-pitched wailing. The rest of them took the incident phlegmatically, the only novelty about it being the strange hour of its happening.

But the hardest part of her punishment was to follow.

"Now this here book goes in the fire!" her father announced when at last his hand was stayed. "And any more that comes home goes after it in the stove. I'll see if you'll mind your pop or not!"

Left alone in her bed, her body quivering, her little soul hot with shame and hatred, the child stifled her sobs in her pillow, her whole heart one bleeding wound.

How could she ever tell Miss Margaret? Surely she would never like her anymore! Never again lay her hand on her hair, or praise her compositions, or call her "honey," or, even, perhaps, allow her to help her on Fridays! And what, then, would be the use of living? If only she could die and be dead like a cat or a bird and not go to hell, she would take the carving knife and kill herself! But there was hell to be taken into consideration. And yet, could hell hold anything worse than the loss of Miss Margaret's kindness? *How* could she tell her of that burned-up book and endure to see her look at her with cold disapproval? Oh, to make such return for her kindness, when she so longed with all her soul to show her how much she loved her!

For the first time in all her schooldays, Tillie went next morning with reluctance to school.

CHAPTER THREE

"What's Hurtin' You, Tillie?"

She meant to make her confession as soon as she reached the schoolhouse—and have it over—but Miss Margaret was busy writing on the blackboard, and Tillie felt an immense relief at the necessary postponement of her ordeal to recess time.

The hours of that morning were very long to her heavy heart, and the minutes dragged to the time of her doom—for nothing but blackness lay beyond the point of the acknowledgment which must turn her teacher's fondness to dislike.

She saw Miss Margaret's eyes upon her several times during the morning, with that look of anxious concern which had so often fed her starved affections. Yes, Miss Margaret evidently could see that she was in trouble and she was feeling sorry for her. But, alas, when she should learn the cause of her misery, how surely would that look turn to coldness and displeasure!

Tillie felt that she was ill preparing the way for her dread confession in the very bad recitations she made all morning. She failed in geography—every question that came to her; she failed to understand Miss Margaret's explanation of compound interest, though the explanation was gone over a third time for her especial benefit; she missed five words in spelling and two questions in United States history!

"Tillie, Tillie!" Miss Margaret solemnly shook her head, as she closed her book at the end of the last recitation before recess. "Too much *Ivanhoe*, I'm afraid! Well, it's my fault, isn't it?"

The little girl's blue eyes gazed up at her with a look of such anguish, that impulsively Miss Margaret drew her to her side, as the rest of the class moved away to their seats.

"What's the matter, dear?" she asked. "Aren't you well? You look pale and ill! What is it, Tillie?"

Tillie's overwrought heart could bear no more. Her head fell on Miss Margaret's shoulder as she broke into wildest crying. Her body quivered with her gasping sobs and her little hands clutched convulsively at Miss Margaret's gown.

"You poor little thing!" whispered Miss Margaret, her arms about the child; "*what's* the matter with you, honey? There, there, don't cry so—tell me what's the matter."

It was such bliss to be petted like this—to feel Miss Margaret's arms about her and hear that loved voice so close to her! For the last time! Never again after this moment would she be liked and caressed! Her heart was breaking and she could not answer for her sobbing.

"What's the matter, dear?' she asked"

"Tillie, dear, sit down here in my chair until I send the other children out to recess—and then you and I can have a talk by ourselves," Miss Margaret said, leading the child a step to her armchair on the platform. She stood beside the chair, holding Tillie's throbbing head to her side, while she tapped the bell which dismissed the children.

"Now," she said, when the door had closed on the last of them and she had seated herself and drawn Tillie to her again, "tell me what you are crying for, little girlie."

"Miss Margaret!" Tillie's words came in hysterical, choking gasps; "you won't never like me no more when I tell you what's happened, Miss Margaret!"

"Why, dear me, Tillie, what on earth is it?"

"I didn't mean to do it, Miss Margaret! And I'll redd up for you, Fridays, still, till it's paid for a'ready, Miss Margaret, if you'll leave me, won't you, please? Oh, won't you never like me no more?"

"My dear little goosie, what *is* the matter with you? Come," she said, taking the little girl's hand reassuringly in both her own, "tell me, child."

A certain note of firmness in her usually drawling Southern voice checked a little the child's hysterical emotion. She gulped the choking lump in her throat and answered.

"I was readin' *Ivanhoe* in bed last night, and pop woke up, and seen my candlelight, and he conceited he'd look once and see what it was, and then he seen me, and he don't uphold to novel-readin', and he—he—"

"Well?" Miss Margaret gently urged her faltering speech.

"He whipped me and—and burnt up your book!"

"Whipped you again!" Miss Margaret's soft voice indignantly exclaimed. "The br—" she checked herself and virtuously closed her lips. "I'm so sorry, Tillie, that I got you into such a scrape!"

Tillie thought Miss Margaret could not have heard her clearly.

"He—burnt up your book yet, Miss Margaret!" she found voice to whisper again.

"Indeed! I ought to make him pay for it!"

"He didn't know it was yourn, Miss Margaret—he don't uphold to novel-readin', and if he'd know it was yourn he'd have you put out of William Penn, so I tole him I lent it off of Elviny Dinkleberger—and I'll help you Fridays till it's paid for a'ready, if you'll leave me, Miss Margaret!"

She lifted pleading eyes to the teacher's face, to see therein a look of anger such as she had never before beheld in that gentle countenance—for Miss Margaret had caught sight of the marks of the strap on Tillie's bare neck, and she was flushed with indignation at the outrage. But Tillie, interpreting the anger to be against herself, turned as white as death, and a look of such hopeless woe came into her face that Miss Margaret suddenly realized the dread apprehension torturing the child.

"Come here to me, you poor little thing!" she tenderly exclaimed, drawing the little girl into her lap and folding her to her heart. "I don't care anything about the *book,* honey! Did you think I would? There, there—don't cry so, Tillie, don't cry. *I* love you, don't you know I do!" and Miss Margaret kissed the child's quivering lips, and with her own fragrant handkerchief wiped the tears from her cheeks, and with her soft, cool fingers smoothed back the hair from her hot forehead.

And this child, who had never known the touch of a mother's hand and lips, was transported in that moment from the suffering of the past night and morning, to a happiness that made this hour stand out to her, in all the years that followed, as the one supreme experience of her childhood.

Ineffable tenderness of the mother heart of woman!

That afternoon, when Tillie got home from school—ten minutes late according to the time allowed her by her father—she was quite unable to go out to help him in the field. Every step of the road home had been a dragging burden to her aching limbs, and the moment she reached the farmhouse, she tumbled in a little heap upon the kitchen settee and lay there, exhausted and white, her eyes shining with fever, her mouth parched with thirst, her head throbbing with pain—feeling utterly indifferent to the consequences of her tardiness and her failure to meet her father in the field.

"Ain't you feelin' good?" her stepmother phlegmatically inquired from across the room, where she sat with a dishpan in her lap, paring potatoes for supper.

"No, ma'am," weakly answered Tillie.

"Pop'll be looking fur you out in the field."

Tillie wearily closed her eyes and did not answer.

Mrs. Getz looked up from her pan and let her glance rest for an instant upon the child's white, pained face. "Are you feelin' too mean to go help pop?"

"Yes, ma'am. I—can't!" gasped Tillie, with a little sob.

"You ain't lookin' good," the woman reluctantly conceded. "Well, I'll leave you lay a while. Mebbe pop used the strap too hard last night. He sayed this dinner that he was some uneasy that he used the strap so hard—but he was that wonderful spited to think you'd set up readin' a novel-book in the nighttime yet! You might of knew you'd ketch an awful lickin' fur doin' such a dumm thing like what that was. Sammy!" she called to her little eight-year-old son, who was playing on the kitchen porch, "you go out and tell pop Tillie she's got sick fur me, and I'm leavin' her lay a while. Now hurry on, or he'll come in here to see, once, ain't she home yet, or what. Go on now!"

Sammy departed on his errand, and Mrs. Getz diligently resumed her potato-paring.

"I don't know what pop'll say to you not comin' out to help," she presently remarked.

Tillie's head moved restlessly, but she did not speak. She was past caring what her father might say or do.

Mrs. Getz thoughtfully considered a doubtful potato, and, concluding at length to discard it, "I guess," she said, throwing it back into the pan, "I'll let that one; it's some poor. Do you feel fur eatin' any supper?" she asked. "I'm havin' fried smashed potatoes and wieners [Frankfort sausages]. Some days I just don't know what to cook all."

Tillie's lips moved, but gave no sound.

"I guess you're right down sick fur all; ain't? I wonder if pop'll have Doc in. He won't want to spend any fur that. But you do look wonderful bad. It's awful onhandy comin' just today. I did feel fur sayin' to pop I'd go to the rewiwal tonight, of he didn't mind. It's a while back a'ready since I was to a meetin'—not even on a funeral. And they say they do now make awful funny up at Bethel rewiwal this week. I was thinkin' I'd go once. But if you can't redd up after supper and help milk and put the childern to bed, I can't go fur all."

No response from Tillie.

Mrs. Getz sighed her disappointment as she went on with her work. Presently she spoke again. "This after, a lady agent come along. She had such a complexion lotion. She talked near a half-hour. She was, now, a beautiful conversationist! I just set and listened. Then she was some spited that I wouldn't buy a box of complexion lotion off of her. But she certainly was, now, a beautiful conversationist!"

The advent of an agent in the neighborhood was always a noteworthy event, and Tillie's utterly indifferent reception of the news that today one had "been along" made Mrs. Getz look at her wonderingly.

"Are you too sick to take interest?" she asked.

The child made no answer. The woman rose to put her potatoes on the stove.

It was an hour later when, as Tillie still lay motionless on the settee, and Mrs. Getz was dishing up the supper and putting it on the table, which stood near the wall at one end of the kitchen, Mr. Getz came in, tired, dirty, and hungry, from the celery beds.

The child opened her eyes at the familiar and often dreaded step, and looked up at him as he came and stood over her.

"What's the matter? What's hurtin' you, Tillie?" he asked, an unwonted kindness in his voice as he saw how ill the little girl looked.

"I don'—know," Tillie whispered, her heavy eyelids falling again.

"You don' know! You can't be so worse if you don' know what's hurtin' you! Have you fever, or the head-ache, or whatever?"

He laid his rough hand on her forehead and passed it over her cheek.

"She's some feverish," he said, turning to his wife, who was busy at the stove. "Full much so!"

"She had the cold a little, and I guess she's took more to it," Mrs. Getz returned, bearing the fried pota-toes across the kitchen to the table.

"I heard the Doc talkin' there's smallpox handy to us, only a mile away at New Canaan," said Getz, a note of anxiety in his voice that made the sick child wearily marvel. Why was he anxious about her? She wondered. It wasn't because he liked her, as Miss Margaret did. He was afraid of catching smallpox himself, perhaps. Or he was afraid she would be unable to help him tomorrow, and maybe for many days, out in the celery beds. That was why he spoke anxiously—not because he liked her and was sorry.

No bitterness was mingled with Tillie's quite matter-of-fact acceptance of these conclusions.

"It would be a good much trouble to us if she was took down with the smallpox," Mrs. Getz's tired voice replied.

"I guess not as much as it would be to *her*," the father said, a rough tenderness in his voice, and something else which Tillie vaguely felt to be a note of pain.

"Are you havin' the Doc in fur her, then?" his wife asked.

"I guess I better, mebbe," the man hesitated. His thrifty mind shrank at the thought of the expense.

He turned again to Tillie and bent over her.

"Can't you tell pop what's hurtin' you, Tillie?"

"No—sir."

Mr. Getz looked doubtfully and rather helplessly at his wife. "It's a bad sign, ain't, when they can't tell what's hurtin' 'em?"

"I don't know what fur sign that is when they don't feel nothin'," she stoically answered, as she dished up her Frankfort sausages.

"If a person would just know oncet!" he exclaimed anxiously. "Anyhow, she's pretty much sick—she looks it so! I guess I better mebbe not take no risks. I'll send fur Doc over. Sammy can go, then."

"All right. Supper's ready now. You can come eat."

She went to the door to call the children in from the porch and the lawn; and Mr. Getz again bent over the child.

"Can you eat along, Tillie?"

Tillie weakly shook her head.

"Don't you feel fur your wittles?"

"No—sir."

"Well, well. I'll send fur the Doc, then, and he can mebbe give you some pills, or what, to make you feel some better; ain't?" he said, again passing his rough hand over her forehead and cheek, with a touch as nearly like a caress as anything Tillie had ever known from him. The tears welled up in her eyes and slowly rolled over her white face, as she felt this unwonted expression of affection.

Her father turned away quickly and went to the table, about which the children were gathering.

"Where's Sammy?" he asked his wife. "I'm sendin' him fur the Doc after supper."

"Where? I guess over," she motioned with her head as she lifted the youngest, a one-year-old boy, into his high chair. "Over" was the family designation for the pump, at which every child of a suitable age was required to wash his face and hands before coming to the table.

While waiting for the arrival of the doctor, after supper, Getz ineffectually tried to force Tillie to eat something. In his genuine anxiety about her and his eagerness for "the Doc's" arrival, he quite forgot about the fee which would have to be paid for the visit.

CHAPTER FOUR

"The Doc" Combines Business and Pleasure

Miss Margaret boarded at the *"hotel"* of New Canaan. As the only other regular boarder was the middle-aged, rugged, unkempt little man known as "the Doc," and as the transient guests were very few and far between, Miss Margaret shared the life of the hotel-keeper's family on an intimate and familiar footing.

The invincible custom of New Canaan of using a bedroom only at night made her unheard-of inclination to sit in her room during the day or before bedtime the subject of so much comment and wonder that, feeling it best to yield to the prejudice, she usually read, sewed, or wrote letters in the kitchen, or, when a fire was lighted, in the combination dining and sitting room.

It was the evening of the day of Tillie's confession about *Ivanhoe*, and Miss Margaret, after the early supper-hour of the country hotel, had gone to the sitting room, removed the chenille cover from the centre-table, uncorked the bottle of fluid sold at the village store as ink, but looking more like raspberry-ade, and settled herself to write, to one deeply interested in everything which interested her, an account of her day and its episode with the little daughter of Jacob Getz.

This room in which she sat, like all other rooms of the district, was too primly neat to be cozy or comfortable. It contained a bright new rag carpet, a luridly painted wooden settee, a sewing-machine, and several uninviting wooden chairs. Margaret often yearned to pull the pieces of furniture out from their stiff, sentinel-like stations against the wall and give to the room that divine touch of homeyness which it lacked. But she did not dare venture upon such a liberty.

Very quickly absorbed in her letter-writing, she did not notice the heavy footsteps which presently sounded across the floor and paused at her chair.

"Now that there writin'—" said a gruff voice at her shoulder; and, startled, she quickly turned in her chair, to find the other boarder, "the Doc," leaning on the back of it, his shaggy head almost on a level with her fair one.

"That there writin'," pursued the doctor, continuing to hold his fat head in unabashed proximity to her own and to her letter, "is wonderful easy to read. Wonderful easy."

Miss Margaret promptly covered her letter with a blotter, corked the raspberry-ade, and rose.

"Done a'ready?" asked the doctor.

"For the present, yes."

"See here oncet, Teacher!"

He suddenly fixed her with his small, keen eyes as he drew from the pocket of his shabby, dusty coat a long, legal-looking paper.

"I have here," he said impressively, "an important dokiment, Teacher, concerning of which I desire to consult you perfessionally."

"Yes?"

"You just stay settin'; I'll fetch a chair and set aside of you and show it to you oncet."

He drew a chair up to the table and Margaret reluctantly sat down, feeling annoyed and disappointed at this interruption of her letter, yet unwilling, in the goodness of her heart, to snub the little man.

The doctor bent near to her and spoke confidentially.

"You see, them swanged fools in the legislature has went to work and passed a act—ag'in' my protest, mind you—compellin' doctors to fill out blanks answerin' to a lot of darn-fool questions 'bout one thing and 'nother, like this here."

He had spread open on the table the paper he had drawn from his pocket. It was soiled from contact with his coat and his hands, and Margaret, instead of touching the sheet, pressed it down with the handle of her pen.

The doctor noticed the act and laughed. "You're wonderful easy kreistled [disgusted]; ain't? I took notice a'ready how when things is some dirty they kreistle you, still. But indeed, Teacher," he gravely added, "it ain't healthy to wash so much and keep so clean as what you do. It's weakenin'. That's why city folks ain't so hearty—they get right into them big, long tubs they have built in their houses upstairs! I seen one oncet in at Doc Hess' in Lancaster. I says to him when I seen it, 'You wouldn't get me into *that*—it's too much like a coffin!' I says. 'It would make a body creepy to get in there.' And he says, 'I'd feel creepy if I *didn't* get in.' 'Yes,' I says, 'that's why you're so thin. You wash yourself away,' I says."

"What's it all about?" Miss Margaret abruptly asked, examining the paper.

"These here's the questions," answered the doctor, tracing them with his thick, dirty forefinger; "and these here's the blank spaces fur to write the answers into. Now you can write better'n me, Teacher; and if you'll just take and write in the answers fur me, why, I'll do a favor fur you sometime if ever you ast it off of me. And if ever you need a doctor, just you call on me, and I'm swanged if I charge you a cent!"

Among the simple population of New Canaan the Doc was considered the most blasphemous man in America, but there seemed to be a sort of general impression in the village that his profanity was, in some way, an eccentricity of genius.

"Thank you," Miss Margaret responded to his offer of free medical services. "I'll fill out the paper for you with pleasure."

She read aloud the first question of the list. "'Where did you attend lectures?'"

Her pen suspended over the paper, she looked at him inquiringly. "Well?" she asked.

"Lekshures be blowed!" he exclaimed. "I ain't never 'tended no lekshures!"

"Oh!" said Miss Margaret, nodding conclusively. "Well, then, let us pass on to the next question. 'To what School of Medicine do you belong?'"

"School?" repeated the doctor; "I went to school right here in this here town—it's better'n thirty years ago, a'ready."

"No," Miss Margaret explained, "that's not the question. 'To what School of *Medicine* do you belong?' Medicine, you know," she repeated, as though talking to a deaf person.

"Oh," said the doctor, "medicine, is it? I never have went to none," he announced defiantly. "I studied medicine in old Doctor Johnson's office and learnt it by practisin' it. That there's the only way to learn any business. Do you suppose you could learn a boy carpenterin' by settin' him down to read books on sawin' boards and a-lekshurin' him on drivin' nails? No more can you make a doctor in no such swanged-fool way like that there!"

"But," said Margaret, "the question means do you practise allopathy, homeopathy, hydropathy, osteopathy—or, for instance, eclecticism? Are you, for example, a homeopathist?"

"Gosh!" said the doctor, looking at her admiringly, "I'm blamed if you don't know more big words than I ever seen in a spellin'-book or heard at a spellin'-bee!

Home-o-pathy? No, sir! When I give a dose to a patient, still, he 'most always generally finds it out, and pretty gosh-hang quick too! When he gits a dose of my herb bitters he knows it good enough. Be sure, I don't give babies, and so forth, doses like them. All such I treat, still, according to home-o-pathy, and not like that swanged fool, Doc Hess, which only last week he give a baby a dose fitten only fur a field-hand—and *he* went to college! Oh, yes! And heerd lekshures too! Natural consequence, the baby up't and died fur 'em. But growed folks they need allopathy."

"Then," said Margaret, "you might be called an eclectic?"

"A eclectic?" the doctor inquiringly repeated, rubbing his nose. "To be sure, I know in a general way what a eclectic *is,* and so forth. But what would *you* mean, anyhow, by a eclectic doctor, so to speak, heh?"

"An eclectic," Margaret explained, "is one who claims to adopt whatever is good and reject whatever is bad in every system or school of medicine."

"If that ain't a description of me yet!" exclaimed the doctor, delighted. "Write 'em down, Teacher! I'm a— now what d'you call 'em?"

"You certainly are a what-do-you-call-'em!" thought Margaret—but she gravely repeated, "An eclectic," and wrote the name in the blank space.

"And here I've been practisin' that there style of medicine fur fifteen years without oncet suspicioning it! That is," he quickly corrected himself, in some confusion, "I haven't, so to speak, called it pretty often a eclectic, you see, gosh hang it! And—*you* understand, don't you, Teacher?"

Margaret understood very well indeed, but she put the question by.

The rest of the blank was filled with less difficulty, and in a few minutes the paper was folded and returned to the doctor's pocket.

"I'm much obliged to you, Teacher," he said heartily. "And mind, now," he added, leaning far back in his chair, crossing his legs, thrusting his thumbs into his vest pockets, and letting his eyes rest upon her, "if ever you want a doctor, I ain't chargin' you nothin'; and leave me tell you somethin','" he said, emphasizing each word by a shake of his forefinger, "Jake Getz and Nathaniel Puntz they're the two school directors that 'most always makes trouble fur the teacher. And I pass you my word that if they get down on you any, and want to chase you off your job, I'm standin' by you—I pass you my word!"

"Thank you. But what would they get down on me for?"

"Well, if Jake Getz saw you standin' up for his childern against his lickin' 'em or makin' 'em work hard; or if you wanted to make 'em take time to learn their books at home when he wants 'em to work—or some such—he'd get awful down on you. And Nathaniel Puntz he's just the *contrary*—he wants hisn spoiled—he's got but the one."

Miss Margaret recalled with a little thrill the loyalty with which Tillie had tried to save her from her father's anger by telling him that Elviny Dinkleberger had lent her *Ivanhoe*. "I suppose I had a narrow escape there," she thought. "Poor little Tillie! She is so conscientious— I can fancy what that lie cost her!"

Gathering up her stationery, she made a movement to rise—but the doctor checked her with a question.

"Say! Not that I want to ast questions too close—but what was you writin', now, in that letter of yourn, about Jake Getz?"

Miss Margaret was scarcely prepared for the question. She stared at the man for an instant, then helplessly laughed at him.

"Well," he said apologetically, "I don't mean to be inquisitive that way—but sometimes I speak unpolite too—fur all I've saw high society a'ready!" he added, on the defensive. "Why, here one time I went in to Lancaster city to see Doc Hess, and he wouldn't have it no other way but I should stay and eat along. 'Och,' I says, 'I don't want to, I'm so common that way, and I know yous are tony and it don't do. I'll just pick a piece [have luncheon] at the tavern,' I says. But no, he says I was to come eat along. So then I did. And his missus she was wonderful fashionable, but she acted just that nice and common with me as my own mother or my wife yet. And that was the first time I have eat what the noospapers calls a course dinner. They was three courses. First they was soup and nothin' else settin' on the table, and then a colored young lady come in with such a silver pan and such a flat, wide knife, and she scraped the crumbs off between every one of them three courses. I felt awful funny. I tell you they was tony. I sayed to the missus, 'I hadn't ought to of came here. I'm not grand enough like yous'; but she sayed, 'It's nothing of the kind, and you're always welcome.' Yes, she made herself that nice and common!" concluded the doctor. "So you see I have saw high society."

"Yes," Miss Margaret assented.

"Say!" he suddenly put another question to her. "Why don't you get married?"

"Well," she parried, "why don't *you?*"

"I was married a'ready. My wife she died fur me. She was layin' three months. She got so sore layin'. It was when we was stoppin' over in Chicago yet. That's out in Illinois. Then, when she died—och," he said despondently, "there fur a while I didn't take no interest in nothin' no more. When your wife dies, you don't feel fur nothin'. Yes, yes," he sighed, "people have often troubles! Oh," he granted, "I went to see other women since. But," shaking his head in discouragement, "it didn't go. I think I'm better off if I stay single. Yes, I stay single yet. Well," he reconsidered the question, his head on one side as he examined the fair lady before him, "if I could get one to suit me oncet."

Miss Margaret grew alarmed. But the doctor complacently continued, "When my wife died fur me I moved fu'ther west, and I got out as fur as Utah yet. That's where they have more'n one wife. I thought, now, that there was a poor practice! One woman would do *me*. Say!" he again fixed her with his eye.

"What?"

"Do you like your job?"

"Well," she tentatively answered, "it's not uninteresting."

"Would you ruther keep your job than quit and get married?"

"That depends—"

"Or," quickly added the doctor, "you might jus' keep on teachin' the school after you was married, if you married someone livin' right here. Ain't? And if you kep' on the right side of the School Board. Unlest you'd ruther marry a town fellah and give up your job out here. Some thinks the women out here has to work too hard; but if they married a man where [who] was well fixed," he said, insinuatingly, "he could hire fur 'em [keep a servant]. Now, there's me. I'm well fixed. I got money plenty."

"You are very fortunate," said Miss Margaret, sympathetically.

"Yes, ain't? And I ain't got no one dependent on me, neither. No brothers, no sisters, no—wife—" he looked at her with an ingratiating smile. "Some says I'm better off that way, but sometimes I think different. Sometimes I think I'd like a wife oncet."

"Yes?" said Miss Margaret.

"Um—m," nodded the doctor. "Yes, and I'm pretty well fixed. I wasn't always so comfortable off. It went a long while till I got to doin' pretty good, and sometimes I got tired waitin' fur my luck to come. It made me ugly dispositioned, my bad luck did. That's how I got in the way of addicting to profane language. I

sayed, still, I wisht, now, the good Lord would try pros-
perity on me fur a while—fur adwersity certainly ain't
makin' me a child of Gawd, I sayed. But now," he
added, rubbing his knees with satisfaction, "I'm fixed
nice. Besides my doctor's fees, I got ten acres, and
three good hommies that'll be cows till a little while
yet. And that there organ in the front room is my
property. Bought it fifteen years ago on the instalment
plan. I leave missus keep it settin' in her parlor fur style
that way. Do you play the organ?"

"I *can*," was Miss Margaret's qualified answer.

"I always liked music—high-class music—like 'Pin-
nyfore.' That's a nopery I heard in Lancaster there one
time at the rooft-garden. That was high-toned music,
you bet. No trash about that. Gimme somepin nice and
ketchy. That's what I like. If it ain't ketchy, I don't take
to it. And so," he added admiringly, "you can play the
organ too!"

"That's one of my distinguished accomplishments,"
said Miss Margaret.

"Well, say!" The doctor leaned forward and took her
into his confidence. "I don't mind if my wife *is* smart, so
long as she don't bother *me* any!"

With this telling climax, the significance of which
Miss Margaret could hardly mistake, the doctor fell
back again in his chair, and regarded with complacency
the comely young woman before him.

But before she could collect her shocked wits to
reply, the entrance of Jake Getz's son, Sammy, interrupted them. He had come into the house at the

"'I don't mind if my wife is smart, so long as she don't bother me any!'"

kitchen door, and, having announced the object of his errand to the landlady, who, by the way, was his father's sister, he was followed into the sitting room by a procession, consisting of his aunt, her husband, and their two little daughters.

Sammy was able to satisfy but meagerly the eager curiosity or interest of the household as to Tillie's illness, and his aunt, cousins, and uncle presently returned to their work in the kitchen or out of doors, while the doctor rose reluctantly to go to the stables to hitch up.

"Pop says to say you should hurry," said Sammy.

"There's time plenty," petulantly answered the doctor. "I conceited I'd stay settin' with you this evening," he said regretfully to Miss Margaret. "But a doctor can't never make no plans to stay no-wheres! Well!" he sighed, "I'll go round back now and hitch a while."

"Sammy," said Miss Margaret, when she found herself alone with the child, "wasn't your mother afraid *you* would get ill, coming over here, on such a cool evening, barefooted?"

"Och, no; she leaves me let my shoes off near till it snows already. The teacher we had last year he used to do worse'n that yet! *He'd wash his feet in the wintertime!*" said Sammy, in the tone of one relating a deed of valor. "I heard Aunty Em speak how he washed 'em as much as oncet a week, still, *in winter!* The Doc he sayed no wonder that feller took cold!"

Miss Margaret gazed at the child with a feeling of fascination. "But, Sammy," she said wonderingly, "your front porches get a weekly bath in winter—do the people of New Canaan wash their porches oftener than they wash themselves?"

"Porches gets dirty," reasoned Sammy. "Folks don't get dirty in wintertime. Summer's the time they get dirty, and then they mebbe wash in the run."

"Oh!" said Miss Margaret.

During the six weeks of her life in Canaan, she had never once seen in this or any other household the least sign of any toilet appointments, except a tin basin at the pump, a roller-towel on the porch, and a small mirror in the kitchen. Toothbrushes, she had learned, were almost unknown in the neighborhood, nearly everyone of more than seventeen years wearing "store-teeth." It was a matter of much speculation to her that these people, who thought it so essential to keep their houses, especially their front porches, immaculately scrubbed, should never feel an equal necessity as to their own persons.

The doctor came to the door and told Sammy he was ready. "I wouldn't do it to go such a muddy night like what this is," he ruefully declared to Miss Margaret, "if I didn't feel it was serious; Jake Getz wouldn't spend any hirin' a doctor, without it was some serious. I'm sorry I got to go."

"Good night, Sammy," said Miss Margaret. "Give Tillie my love; and if she is not able to come to school tomorrow, I shall go to see her."

CHAPTER FIVE

"Novels Ain't Moral, Doc!"

Tillie still lay on the kitchen settee, her father sitting at her side, when the doctor and Sammy arrived. The other children had all been put to bed, and Mrs. Getz, seated at the kitchen table, was working on a pile of mending by the light of a small lamp.

The doctor's verdict, when he had examined his patient's tongue, felt her pulse, and taken her temperature, was not clear.

"She's got a high fever. That's all the fu'ther I can go now. What it may turn to till morning, I can't tell *till* morning. Give her these powders every hour, without she's sleeping. That's the most that she needs just now."

"Yes, if she can keep them powders down," said Mr. Getz, doubtfully. "She can't keep nothin' with her."

"Well, keep on giving them, anyhow. She's a pretty sick child."

"You ain't no fears of smallpox, are you?" Mrs. Getz inquired. "Mister was afraid it might mebbe be smallpox," she said, indicating her husband by the epithet.

"Not that you say that I sayed it was!" Mr. Getz warned the doctor. "We don't want no report put out! But is they any symptoms?"

"Och, no," the doctor reassured them. "It ain't smallpox. What did you give her that she couldn't keep with her?"

"I fed some boiled milk to her."

"Did she drink tea?" he inquired, looking profound.

"We don't drink no store tea," Mrs. Getz answered him. "We drink peppermint tea fur supper, still. Tillie she didn't drink none this evening. Some says store tea's bad fur the nerves. I ain't got no nerves," she went on placidly. "Leastways, I ain't never felt none, so fur. Mister he likes the peppermint."

"And it comes cheaper," said Mister.

"Mebbe you've been leavin' Tillie work too much in the hot sun out in the fields with you?" the doctor shot a keen glance at the father; for Jake Getz was known to all Canaan Township as a man that got more work out of his wife and children than any other farmer in the district.

"After school, some," Mr. Getz replied. "But not fur long at a time, fur it gets late a'ready till she gets home. Anyhow, it's healthy fur her workin' in the fields. I guess," he speculated, "it was her settin' up in bed readin' last night done it. I don't know right how long it went that she was readin' before I seen the light, but it was near morning a'ready, and she'd burned near a whole candle out."

"And mebbe you punished her?" the doctor inquired, holding his hand to Tillie's temples.

"Well," nodded Mr. Getz, "I guess she won't be doin' somepin like that soon again. I think, still, I mebbe used the strap too hard, her bein' a girl that way. But a body's got to learn 'em when they're young, you know. And here it was a *novel-book*! She borrowed the loan of it off of Elviny Dinkleberger! I chucked it in the fire! I don't uphold to novel-readin'!"

"Well, now," argued the doctor, settling back in his chair, crossing his legs, and thrusting his thumbs into the armholes of his vest, "some chance times I read in such a 'Home Companion' paper, and here this winter I read a piece in nine chapters. I make no doubt that was a novel. Leastways, I guess you'd call it a novel. And that piece," he said impressively, "wouldn't hurt nobody! It learns you. That piece," he insisted, "was got up by a moral person."

"Then I guess it wasn't no novel, Doc," Mr. Getz firmly maintained. "Anybody knows novels ain't moral. Anyhow, I ain't havin' none in my house. If I see any, they get burnt up."

"It's a pity you burnt it up, Jake. I like to come by somepin like that, still, to pass the time when there ain't much doin'. How did Elviny Dinkleberger come by such a novel?"

"I don't know. If I see her pop, I'll tell him he better put a stop to such behaviors."

Tillie stirred restlessly on her pillow.

"What was the subjeck of that there novel, Tillie?" the doctor asked.

"Its subjeck was *Iwanhoe*," Mr. Getz answered. "Yes, I chucked it right in the stove."

"*Iwanhoe!*" exclaimed the doctor. "Why, Elviny must of borrowed the loan of that off of Teacher—I seen Teacher have it."

Tillie turned pleading eyes upon his face, but he did not see her.

"Do you mean to say," demanded Mr. Getz, "that Teacher lends *novels* to the scholars!"

"Och!" said the doctor, suddenly catching the frantic appeal of Tillie's eyes, and answering it with ready invention, "what am I talkin' about! It was Elviny lent it to Aunty Em's little Rebecca at the *hotel*, and Teacher was tellin' Rebecca she mustn't read it, but give it back right aways to Elviny."

"Well!" said Mr. Getz, "a teacher that would lend novels to the scholars wouldn't stay long at William Penn if *my* wote could put her out! And there's them on the Board that thinks just like what I think!"

"To be sure!" the doctor soothed him. "*To* be sure! Yes," he romanced, "Rebecca she lent that book off of Elviny Dinkleberger, and Teacher she tole Rebecca to give it back."

"I'll speak somepin to Elviny's pop, first time I see him, how Elviny's lendin' a novel to the scholars!" affirmed Mr. Getz.

"You needn't trouble," said the doctor, coolly. "Elviny's pop he *give* Elviny that there book last Christmas. I don't know what he'll think, Jake, at your burnin' it up."

Tillie was gazing at the doctor, now, half in bewilderment, half in passionate gratitude.

"If Tillie did get smallpox," Mrs. Getz here broke in, "would she mebbe have to be took to the pest-house?"

Tillie started, and her feverish eyes sought in the face of the doctor to know what dreadful place a "pest-house" might be.

"Whether she'd have to be took to the pest-house?" the doctor inquiringly repeated. "Yes, if she took the smallpox. But she ain't takin' it. You needn't worry."

"Doctors don't know near as much now as what they used to, still," Mr. Getz affirmed. "They didn't *have* to have no such pest-houses when I was a boy. Leastways, they didn't have 'em. And they didn't never ketch such diseases like 'pendycitis and grip and them."

"Do you mean to say, Jake Getz, that you pass it as your opinion us doctors don't know more now than what they used to know thirty years ago, when you was a boy?"

"Of course they don't," was the dogmatic rejoinder. "Nor nobody knows as much now as they did in ancient times a'ready. I mean back in Bible times."

"Do you mean to say," hotly argued the doctor, "that they had automobiles in them days?"

"To be sure I do! Automobiles and all the other lost sciences!"

"Well," said the doctor, restraining his scorn with a mighty effort, "I'd like to see you prove it oncet!"

"I can prove it right out of the Bible! Do you want better proof than that, Doc? The Bible says in so many

words, 'There's nothing new under the sun.' There!
You can't come over that there, can you? You don't
consider into them things enough, Doc. You ain't a
religious man, that's the trouble!"

"I got religion a plenty, but I don't hold to no *sich*
dumm thoughts!"

"Did you get your religion at Bethel rewiwal?" Mrs.
Getz quickly asked, glancing up from the little stocking
she was darning, to look with some interest at the doctor. "I wanted to go over oncet before the rewiwal's
done. But now Tillie's sick, mebbe I won't get to go fur
all. When they have rewiwals at Bethel they always make
so! And," she added, resuming her darning, "I like to
see 'em jump that way. My, but they jump, now, when
they get happy! But I didn't get to go this year yet."

"Well, and don't you get affected too?" the doctor
asked, "and go out to the mourners' bench?"

"If I do? No, I go just to see 'em jump," she monoto-
nously repeated. "I wasn't never conwerted. Mister he's
a hard Evangelical, you know."

"And what does he think of your unconwerted state?"
the doctor jocularly inquired.

"What he thinks? There's nothing to think," was the
stolid answer.

"Up there to Bethel rewiwal," said Mr. Getz, "they
don't stay conwerted. Till rewiwal's over, they're off
church again."

"It made awful funny down there this two weeks
back," repeated Mrs. Getz. "They jumped so. Now
there's the Lutherans, they don't make nothin' when

they conwert themselves. They don't jump nor nothin'. I don't like their meetin's. It's onhandy Tillie got sick fur me just now. I did want to go oncet. Here's all this mendin' she could have did, too. She's handier at sewin' than what I am, still. I always had so much other work, I never come at sewin', and I'm some dopplig at it."

"Yes? Yes," said the doctor, rising to go. "Well, Tillie, good-by, and don't set up nights any more readin' novels," he laughed.

"She ain't likely to," said her father. "My childern don't generally do somepin like that again after I once ketch 'em at it. Ain't so, Tillie? Well, then, Doc, you think she ain't serious?"

"I said I can't tell till I've saw her again a'ready."

"How long will it go till you come again?"

"Well," the doctor considered, "it looks some fur fallin' weather—ain't? If it rains and the roads are muddy till morning, so's I can't drive fast, I won't mebbe be here till ten o'clock."

"Oh, doctor," whispered Tillie, in a tone of distress, "can't I go to school? Can't I? I'll be well enough, won't I? It's Friday tomorrow, and I—I want to go!" she sobbed. "I want to go to Miss Margaret!"

"No, you can't go to school tomorrow, Tillie," her father said, "even if you're some better; I'm keepin' you home to lay still one day anyhow."

"But I don't want to stay home!" the child exclaimed, casting off the shawl with which her father had covered her and throwing out her arms. "I want to go to school!

I want to, pop!" she sobbed, almost screaming. "I want to go to Miss Margaret! I will, I will!"

"Tillie—Tillie!" her father soothed her in that unwonted tone of gentleness that sounded so strange to her. His face had turned pale at her outcries, delirious they seemed to him, coming from his usually meek and submissive child. "There now," he said, drawing the cover over her again; "now lay still and be a good girl, ain't you will?"

"Will you leave me go to school tomorrow?" she pleaded piteously. "*Dare* I go to school tomorrow?"

"No, you dassent, Tillie. But if you're a good girl, mebbe I'll leave Sammy ast Teacher to come to see you after school."

"Oh, pop!" breathed the child ecstatically, as in supreme contentment she sank back again on her pillow. "I wonder will she come? Do you think she will come to see me, mebbe?"

"To be sure will she."

"Now think," said the doctor, "how much she sets store by Teacher! And a lot of 'em's the same way—girls *and* boys."

"I didn't know she was so much fur Teacher," said Mr. Getz. "She never spoke nothin'."

"She never spoke nothin' to me about it neither," said Mrs. Getz.

"Well, I'll give you all good-by, then," said the doctor; and he went away.

On his slow journey home through the mud he mused on the inevitable clash which he foresaw must

some day come between the warmhearted teacher
(whom little Tillie so loved, and who so injudiciously
lent her "novel-books") and the stern and influential
school director, Jacob Getz.

"There *my* chanct comes in," thought the doctor;
"there's where I mebbe put in my jaw and pop the
question—just when Jake Getz is makin' her trouble
and she's gettin' chased off her job. I passed my word
I'd stand by her, and, by gum, I'll do it! When she's out
of a job—that's the time she'll be dead easy! Ain't?
She's the most allurin' female I seen since my wife up't
and died fur me!"

CHAPTER SIX

JAKE GETZ IN A QUANDARY

TILLIE'S ILLNESS, THOUGH SEVERE WHILE IT LASTED, proved to be a matter of only a few days' confinement to bed; and fortunately for her, it was while she was still too weak and ill to be called to account for her misdeed that her father discovered her deception as to the owner of *Ivanhoe*. At least he found out, in talking with Elviny Dinkleberger and her father at the Lancaster market, that the girl was innocent of ever having owned or even seen the book, and that, consequently, she had of course never lent it either to Rebecca Wackernagel at the hotel or to Tillie.

Despite his rigorous dealings with his family (which, being the outcome of the Pennsylvania Dutch faith in the Divine right of the head of the house, were entirely conscientious), Jacob Getz was strongly and deeply attached to his wife and children; and his alarm at Tillie's illness, coming directly upon his severe punishment of her, had softened him sufficiently to temper

59

his wrath at finding that she had told him what was not true.

What her object could have been in shielding the real owner of the book he could not guess. His suspicions did not turn upon the teacher, because, in the first place, he would have seen no reason why Tillie should wish to shield her, and, in the second, it was inconceivable that a teacher at William Penn should set out so to pervert the young whom trusting parents placed under her care. There never had been a novel-reading teacher at William Penn. The Board would as soon have elected an opium-eater.

Where had Tillie obtained that book? And why had she put the blame on Elviny, who was her little friend? The Doc, evidently, was in league with Tillie! What could it mean? Jake Getz was not used to dealing with complications and mysteries. He pondered the case heavily.

When he went home from market, he did not tell Tillie of his discovery, for the doctor had ordered that she be kept quiet.

Not until a week later, when she was well enough to be out of bed, did he venture to tell her he had caught her telling a falsehood.

He could not know that the white face of terror which she turned to him was fear for Miss Margaret and not, for once, apprehension of the strap.

"I ain't whippin' you this time," he gruffly said, "if you tell me the truth whose that there book was."

Tillie did not speak. She was resting in the wooden rocking chair by the kitchen window, a pillow at her head and a shawl over her knees. Her stepmother was busy at the table with her Saturday baking; Sammy was giving the porch its Saturday cleaning, and the other children, too little to work, were playing outdoors; even the baby, bundled up in its cart, was out on the grass plot.

"Do you hear me, Tillie? Whose book was that there?"

Tillie's head hung low and her very lips were white. She did not answer.

"You're goin' to act stubborn to *me!*" her father incredulously exclaimed, and the woman at the table turned and stared in dull amazement at this unheard-of defiance of the head of the family. "Tillie!" he grasped her roughly by the arm and shook her. "Answer to me!"

Tillie's chest rose and fell tumultuously. But she kept her eyes downcast and her lips closed.

"Fur why don't you want to tell, then?"

"I—can't, pop!"

"Can't! If you wasn't sick I'd soon learn you if you can't! Now you might as well tell me right aways, fur I'll make you tell me *some* time!"

Tillie's lips quivered and the tears rolled slowly over her white cheeks.

"Fur why did you say it was Elviny?"

"She was the only person I thought to say."

"But fur why didn't you say the person it *was? *Answer to me!" he commanded.

Tillie curved her arm over her face and sobbed. She was still too weak from her fever to bear the strain of this unequal contest of wills.

"Well," concluded her father, his anger baffled and impotent before the child's weakness, "I won't bother you with it no more *now*. But you just wait till you're well oncet! We'll see then if you'll tell me what I ast you or no!"

"Here's the Doc," announced Mrs. Getz, as the sound of wheels was heard outside the gate.

"Well," her husband said indignantly as he rose and went to the door, "I just wonder what he's got to say fur hisself, lyin' to me like what he done!"

"Hello, Jake!" was the doctor's breezy greeting as he walked into the kitchen, followed by a brood of curious little Getzes, to whom the doctor's daily visits were an exciting episode. "Howdy-do, missus," he briskly addressed the mother of the brood, pushing his hat to the back of his head in lieu of raising it. "And how's the patient?" he inquired with a suddenly professional air and tone. "Some better, heh? *Heh?* Been cryin'! What fur?" he demanded, turning to Mr. Getz. "Say, Jake, you ain't been badgerin' this kid again fur somepin? She'll be havin' a *relapse* if you don't leave her be!"

"It's *you* I'm wantin' to badger, Doc Weaver!" retorted Mr. Getz. "What fur did you lie to me about that there piece entitled *Iwanhoe?*"

"You and your *Iwanhoe* be blowed! Are you tormentin' this here kid about *that* yet? A body'd think you'd want to change that subjec', Jake Getz!"

"Not till I find from you, Doc, whose that there novel-book was, and why you tole me it was Elviny Dinkleberger's!"

"That's easy tole," responded the doctor. "That there book belonged to—"

"No, Doc, no, no!" came a pleading cry from Tillie. "Don't tell, Doc, please don't tell!"

"Never you mind, Tillie, *that's* all right. Look here, Jake Getz!" The doctor turned his sharp little eyes upon the face of the father grown dark with anger at his child's undutiful interference. "You're got this here little girl worked up to the werge of a *relapse!* I tole you she must be kep' quiet and not worked up still!"

"All right. I'm leavin' *her* alone—till she's well oncet! You just answer fur *yourself* and tell why you lied to me!"

"Well, Jake, it was this here way. That there book belonged to *me* and Tillie lent it off of me. That's how! Ain't Tillie?"

Mr. Getz stared in stupefied wonder, while Mrs. Getz, too, looked on with a dull interest, as she leaned her back against the sink and dried her hands upon her apron.

As for Tillie, a great throb of relief thrilled through her as she heard the doctor utter this Napoleonic lie—only to be followed the next instant by an overwhelming sense of her own wickedness in thus conniving with fraud. Abysses of iniquity seemed to yawn at her feet, and she gazed with horror into their black depths. How could she ever again hold up her head.

But—Miss Margaret, at least, was safe from the School Board's wrath and indignation, and how unimportant, compared with that, was her own soul's salvation!

"Why didn't Tillie say it was yourn?" Mr. Getz presently found voice to ask.

"I tole her if she left it get put out I am addicted to novel readin'," said the doctor glibly, and with evident relish, "it might spoil my practice some. And Tillie she's that kind-hearted she was sorry fur me!"

"And so you put her up to say it was Elviny's! You put her up to tell lies to her pop!"

"Well, I never thought you'd foller it up any, Jake, and try to get *Elviny* into trouble."

"Doc, I always knowed you was a *blasphemer* and that you didn't have no religion. But I thought you had anyhow morals. And I didn't think, now, you was a coward that way, to get behind a child and lie out of your own evil deeds!"

"I'm that much a coward and a *blasphemer*, Jake, that I'm goin' to add the cost of that there book of mine where you burnt up, to your doctor's bill, unlest you pass me your promise you'll drop this here subjec' and not bother Tillie with it no more."

The doctor had driven his victim into a corner. To yield a point in family discipline or to pay the price of the property he had destroyed—one of the two he must do. It was a most untoward predicament for Jacob Getz.

"You had no right to lend that there book to Tillie, Doc, and I ain't payin' you a cent fur it!" he maintained.

"I jus' mean, Jake, I'll make out my bill easy or stiff accordin' to the way you pass your promise."

"If my word was no more better'n yours, Doc, my passin' my promise wouldn't help much!"

"That's all right, Jake. I don't set up to be religious and moral. I ain't sayed my prayers since I am old enough a'ready to know how likely I was, still, to kneel on a tack!"

"It's no wonder you was put off of church!" was the biting retort.

"Hold up there, Jake. I wasn't put off. I *went* off. I took myself off of church before the brethren had a chanct to *put* me off."

"Sammy!" Mr. Getz suddenly and sharply admonished his little son, who was sharpening his slate-pencil on the windowsill with a table-knife, "you stop right aways sharpenin' that pencil! You dassent sharpen your slate-pencils, do you hear? It wastes 'em so!"

Sammy hastily laid down the knife and thrust the pencil into his pocket.

Mr. Getz turned again to the doctor and inquired irritably, "What is it to *you* if I teach my own child to mind me or not, I'd like to know?"

"Because she's been bothered into a sickness with this here thing a'ready, and it's time it stopped now!"

"It was you started it, leavin' her lend the book off of you!"

"That's why I feel fur sparin' her some more trouble, seein' I was the instrument in the hands of Providence fur gettin' her into all this here mess. See?"

"I can't be sure when *to* know if you're lyin' or not," said Mr. Getz helplessly.

"Mebbe you can't, Jake. Sometimes I'm swanged if I'm sure, still, myself. But there's one thing you *kin* be cock-sure of—and that's a big doctor-bill unlest you do what I sayed."

"Now that I know who she lent the book off of there ain't nothin' to bother her about," sullenly granted Mr. Getz. "And as fur punishment—she's had punishment a-plenty, I guess, in her bein' so sick."

"All right," the doctor said magnanimously. "There's one thing I'll give you, Jake: you're a man of your word, if you *are* a Dutch hog!"

"A—*whatever?*" Mr. Getz angrily demanded.

"And I don't see," the doctor complacently continued, rising and pulling his hat down to his eyebrows, preparatory to leaving, "where Tillie gets her fibbin' from. Certainly not from her pop."

"I don't mind her ever tellin' me no lie before."

"Och, Jake, you drive your children to lie to you, the way you bring 'em up to be afraid of you. They *got* to lie, now and again, to a feller like you! Well, well," he soothingly added as he saw the black look in the father's face at the airing of such views in the presence of his children, "never mind, Jake, it's all in the day's work!"

He turned for a parting glance at Tillie. "She's better. She'll be well till a day or two, now, and back to school—*if* she's kep' quiet, and her mind ain't bothered any. Now, *good-*by to yous."

CHAPTER SEVEN

"The Last Days of Pump-eye"

FOR A LONG TIME AFTER HER UNHAPPY EXPERIENCES with *Ivanhoe* Tillie did not again venture to transgress against her father's prohibition of novels. But her fear of the family strap, although great, did not equal the keenness of her mental hunger, and was not sufficient, therefore, to put a permanent check upon her secret midnight reading, though it did lead her to take every precaution against detection. Miss Margaret continued to lend her hooks and magazines from time to time, and in spite of the child's reluctance to risk involving the teacher in trouble with the School Board through her father, she accepted them. And so during all this winter, through her love for books and her passionate devotion to her teacher, the little girl reveled in feasts of fancy and emotion and this term at school was the first season of real happiness her young life had ever known.

Once on her return from school the weight of a heavy volume had proved too great a strain on her worn and thin undergarment during the long walk home; the skirt had torn away from the hand, and as she entered the kitchen, her stepmother discovered the book.

Tillie pleaded with her not to tell her father, and perhaps she might have succeeded in gaining a promise of secrecy had it not happened that just at the critical moment her father walked into the kitchen. Of course, then the book was handed over to him, and Tillie with it.

"Did you lend this off the Doc again?" her father sternly demanded, the fated book in one hand and Tillie's shoulder grasped in the other.

Tillie hated to utter the lie. She hoped she had modified her wickedness a bit by answering with a nod of her head.

"What's he mean, throwin' away so much money on books?" Mr. Getz took time in his anger to wonder. He read the title, "*Last Days of Pump-eye.* Well!" he exclaimed, "this here's the last *hour* of this here 'Pump-eye!' In the stove she goes! I don't owe the Doc no doctor's bill *now,* and I'd like to see him make me pay him fur these here novels he leaves you lend off of him!"

"Please, please, pop!" Tillie gasped, "don't burn it. Give it back to—him! I won't read it—I won't bring home no more books of—hisn! Only, please, pop, don't burn it—please!"

For answer, he drew her with him as he strode to the fireplace. "I'm burnin' every book you bring home, do you hear?" he exclaimed; but before he could make good his words, the kitchen door was suddenly opened, and Sammy's head was poked in, with the announcement, "The Doc's buggy's comin' up the road!" The door banged shut again, but instantly Tillie wrenched her shoulder free from her father's hand, flew out of doors and dashed across the "yard" to the front gate. Her father's voice followed her, calling to her from the porch to "come right aways back here!" Unheeding, she frantically waved to the doctor in his approaching buggy. Sammy, with a bevy of small brothers and sisters, to whom, no less than to their parents, the passing of a "team" was an event not to be missed, were all crowded close to the fence.

"Someone sick again?" inquired the doctor as he drew up at Tillie's side.

"No, Doc—but," Tillie could hardly get her breath to speak, "pop's goin' to burn up *Last Days of Pompeii*; it's Miss Margaret's, and he thinks it's yourn; come in and take it, Doc—*please*—and give it back to Miss Margaret, won't you?"

"Sure!" The doctor was out of his buggy at her side in an instant.

"Oh!" breathed Tillie, "here's pop comin' with the book!"

"See me fix him!'" chuckled the doctor. "He's so dumm he'll b'lee' most anything. If I have much more dealin's with your pop, Tillie, I'll be ketchin' on to how them novels is got up myself. And then mebbe I'll *let* doctorin', and go to novel-writin'!"

The doctor laughed with relish of his own joke, as Mr. Getz, grim with anger, stalked up to the buggy.

"Look-ahere!" His voice was menacing as he held out the open book for Tillie's inspection, and the child turned cold as she read on the fly-leaf,

"Margaret Lind.
"From A. C. L.   Christmas, 18—"

"You sayed the Doc give it to you! Did you lend that other 'n' off of Teacher too? Answer to me! I'll have her chased off of William Penn! I'll bring it up at next Board meetin'!"

"Hold your whiskers, Jake, or they'll blow off! You're talkin' through your hat! Don't be so dumm! Teacher she gev me that there book because she passed me her opinion she don't stand by novel-readin'. She was goin' to throw out that there book and I says I'd take it if she didn't want it. So then I left Tillie borrow the loan of it."

"So that's how you come by it, is it?" Mr. Getz eyed the doctor with suspicion. "How did you come by that there *Iwanhoe?*"

"That there I bought at the second-hand bookstore in there at Lancaster one time. I ain't just so much fur books, but now and again I like to buy one too, when I see 'em cheap."

"Well, here!" Mr. Getz tossed the book into the buggy. "Take your old 'Pump-eye.' And clear out. If I can't make you stop tryin' to spoil my child fur me, I can anyways learn *her* what she'll get oncet, if she don't mind!"

Again his hand grasped Tillie's shoulder as he turned her about to take her into the house.

"You better watch out, Jake Getz, or you'll have another doctor's bill to pay!" the doctor warningly called after him. "That girl of yourn ain't strong enough to stand your rough handlin', and you'll find it out someday—to your *regret*! You'd better go round back and let off your feelin's choppin' wood fur missus, 'stead of hittin' that little girl, you big dopple!"

Mr. Getz stalked on without deigning to reply, thrusting Tillie ahead of him. The doctor jumped into his buggy and drove off.

His warning, however, was not wholly lost upon the father. Tillie's recent illness had awakened remorse for the severe punishment he had given her on the eve of it; and it had also touched his purse; and so, though she did not escape punishment for this second and, therefore, aggravated offense, it was meted out in stinted measure. And indeed, in her relief and thankfulness at again saving Miss Margaret, the child scarcely felt the few light blows which, in order that parental authority be maintained, her father forced himself to inflict upon her.

In spite of these mishaps, however, Tillie continued to devour all the books she could lay hold of and to run perilous risks for the sake of the delight she found in them.

Miss Margaret stood to her for an image of every heroine of whom she read in prose or verse, and for the realization of all the romantic daydreams in which, as an escape from the joyless and sordid life of her home, she was learning to live and move and have her being.

Therefore it came to her as a heavy blow indeed when, just after the Christmas holidays, her father announced to her on the first morning of the reopening of school, "You best make good use of your time from now on, Tillie, fur next spring I'm takin' you out of school."

Tillie's face turned white, and her heart thumped in her breast so that she could not speak.

"You're comin' twelve year old," her father continued, "and you're enough educated, now, to do you. Me and mom needs you at home."

It never occurred to Tillie to question or discuss a decision of her father's. When he spoke it was a finality and one might as well rebel at the falling of the snow or rain. Tillie's woe was utterly hopeless.

Her dreary, drooping aspect in the next few days was noticed by Miss Margaret.

"Pop's takin' me out of school next spring," she heart-brokenly said when questioned. "And when I can't see you every day, Miss Margaret, I won't feel for nothin' no more. And I thought to get more educated than what I am yet. I thought to go to school till I was anyways fourteen."

So keenly did Miss Margaret feel the outrage and wrong of Tillie's arrested education, when her father could well afford to keep her in school until she was grown, if he would; so stirred was her warm Southern blood at the thought of the fate to which poor Tillie seemed doomed—the fate of a household drudge with not a moment's leisure from sunrise to night for a thought above the grubbing existence of a domestic beast of burden (thus it all looked to this woman from Kentucky), that she determined, cost what it might, to go herself to appeal to Mr. Getz.

"He will have me 'chased off of William Penn,'" she ruefully told herself. "And the loss just now of my munificent salary of thirty-five dollars a month would be inconvenient. 'The Doc' said he would 'stand by' me. But that might be more inconvenient still!" she thought, with a little shudder. "I suppose this is an impolitic step for me to take. But policy 'be blowed,' as the doctor would say! What are we in this world for but to help one another? I *must* try to help little Tillie— bless her!"

So the following Monday afternoon after school, found Miss Margaret, in a not very complacent or confident frame of mind, walking with Tillie and her younger brother and sister out over the snow-covered road to the Getz farm to face the redoubtable head of the family.

CHAPTER EIGHT

MISS MARGARET'S ERRAND

IT WAS HALF-PAST FOUR O'CLOCK WHEN THEY REACHED the farmhouse, and they found the weary, dreary mother of the family cleaning fish at the kitchen sink, one baby pulling at her skirts, another sprawling on the floor at her feet.

Miss Margaret inquired whether she might see Mr. Getz.

"If you kin? Yes, I guess," Mrs. Getz dully responded. "Sammy, you go to the barn and tell pop Teacher's here and wants to speak somepin to him. Mister's out back," she explained to Miss Margaret, "choppin' wood."

Sammy departed, and Miss Margaret sat down in the chair which Tillie brought to her. Mrs. Getz went on with her work at the sink, while Tillie set to work at once on a crock of potatoes waiting to be pared.

"You are getting supper very early, aren't you?' Miss Margaret asked, with a friendly attempt to make conversation.

"No, we're some late. And I don't get it ready yet, I just start it. We're getting strangers fur supper."

"Are you?"

"Yes. Some of Mister's folks from East Bethel."

"And are they strangers to you?"

Mrs. Getz paused in her scraping of the fish to consider the question.

"If they're strangers to us? Och, no. We knowed them this long time a'ready. Us we're well acquainted. But to be sure they don't live with us, so we say strangers is comin'. You don't talk like us; ain't?"

"N—not exactly."

"I do think now (you must excuse me sayin' so) but you do talk awful funny," Mrs. Getz smiled feebly.

"I suppose I do," Miss Margaret sympathetically replied.

Mr. Getz now came into the room, and Miss Margaret rose to greet him.

"I'm much obliged to meet you," he said awkwardly as he shook hands with her.

He glanced at the clock on the mantel, then turned to speak to Tillie.

"Are yous home long a'ready?" he inquired.

"Not so very long," Tillie answered with an apprehensive glance at the clock.

"You're some late," he said, with a threatening little nod as he drew up a chair in front of the teacher.

"It's my fault," Miss Margaret hastened to say. "I made the children wait to bring me out here."

"Well," conceded Mr. Getz, "then we'll leave it go this time."

Miss Margaret now bent her mind to the difficult task of persuading this stubborn Pennsylvania Dutchman to accept her views as to what was for the highest and best good of his daughter. Eloquently she pointed out to him that Tillie being a child of unusual ability, it would be much better for her to have an education than to be forced to spend her days in farmhouse drudgery.

But her point of view, being entirely novel, did not at all appeal to him.

"I never thought to leave her go to school after she was twelve. That's long enough fur a girl; a female don't need much book-knowledge. It don't help her none to keep house fur her mister."

"But she could become a teacher and then she could earn money," Miss Margaret argued, knowing the force of this point with Mr. Getz.

"But look at all them years she'd have to spend learnin' herself to be intelligent enough fur to be a teacher, when she might be helpin' me and mom."

"But she could help you by paying board here when she becomes the New Canaan teacher."

"That's so too," granted Mr. Getz; and Margaret grew faintly hopeful.

"But," he added, after a moment's heavy weighing of the matter, "it would take too long to get her enough *educated* fur to be a teacher, and I'm one of them," he maintained, "that holds a child is born to help the parent, and not contrarywise—that the parent must do everything fur the child that way."

"If you love your children, you must wish for their highest good," she suggested, "and not trample on their best interests."

"But they have the right to work for their parents," he insisted. "You needn't plague me to leave Tillie stay in school, Teacher. I ain't leavin' her!"

"Do you think you have a right to bring children into the world only to crush everything in them that is worthwhile?" Margaret dared to say to him, her face flushed, her eyes bright with the intensity of her feelings.

"That's all blamed foolishness!" Jake Getz affirmed.

"Do you think that your daughter, when she is grown and realizes all that she has lost, will 'rise up and call you blessed?'" she persisted.

"Do I think? Well, what I think is that it's a good bit more particular that till she's growed she's been learnt to work and serve them that raised her. And what I think is that a person ain't fit to be a teacher of the young that sides along with the childern ag'in' their parents."

Miss Margaret felt that it was time she took her leave.

"Look-ahere oncet, Teacher!" Mr. Getz suddenly said, fixing on her a suspicious and searching look, "do you uphold to novel-readin'?"

Miss Margaret hesitated perceptibly. She must shield Tillie even more than herself. "What a question to ask of the teacher at William Penn!" she gravely answered.

"I know it ain't such a wery polite question," returned Mr. Getz, half apologetically. "But the way you side along with childern ag'in' their parents suspicions me that the Doc was lyin' when he sayed them novel-books was hisn. Now was they hisn or was they yourn?"

Miss Margaret rose with a look and air of injury. "Mr. Getz, no one ever before asked me such questions.

Indeed," she said, in a tone of virtuous primness, "I can't answer such questions."

"All the same," sullenly asserted Mr. Getz, "I wouldn't put it a-past you after the way you passed your opinion to me this after!"

"I must be going," returned Miss Margaret with dignity.

Mrs. Getz came forward from the stove with a look and manner of apology for her husband's rudeness to the visitor.

"What's your hurry? Can't you stay and eat along? We're not anyways tired of you."

"Thank you. But they will be waiting for me at the hotel," said Miss Margaret gently.

Tillie, a bit frightened, also hovered near, her wistful little face pale. Miss Margaret drew her to her and held her at her side, as she looked up into the face of Mr. Getz.

"I am very, very sorry, Mr. Getz, that my visit has proved so fruitless. You don't realize what a mistake you are making."

"That ain't the way a teacher had ought to talk before a scholar to its parent!" indignantly retorted Mr. Getz. "And I'm pretty near sure it was all the time *you* where lent them books to Tillie—corruptin' the young! I can tell you right now, I ain't wotin' fur you at next election! And the way I wote is the way two other members always wotes still—and so you'll lose your job at William Penn! That's what you get fur tryin' to interfere between a parent and a scholar! I hope it'll learn you!"

"And when is the next election?" imperturbably asked Miss Margaret.

"Next month on the twenty-fifth of February. Then you'll see oncet!"

"According to the terms of my agreement with the Board I hold my position until the first of April unless the Board can show reasons why it should be taken from me. What reasons can you show?"

"That you side along with the—"

"That I try to persuade you not to take your child out of school when you can well afford to keep her there. That's what you have to tell the Board."

Mr. Getz stared at her, rather baffled. The children also stared in wide-eyed curiosity, realizing with wonder that Teacher was "talkin' up to pop!" It was a novel and interesting spectacle.

"Well, anyways," continued Mr. Getz, rallying, "I'll bring it up in Board meeting that you mebbe leave the scholars borry the loan of novels off of you."

"But you can't prove it. I shall hold the Board to their contract. They can't break it."

Miss Margaret was taking very high ground, of which, in fact, she was not at all sure.

Mr. Getz gazed at her with mingled anger and fascination. Here was certainly a new species of woman! Never before had any teacher at William Penn failed to cringe to his authority as a director.

"This much I *kin* say," he finally declared. "Mebbe you kin hold us to that there contract, but you won't, anyways, be elected to come back here next term!

That's sure! You'll have to look out fur another place till September a'ready. And we won't give you no *recommend*, neither, to get yourself another school with!"

Just here it was that Miss Margaret had her triumph, which she was quite human enough to thoroughly enjoy. "You won't have a chance to reëlect me, for I am going to resign at the end of the term. I am going to be married the week after school closes."

Never had Mr. Getz felt himself so foiled. Never before had any one subject in any degree to his authority so neatly eluded a reckoning at his hands. A tingling sensation ran along his arm and he had to restrain his impulse to lift it, grasp this slender creature standing so fearlessly before him, and thoroughly shake her.

"Who's the party?" asked Mrs. Getz, curiously. "It never got put out that you was promised. I ain't heard you had any steady comp'ny. To be sure, some says the Doc likes you pretty good. Is it now, mebbe, the Doc? But no," she shook her head; "Mister's sister Em at the *hotel* would have tole me. Is it someone where lives around here?"

"I don't mind telling you," Miss Margaret graciously answered, realizing that her reply would greatly increase Mr. Getz's sense of defeat. "It is Mr. Lansing, a nephew of the State Superintendent of schools and a professor at the Millersville Normal School."

"Well, now just look!" Mrs. Getz exclaimed wonderingly. "Such a tony party! The State Superintendent's nephew! That's even a more way-up person than

"I am going to be married the week after school closes"

what the county superintendent is! Ain't? Well, who'd
'a' thought!"

"Miss Margaret!" Tillie breathed, gazing up at her,
her eyes wide and strained with distress, "if you go away
and get married, won't I *never* see you no more?"

"But, dear, I shall live so near—at the Normal School
only a few miles away. You can come to see me often."

"But pop won't leave me, Miss Margaret—it costs too
expensive to go wisiting, and I got to help with the
work, still. O Miss Margaret!" Tillie sobbed, as Margaret
sat down and held the clinging child to her, "I'll never
see you no more after you go away!"

"Tillie, dear!" Margaret tried to soothe her. "I'll
come to see *you,* then, if you can't come to see me. Listen, Tillie—I've just thought of something."

Suddenly she put the little girl from her and
stood up.

"Let me take Tillie to live with me next fall at the
Normal School. Won't you do that, Mr. Getz?" she
urged him. "She could go to the preparatory school,
and if we stay at Millersville, Dr. Lansing and I would try
to have her go through the Normal School and graduate. *Will* you consent to it, Mr. Getz?"

"And who'd be payin' fur all this here?" Mr. Getz
ironically inquired.

"Tillie could earn her own way as my little maid—
helping me keep my few rooms in the Normal School
building and doing my mending and darning for me.
And you know after she was graduated she could earn
her living as a teacher."

Margaret saw the look of feverish eagerness with which Tillie heard this proposal and awaited the outcome. Before her husband could answer, Mrs. Getz offered a weak protest.

"I hear the girls hired in town have to set away back in the kitchen and never dare set front—always away back, still. Tillie wouldn't like that. Nobody would."

"But I shall live in a small suite of rooms at the school—a library, a bedroom, a bathroom, and a small room next to mine that can be Tillie's bedroom. We shall take our meals in the school dining room."

"Well, that mebbe she wouldn't mind. But 'way back she wouldn't be satisfied to set. That's why the country girls don't like to hire in town, because they dassent set front with the missus. Here last market-day Sophy Haberbush she conceited she'd like oncet to hire out in town, and she ast me would I go with her after market to see a lady that adwertised in the noospaper fur a girl, and I sayed no, I wouldn't mind. So I went along. But Sophy she wouldn't take the place fur all. She ast the lady could she have her country company, Sundays—he was her company fur four years now and she wouldn't like to give him up neither. She tole the lady her company goes, still, as early as eleven. But the lady sayed her house must be darkened and locked at half-past ten a'ready. She ast me was I Sophy's mother and I sayed no, I'm nothin' to her but a neighbor woman. And she tole Sophy, when they eat, still, Sophy she couldn't eat along. I guess she thought Sophy Haberbush wasn't good enough. But she's as good as any person. Her mother's name is Smith before she was married, and them Smiths was well fixed. She sayed Sophy'd have to go in and out the back way and never out the front. Why, they say some of the town people's that proud, if the front door-bell rings and the missus is standin' right there by it, she won't open that there front door but wants her hired girl to come clear from the kitchen to open it. Yes, you mightn't b'lee me, but I heerd that a'ready. And Mary Hertzog she tole me when she hired out there fur a while one winter in town, why, one day she went to the missus and she says, 'There's two ladies in the parlor and I tole 'em you was helpin' in the kitchen,' and the missus she ast her, 'What fur did you tell 'em that? Why, I'm that ashamed I don't know how to walk in the par-lor!' And Mary she ast the colored gentleman that worked there, what, now, did the missus mean? And he sayed, 'Well, Mary, you've a heap to learn about the laws of society. Don't you know you must always leave on the ladies ain't doin' nothin'?' Mary sayed that colored gentleman was so wonderful intelligent that way. He'd been a restaurant waiter there fur a while and so was throwed in with the best people, and he was, now, that tony and high-minded! Och, I wouldn't hire in town! To be sure, Mister can do what he wants. Well," she added, "it's a quarter till five—I guess I'll put the peppermint on a while. Mister's folks'll be here till five."

She moved away to the stove, and Margaret resumed her assault upon the stubborn ignorance of the father.

"Think, Mr. Getz, what a difference all this would make in Tillie's life," she urged.

"And you'd be learnin' her all them years to up and sass her pop when she was growed and earnin' her own livin'!" he objected.

"I certainly would not."

"And all them years till she graduated she'd be no use to us where owns her," he said, as though his child were an item of live stock on the farm.

"She could come home to you in the summer vacations," Margaret suggested.

"Yes, and she'd come that spoilt we couldn't get no work out of her. No, if I hire her out winters, it'll be where I kin draw her wages myself—where's my right as her parent. What does a body have childern fur? To get no use out of 'em? It ain't no good you're plaguin' me. I ain't leavin' her go. Tillie!" he commanded the child with a twirl of his thumb and a motion of his head; "go set the supper table!"

Margaret laid her arm about Tillie's shoulder. "Well, dear," she said sorrowfully, "we must give it all up, I suppose. But don't lose heart, Tillie. I shall not go out of your life. At least we can write to each other. Now," she concluded, bending and kissing her, "I must go, but you and I shall have some talks before you stop school, and before I go away from New Canaan."

She pressed her lips to Tillie's in a long kiss, while the child clung to her in passionate devotion. Mr. Getz looked on with dull bewilderment. He knew, in a vague way, that every word the teacher spoke to the child, no less than those useless caresses, was "siding along with the scholar ag'in' the parent," and yet he could not definitely have stated just how. He was quite sure that she would not dare so to defy him did she not know that she had the whip-handle in the fact that she did not want her "job" next year, and that the Board could not, except for definite offenses, break their contract with her. It was only in view of these considerations that she played her game of "plaguing" him by championing Tillie. Jacob Getz was incapable of recognizing in the teacher's attitude toward his child an unselfish interest and love.

So, in dogged, sullen silence, he saw this extraordinary young woman take her leave and pass out of his house.

CHAPTER NINE

"I'LL DO MY DARN BEST, TEACHER!"

IT SOON "GOT PUT OUT" IN NEW CANAAN THAT MISS Margaret was "promised," and the doctor was surprised to find how much the news depressed him.

"I didn't know, now, how much I was stuck on her! To think I can't have her even if I do want her" (up to this time he had had moments now and then of not feeling absolutely sure of his inclination), "and that she's promised to one of them tony Millersville Normal professors! If it don't beat all! Well," he drew a long, deep sigh as, lounging back in his buggy, he let his horse jog at his own gait along the muddy country road, "I jus' don't feel fur *nothin'* today. She was now certainly a sweet lady," he thought pensively, as though alluding to one who had died. "If there's one sek I do now like, it's the female—and she was certainly a nice party!"

In the course of her career at William Penn, Miss Margaret had developed such a genuine fondness, for the shaggy, good-natured, generous, and unscrupulous little doctor, that before she abandoned her post at the end of the term, and shook the dust of New Canaan from her feet, she took him into her confidence and begged him to take care of Tillie.

"She is an uncommon child, doctor, and she must— I am determined that she must—be rescued from the life to which that father of hers would condemn her. You must help me to bring it about."

"Nothin' I like better, Teacher, than gettin' ahead of Jake Getz," the doctor readily agreed. "Or obligin' *you*. To tell you the truth—and it don't do no harm to say it now—if you hadn't been promised, I was a-goin' to ast you myself! You took notice I gave you an inwitation there last week to go buggy-ridin' with me. That was leadin' up to it. After that Sunday night you left me set up with you, I never conceited you was promised a'ready to somebody else—and you even left me set with my feet on your chair-rounds!" The doctor's tone was a bit injured.

"Am I to understand," inquired Miss Margaret, won-deringly, "that the permission to sit with one's feet on the rounds of a lady's chair is taken in New Canaan as an indication of her favor—and even of her inclination to matrimony?"

"It's looked to as meanin' gettin' down to *biz!*" the doctor affirmed.

"Then," meekly, "I humbly apologize."

"That's all right," generously granted the doctor, "if you didn't know no better. But to be sure, I'm some disappointed."

"I'm sorry for that!"

"Would you of mebbe said yes, if you hadn't of been promised a'ready to one of them tony Millersville Normal professors," the doctor inquired curiously—"me bein' a professional gentleman that way?"

"I'm sure," replied this daughter of Eve, who wished to use the doctor in her plans for Tillie, "I should have been highly honored."

The rueful, injured look on the doctor's face cleared to flattered complacency. "Well," he said, "I'd like wery well to do what you ast off of me fur little Tillie Getz. But, Teacher, what can a body do against a feller like Jake Getz? A body can't come between a man and his own offspring."

"I know it," replied Margaret, sadly. "But just keep a little watch over Tillie and help her whenever you see that you can. Won't you? Promise me that you will. You have several times helped her out of trouble this winter. There may be other similar opportunities. Between us, doctor, we may be able to make something of Tillie."

The doctor shook his head. "I'll do my darn best, Teacher, but Jake Getz he's that wonderful set. A little girl like Tillie couldn't never make no headway with Jake Getz standin' in her road. But anyways, Teacher, I pass you my promise I'll do what I can."

Miss Margaret's parting advice and promises to Tillie so fired the girl's ambition and determination that some of the sting and anguish of parting from her who stood to the child for all the mother-love that her life had missed, was taken away in the burning purpose with which she found herself imbued, to bend her every thought and act in all the years to come to the reaching of that glorious goal which her idolized teacher set before her.

"As soon as you are old enough," Miss Margaret admonished her, "you must assert yourself. Take your rights—your right to an education, to some girlish pleasures, to a little liberty. No matter what you have to suffer in the struggle, *fight it out,* for you will suffer more in the end if you let yourself be defrauded of everything which makes it worthwhile to have been born. Don't let yourself be sacrificed for those who not only will never appreciate it, but who will never be worth it. I think I do you no harm by telling you that you are worth all the rest of your family put together. The self-sacrifice which pampers the selfishness of others is *not* creditable. It is weak. It is unworthy. Remember what I say to you—make a fight for your rights, just as soon as you are old enough—your right to be a woman instead of a chattel and a drudge. And meantime, make up for your rebellion by being as obedient and helpful and affectionate to your parents as you can be, without destroying yourself."

Such sentiments and ideas were almost a foreign language to Tillie, and yet, intuitively, she understood the import of them. In her loneliness, after Miss Margaret's departure, she treasured and brooded over them day and night; and very much as the primitive Christian courted martyrdom, her mind dwelt, with ever-growing resolution, upon the thought of the heroic courage with which, in the years to come, she would surely obey them.

Miss Margaret had promised Tillie that she would write to her, and the child, overlooking the serious difficulties in the way, had eagerly promised in return to answer her letters.

Once a week Mr. Getz called for mail at the village store, and Miss Margaret's first letter was laboriously read by him on his way out to the farm.

He found it, on the whole, uninteresting, but he vaguely gathered from one or two sentences that the teacher, even at the distance of five miles, was still trying to "plague" him by "siding along with his child ag'in' her parent."

"See here oncet," he said to Tillie, striding to the kitchen stove on his return home, the letter in his hand: "this here goes after them novel-books, in the fire! I ain't leavin' that there woman spoil you with no such letters like this here. Now you know!"

The gleam of actual wickedness in Tillie's usually soft eyes, as she saw that longed-for letter tossed into the flames, would have startled her father had he seen it. The girl trembled from head to foot and turned a deathly white.

"I hate you, hate you, hate you!" her hot heart was saying as she literally glared at her tormentor. "I'll never forget this—never, never; I'll make you suffer for it—I will, I will!"

But her white lips were dumb, and her impotent passion, having no other outlet, could only tear and bruise her own heart as all the long morning she worked in a blind fury at her household tasks.

But after dinner she did an unheard-of thing. Without asking permission, or giving any explanation to either her father or her stepmother, she deliberately abandoned her usual Saturday afternoon work of cleaning up (she said to herself that she did not care if the house rotted), and dressing herself, she walked straight through the kitchen before her stepmother's very eyes, and out of the house.

Her father was out in the fields when she undertook this high-handed step; and her mother was so dumb with amazement at such unusual behavior that she offered but a weak protest.

"What'll pop say to your doin' somepin like this here!" she called querulously after Tillie as she followed her across the kitchen to the door. "He'll whip you, Tillie; and here's all the sweepin' to be did—"

There was a strange gleam in Tillie's eyes before which the woman shrank and held her peace. The girl swept past her, almost walked over several of the children sprawling on the porch, and went out of the gate and up the road toward the village.

"What's the matter of her anyways?" the woman wonderingly said to herself as she went back to her work. "Is it that she's so spited about that letter pop burnt up? But what's a letter to get spited about? There was enough worse things 'n that that she took off her pop without actin' like this. Och, but he'll whip her if he gets in here before she comes back. Where's she

"The girl swept past her"

goin' to, I wonder! Well, I never did! I would not be *her* if her pop finds how she went off and let her work! I wonder shall I mebbe tell him on her or not, if he don't get in till she's home a'ready?"

She meditated upon this problem of domestic economy as she mechanically did her chores, her reflections on Tillie taking an unfriendly color as she felt the weight of her stepdaughter's abandoned tasks added to the already heavy burden of her own.

It was to see the doctor that Tillie had set out for the village hotel. He was the only person in all her little world to whom she felt she could turn for help in her suffering. Her "Aunty Em," the landlady at the hotel, was, she knew, very fond of her; but Tillie never thought of appealing to her in her trouble.

"I never thought when I promised Miss Margaret I'd write to her still where I'd get the stamps from, and the paper and envelopes," Tillie explained to the doctor as they sat in confidential consultation in the hotel parlor, the child's white face of distress a challenge to his faithful remembrance of his promise to the teacher. "And now I got to find some way to let her know I didn't see her letter to me. Doc, will you write and tell her for me!" she pleaded.

"My handwritin' ain't just so plain that way, Tillie. But I'll give you all the paper and envelopes and stamps you want to write on yourself to her."

"Oh, Doc!" Tillie gazed at him in fervent gratitude. "But mebbe I hadn't ought to take 'em when I can't pay you."

"That's all right. If it'll make you feel some easier, you kin pay me when you're growed up and teachin'. Your Miss Margaret she's bound to make a teacher out of you—or anyways a *educated* person. And then you kin pay me when you're got your nice education to make your livin' with."

"That's what we'll do then!" Tillie joyfully accepted this proposal. "I'll keep account and pay you back every cent, Doc, when I'm earnin' my own livin'."

"All right. *That*'s settled then. Now, fur your gettin' your letters, still, from Teacher. How are we goin' to work that there? I'll tell you, Tillie!" he slapped the table as an idea came to him. "You write her off a letter and tell her she must write her letters to you in an envelope directed to *me*. And I'll see as you get 'em all right, you bet! Ain't?"

"Oh, Doc!" Tillie was affectionately grateful. "You are so kind to me! What would I do without you?" Tears choked her voice, filled her eyes, and rolled down her face.

"Och, that's all right," he patted her shoulder. "Ain't no better fun goin' fur me than gettin' ahead of that mean old Jake Getz!"

Tillie drew back a bit shocked; but she did not protest.

Carrying in her bosom a stamped envelope, a sheet of paper and a pencil, the child walked home in a very different frame of mind from that in which she had started out. She shuddered as she remembered how wickedly rebellious had been her mood that morning. Never before had such hot and dreadful feelings and

thoughts burned in her heart and brain. In an undefined way, the growing girl realized that such a state of
mind and heart was unworthy her sacred friendship
with Miss Margaret.

"I want to be like her—and she was never ugly in her
feelings like what I was all morning!"

When she reached home, she so effectually made
up for lost time in the vigor with which she attacked
the Saturday cleaning that Mrs. Getz, with unusual
forbearance, decided not to tell her father of her
insubordination.

Tillie wrote her first letter to Miss Margaret, by stealth,
at midnight.

CHAPTER TEN

ADAM SCHUNK'S FUNERAL

A CRUCIAL STRUGGLE WITH HER FATHER, TO WHICH both Tillie and Miss Margaret had fearfully looked forward, came about much sooner than Tillie had anticipated. The occasion of it, too, was not at all what she had expected and even planned it to be.

It was her conversion, just a year after she had been taken out of school, to the ascetic faith of the New Mennonites that precipitated the crisis, this conversion being wrought by a sermon which she heard at the funeral of a neighboring farmer.

A funeral among the farmers of Lancaster County is a festive occasion, the most popular form of dissipation known, bringing the whole population forth as in some regions they turn out to a circus.

Adam Schunk's death, having been caused by his own hand in a fit of despair over the loss of some money he had unsuccessfully invested, was so sudden and shocking that the effect produced on Canaan Township was profound, not to say awful.

As for Tillie, it was the first event of the kind that had ever come within her experience, and the religious sentiments in which she had been reared aroused in her, in common with the rest of the community, a superstitious fear before this sudden and solemn calling to judgment of one whom they had all known so familiarly, and who had so wickedly taken his own life.

During the funeral at the farmhouse, she sat in the crowded parlor where the coffin stood, and though surrounded by people, she felt strangely alone with this weird mystery of Death which for the first time she was realizing.

Her mother was in the kitchen with the other farmers' wives of the neighborhood who were helping to prepare the immense quantity of food necessary to feed the large crowd that always attended a funeral, every one of whom, by the etiquette of the county, remained to supper after the services.

Her father, being among the hired hostlers of the occasion, was outside in the barn. Mr. Getz was head hostler at every funeral of the district, being detailed to assist and superintend the work of the other half dozen men employed to take charge of the "teams" that belonged to the funeral guests, who came in families, companies, and crowds. That so well-to-do a farmer as Jake Getz, one who owned his farm "clear," should make a practice of hiring out as a funeral hostler, with the humbler farmers who only rented the land they tilled, was one of the facts which gave him his reputation for being "keen on the penny."

Adam Schunk, deceased, had been an "Evangelical," but his wife being a New Mennonite, a sect largely prevailing in southeastern Pennsylvania, the funeral services were conducted by two ministers, one of them a New Mennonite and the other an Evangelical. It was the sermon of the New Mennonite that led to Tillie's conversion.

The New Mennonites being the most puritanic and exclusive of all sects, earnestly regarding themselves as the custodians of the only absolutely true light, their ministers insist on certain prerogatives as the condition of giving their services at a funeral. A New Mennonite preacher will not consent to preach after a "World's preacher"—he must have first voice. It was therefore the somber doctrine of fear preached by the Reverend Brother Abram Underwocht which did its work upon Tillie's conscience so completely that the gentler Gospel set forth afterward by the Evangelical brother was scarcely heeded.

The Reverend Brother Abram Underwocht, in the "plain" garb of the Mennonite sect, took his place at the foot of the stairway opening out of the sitting room, and gave expression to his own profound sense of the solemnity of the occasion by a question introductory to his sermon, and asked in a tone of heavy import: "If this ain't a blow, what is it?"

Handkerchiefs were promptly produced and agitated faces hidden therein.

Why this was a "blow" of more than usual force, Brother Underwocht proceeded to explain in a blood-curdling talk of more than an hour's length, in which he set forth the New Mennonite doctrine that none outside of the only true faith of Christ, as held and taught by the New Mennonites, could be saved from the fire which cannot be quenched. With the heroism born of deep conviction, he stoically disregarded the feelings of the bereaved family, and affirmed that the deceased having belonged to one of "the World's churches," no hope could be entertained for him, nor could his grieving widow look forward to meeting him again in the heavenly home to which she, a saved New Mennonite, was destined.

Taking advantage of the fact that at least one third of those present were non-Mennonites, Brother Underwocht followed the usual course of the preachers of his sect on such an occasion, and made of his funeral sermon an exposition of the whole field of New Mennonite faith and practice. Beginning in the Garden of Eden, he graphically described that renowned locality as a type of the Paradise from which Adam Schunk and others who did not "give themselves up" were excluded.

"It must have been a magnificent scenery to Almighty Gawd," he said, referring to the beauties of man's first Paradise. "But how soon to be snatched by sin from man's mortal vision, when Eve started that conversation with the enemy of her soul! Beloved, that was an unfortunate circumstance! And you that are still out of Christ and in the world, have need to pray fur Gawd's help, his aid, and his assistance, to enable you to overcome the

enemy who that day was turned loose upon the world—
that Gawd may see fit to have you when you're done
here a'ready. Heed the solemn warning of this poor
soul now laying before you cold in death!

> Know that you're a transient creature,
> Soon to fade and pass away.

"Even Lazarus, where [who] was raised to life, was
not raised fur never to die no more!"

The only comfort he could offer to this stricken
household was that *he* knew how bad they felt, having
had a brother who had died with equal suddenness
and also without hope, as he "had suosode hisself with
a gun."

This lengthy sermon was followed by a hymn, sung a
line at a time at the preacher's dictation:

> The body we now to the grave will commit,
> To there see corruption till Jesus sees fit
> A spirit'al body for it to prepare,
> Which henceforth then shall immortality wear.

The New Mennonites being forbidden by the "Rules
of the Meeting" ever to hear a prayer or sermon by one
who is not "a member," it was necessary, at the end of the
Reverend Abram Underwocht's sermon, for all the Mennonites present to retire to a room apart and sit behind
closed doors, while the Evangelical brother put forth his
false doctrine.

So religiously stirred was Tillie by the occasion that she was strongly tempted to rise and follow into the kitchen those who were thus retiring from the sound of the false teacher's voice. But her conversion not yet being complete, she kept her place.

No doubt it was not so much the character of Brother Underwocht's New Mennonite sermon which effected this state in Tillie as that the spiritual condition of the young girl, just awakening to her womanhood, with all its mysterious craving, its religious brooding, its emotional susceptibility, led her to respond with her whole soul to the first appeal to her feelings.

Absorbed in her mournful contemplation of her own deep "conviction of sin," she did not heed the singing, led by the Evangelical brother, of the hymn,

Rock of Ages, *clept* for me,

nor did she hear a word of his discourse.

At the conclusion of the house services, and before the journey to the graveyard, the supper was served, first to the mourners, and then to all those who expected to follow the body to the grave. The third table, for those who had prepared the meal, and the fourth, for the hostlers, were set after the departure of the funeral procession.

Convention has prescribed that the funeral meal shall consist invariably of cold meat, cheese, all sorts of stewed dried fruits, pickles, "lemon rice" (a dish never omitted), and coffee.

As no one household possesses enough dishes for such an occasion, two chests of dishes owned by the Mennonite church are sent to the house of mourning whenever needed by a member of the Meeting.

The Mennonites present suffered a shock to their feelings upon the appearance of the widow of the deceased Adam Schunk, for—unprecedented circumstance! She wore over her black Mennonite hood a crape veil! This was an innovation nothing short of revolutionary, and the brethren and sisters, to whom their prescribed form of dress was sacred, were bewildered to know how they ought to regard such a digression from their rigid customs.

"I guess Mandy's proud of herself with her weil," Tillie's stepmother whispered to her as she gave the girl a tray of coffee cups to deliver about the table.

But Tillie's thoughts were inward bent, and she heeded not what went on about her. Fear of death and the judgment, a longing to find the peace which could come only with an assured sense of her salvation, darkness as to how that peace might be found, a sense of the weakness of her flesh and spirit before her father's undoubted opposition to her "turning plain," as well as his certain refusal to supply the wherewithal for her Mennonite garb, should she indeed be led of the Spirit to "give herself up"—all these warring thoughts and emotions stamped their lines upon the girl's sweet, troubled countenance, as, blind and deaf to her surroundings, she lent her helping hand almost as one acting in a trance.

CHAPTER ELEVEN

"Pop! I Feel to Be Plain"

THE PSYCHICAL AND, CONSIDERING THE CRITICAL AGE of the young girl, the physiological processes by which Tillie was finally led to her conversion it is not necessary to analyze; for the experience is too universal, and differs too slightly in individual cases, to require comment. Perhaps in Tillie's case it was a more intense and permanent emotion than with the average convert. Otherwise, deep and earnest though it was with her, it was not unique.

The New Mennonite sermon which had been the instrument to determine the channel in which should flow the emotional tide of her awakening womanhood, had convinced her that if she would be saved, she dare not compromise with the world by joining one of those churches as, for instance, the Methodist or the Evangelical, which permitted every sort of worldly indulgence—fashionable dress, attendance at the circus, voting at the polls, musical instruments, "pleasure-seeking," and many other things which the

Word of God forbade. She must give herself up to the Lord absolutely and entirely, forswearing all the world's allurements. The New Mennonites alone, of all the Christian sects, lived up to this scriptural ideal, and with them Tillie would cast her lot.

This austere body of Christians could not so easily have won her heart had it forbidden her cherished ambition, constantly encouraged and stimulated by Miss Margaret, to educate herself. Fortunately for her peace of mind, the New Mennonites were not, like the Amish, "enemies to education," though to be sure, as the preacher, Brother Abram Underwocht, reminded her in her private talk with him, "To be dressy, or *too* well educated, or stylish, didn't belong to Christ and the apostles; they were plain folks."

It was in the lull of work that came, even in the Getz family, on Sunday afternoon, that Tillie, summoning to her aid all the fervor of her newfound faith, ventured to face the ordeal of opening up with her father the subject of her conversion.

He was sitting on the kitchen porch, dozing over a big Bible spread open on his knee. The children were playing on the lawn, and Mrs. Getz was taking her Sunday afternoon nap on the kitchen settee.

Tillie seated herself on the porch step at her father's feet. Her eyes were clear and bright, but her face burned, and her heart beat heavily in her heaving bosom.

"Pop!" she timidly roused him from his dozing.

"Heh?" he muttered gruffly, opening his eyes and lifting his head.

"Pop, I got to speak somepin to you."

An unusual note in her voice arrested him, and, wide awake now, he looked down at her inquiringly.

"Well? What, then?"

"Pop! I feel to be plain."

"*You!* Feel fur turnin' plain! Why, you ain't old enough to know the meanin' of it! What d'you want about that there theology?"

"I'm fourteen, pop. And the Spirit has led me to see the light. I have gave myself up," she affirmed quietly, but with a quiver in her voice.

"You have gave yourself up!" her father incredulously repeated.

"Yes, sir. And I'm loosed of all things that belong to the world. And now I feel fur wearin' the plain dress, fur that's according to Scripture, which says, 'all is wanity!'"

Never before in her life had Tillie spoken so many words to her father at one time, and he stared at her in astonishment.

"Yes, you're growin' up, that's so. I ain't noticed how fast you was growin'. It don't seem no time since you was born. But it's fourteen years back a'ready—yes, that's so. Well, Tillie, if you feel fur joinin' church, you're got to join on to the Evangelicals. I ain't leavin' you follow no such nonsense as to turn plain. That don't belong to us Getzes. We're Evangelicals this long time a'ready."

"Aunty Em was a Getz, and *she's* gave herself up long ago."

"Well, she's the only one by the name Getz that I ever knowed to be so foolish! I'm an Evangelical, and what's good enough fur your pop will do *you*, I guess!"

"The Evangelicals ain't according to Scripture, pop. They have wine at the Communion, and the Bible says, 'Taste not, handle not,' and 'Look not upon the wine when it is red.'"

That she should criticize the Evangelicals and pronounce them unscriptural was disintegrating to all his ideas of the subjection of children. His sunburned face grew darker.

"Mebbe you don't twist that there Book! Gawd he wouldn't of created wine to be made if it would be wrong fur to look at it! You can't come over that, can you? Them Scripture you spoke, just mean not to drink to drunkenness, nor eat to gluttonness. But," he sternly added, "it ain't fur you to answer up to your pop! I ain't leavin' you dress plain—and that's all that's to say!"

"I got to do it, pop," Tillie's low voice answered. "I must obey to Christ."

"What you sayin' to me? That you got to do somepin I tole you you haven't the dare to do? Are you sayin' that to *me*, Tillie? Heh?"

"I got to obey to Christ," she repeated, her face paling.

"You think! Well, we'll see about that oncet! You leave me see you obeyin' to anyone before your pop, and you'll soon get learnt better! How do you bring it out that the Scripture says, 'Childern, obey your parents?'"

"'Obey your parents in the Lord,'" Tillie amended.

"Well, you'll be obeyin' to the Scripture *and* your parent by joinin' the Evangelicals. D'you understand?"

"The Evangelicals don't hold to Scripture, pop. They enlist. And we don't read of Christ takin' any interest in war."

"Yes, but in the Old Dispensation them old kings did it, and certainly they was good men! They're in the Bible!"

"But we're livin' under the New Dispensation. And a many things is changed to what they were under the Old. Pop, I can't dress fashionable anymore."

"Now, look here, Tillie, I oughtn't argy no words with you, fur you're my child and you're got the right to mind me just because I say it. But can't you see the inconsistentness of the plain people? Now a New Mennonite he says his conscience won't leave him wear grand [wear worldly dress] but he'll make his livin' in Lancaster city by keepin' a jew'lry store. And yet them Mennonites won't leave a sister keep a millinery shop!"

"But," Tillie tried to hold her ground, "there's watches, pop, and clocks that jew'lers sells. They're useful. We got to have watches and clocks. Millinery is only pleasing to the eye."

"Well, the women couldn't go bareheaded neither, could they? And is earrings and such things like them useful? And all them fancy things they keep in their dry goods stores? Och, they're awful inconsistent that way! I ain't got no use fur New Mennonites! Why, here one day, when your mom was livin' yet, I owed a New

Mennonite six cents, and I handed him a dime and he couldn't change it out, but he sayed he'd send me the four cents. Well, I waited and waited, and he never sent it. Then I bought such a postal card and wrote it in town to him yet. And that didn't fetch the four cents neither. I wrote to him backward and forward till I had wrote three cards a'ready, and then I seen I wouldn't gain nothin' by writin' one more if he did pay me, and if he didn't pay I'd lose that other cent yet. So I let it. Now that's a New Mennonite fur you! Do you call that consistentness?"

"But it's the Word of Gawd I go by, pop, not by the weak brethren."

"Well, you'll go by your pop's word and not join to them New Mennonites! Now I don't want to hear no more!"

"Won't you buy me the plain garb, pop?"

"Buy you the plain garb! Now look here, Tillie. If ever you ast me again to leave you join to anything but the Evangelicals, or speak somepin to me about buyin' you the plain garb, I'm usin' the strap. Do you hear me?"

"Pop," said Tillie, solemnly, her face very white, "I'll always obey to you where I can—where I think it's right to. But if you won't buy me the plain dress and cap, Aunty Em Wackernagel's going to. She says she never knew what happiness it was to be had in this life till she gave herself up and dressed plain and loosed herself from all worldly things. And I feel just like her."

"All right—just you come wearin' them Mennonite costumes 'round me oncet! I'll burn 'em up like what

I burned up them novels where you lent off of your teacher! And I'll punish you so's you won't try it a second time to do what I tell you you haven't the dare to do!"

The color flowed back into Tillie's white face as he spoke. She was crimson now as she rose from the porch step and turned away from him to go into the house.

Jake Getz realized, as with a sort of dull wonder his eyes followed her, that there was a something in his daughter's face this day, and in the bearing of her young frame as she walked before him, which he was not wont to see, which he did not understand, and with which he felt he could not cope. The vague sense of uneasiness which it gave him strengthened his resolve to crush, with a strong hand, this budding insubordination.

Two uneventful weeks passed by, during which Tillie's quiet and dutiful demeanor almost disarmed her father's threatening watchfulness of her; so that when, one Sunday afternoon, at four o'clock, she returned from a walk to her Aunty Em Wackernagel's, clad in the meek garb of the New Mennonites, his amazement at her intrepidity was even greater than his anger.

The younger children, in high glee at what to them was a most comical transformation in their elder sister, danced around her with shrieks of laughter, crying out at the funny white cap which she wore, and the prim little three-cornered cape falling over her bosom, designed modestly to cover the vanity of woman's alluring form.

Mrs. Getz, mechanically moving about the kitchen to get the supper, paused in her work only long enough to remark with stupid astonishment, "Did you, now, get religion, Tillie?"

"Yes, ma'am. I've gave myself up."

"Where did you come by the plain dress?"

"Aunty Em bought it for me and helped me make it."

Her father had followed her in from the porch and now came up to her as she stood in the middle of the kitchen. The children scattered at his approach.

"You go upstairs and take them clo'es off!" he commanded. "I ain't leavin' you wear 'em one hour in this house!"

"I have no others to put on, pop," Tillie gently answered, her soft eyes meeting his with an absence of fear which puzzled and baffled him.

"Where's your others, then?"

"I've let 'em at Aunty Em's. She took 'em in exchange for my plain dress. She says she can use 'em on 'Manda and Rebecca."

"Then you walk yourself right back over to the *hotel* and get 'em back off of her, and let them clo'es you got on. Go!" he roughly pointed to the door.

"She wouldn't give 'em back to me. She'd know I hadn't ought to yield up to temptation, and she'd help me to resist by refusing me my fashionable clo'es."

"You tell her if you come back home without 'em, I'm whippin' you! She'll give 'em to you then."

"She'd say my love to Christ ought not to be so weak but I can bear anything you want to do to me, pop. She had to take an awful lot off of gran'pop when she turned plain. Pop," she added earnestly, "no matter what you do to me, I ain't givin' 'way; I'm standin' firm to serve Christ!"

"We'll see oncet!" her father grimly answered, striding across the room and taking his strap from its corner in the kitchen cupboard he grasped Tillie's slender shoulder and lifted his heavy arm.

And now for the first time in her life his wife interposed a word against his brutality.

"Jake!"

In astonishment he turned to her. She was as pale as her stepdaughter.

"Jake! If she *has* got religion, you'll have awful bad luck if you try to get her away from it!"

"I ain't sayin' she can't get *religion* if she wants! To be sure, I brung her up to be a Christian. But I don't hold to this here nonsense of turnin' plain, and I tole her so, and she's got to obey to me or I'll learn her!"

"You'll have bad luck if you whip her fur somepin like this here," his wife repeated. "Don't you mind how when Aunty Em turned plain and gran'pop he acted to her so ugly that way, it didn't rain fur two weeks and his crops was spoilt, and he got that boil yet on his neck? Yes, you'll see oncet," she warned him, "if you use the strap fur somepin like what this is, what you'll mebbe come by yet!"

"Och, you're foolish!" he answered, but his tone was not confident. His raised arm dropped to his side and he looked uneasily into Tillie's face, while he still kept his painful grasp of her shoulder.

The soft bright eyes of the young girl met his, not with defiance, but with a light in them that somehow brought before his mind the look her mother had worn the night she died. Superstition was in his blood, and he shuddered inwardly at his uncanny sense of mystery before this unfamiliar, illumined countenance of his daughter. The exalted soul of the girl cast a spell which even *his* unsensitive spirit could keenly feel, and something stirred in his breast—the latent sense of affectionate, protecting fatherhood.

Tillie saw and felt this sudden change in him. She lifted her free hand and laid it on his arm, her lips quivering. "Father!" she half whispered.

She had never called him that before, and it seemed strangely to bring home to him what, in this crisis of his child's life, was due to her from him, her only living parent.

Suddenly he released her shoulder and tossed away the strap. "I see I wouldn't be doin' right to oppose you in this here, Tillie. Well, I'm glad, fur all, that I ain't whippin' you. It goes ag'in' me to hit you since you was sick that time. You're gettin' full big, too, to be punished that there way, fur all I always sayed still I'd never leave a child of mine get ahead of me, no matter how big they was, so long as they lived off of me. But this here's different. You're feelin' conscientious about this here matter, and I ain't hinderin' you."

To Tillie's unspeakable amazement, he laid his hand on her head and held it there for an instant. "Gawd bless you, my daughter, and help you to serve the Lord acceptable!"

So that crisis was past.

But Tillie knew, that night, as she rubbed witch hazel on her sore shoulder, that a far worse struggle was before her. In seeking to carry out the determination that burned in her heart to get an education, no aid could come to her as it had today, from her father's sense of religious awe. Would she be able, she wondered, to stand firm against his opposition when, a second time, it came to an issue between them?

*"'Gawd bless you, my daughter, and help
you to serve the Lord acceptable!'"*

→ CHAPTER TWELVE ←

ABSALOM KEEPS COMPANY

TILLIE WROTE TO MISS MARGARET (SHE COULD NOT learn to call her Mrs. Lansing) how that she had "given herself up and turned plain," and Miss Margaret, seeing how sacred this experience was to the young girl, treated the subject with all respect and even reverence.

The correspondence between these two, together with the books which from time to time came to the girl from her faithful friend, did more toward Tillie's growth and development along lines of which her parents had no suspicion, than all the schooling at William Penn, under the instruction of the average "Millersville Normal," could ever have accomplished.

And her tongue, though still very provincial, soon lost much of its native dialect, through her constant reading and study.

Of course whenever her father discovered her with her books he made her suffer.

"You're got education enough a'ready," he would insist. "And too much fur your own good. Look at

116

me—I was only *educated* with a Testament and a spelling book and a slate. We had no such a blackboards even, to recite on. And do *I* look as if I need to know any more'n what I know a'ready?"

Tillie bore her punishments like a martyr—and continued surreptitiously to read and to study whenever and whatever she could; and not even the extreme conscientiousness of a New Mennonite faltered at this filial disobedience. She obeyed her father implicitly, however tyrannical he was, to the point where he bade her suppress and kill all the best that God had given her of mind and heart. Then she revolted; and she never for an instant doubted her entire justification in eluding or defying his authority.

There was another influence besides her books and Miss Margaret's letters which, unconsciously to herself, was educating Tillie at this time. Her growing fondness for stealing off to the woods not far from the farm, of climbing to the hilltop beyond the creek, or walking over the fields under the wide sky—not only in the spring and summer, but at all times of the year—was yielding her a richness, a depth and breadth, of experience that nothing else could have given her.

A nature deeply sensitive to the mysterious appeal of sky and green earth, of deep, shady forest and glistening water, when unfolding in daily touch with these things, will learn to see life with a broader, saner mind and catch glimpses and vistas of truth with a clearer vision than can ever come to one whose most susceptible years are spent walled in and over-topped by the houses of the city that shut out and stifle "the larger thought of God." And Tillie, in spite of her narrowing New Mennonite "convictions," did reach through her growing love for and intimacy with Nature a plane of thought and feeling which was immeasurably above her perfunctory creed.

Sometimes the emotions excited by her solitary walks gave the young girl greater pain than happiness—yet it was a pain she would not have been spared, for she knew, though the knowledge was never formulated in her thought, that in some precious, intimate way her suffering set her apart and above the villagers and farm-ing people about her—those whose placid, contented eyes never strayed from the potato-patch to the distant hills, or lifted themselves from the goodly tobacco fields to the wide blue heavens.

Thus, cramped and crushing as much of her life was, it had—as all conditions must have—its compensations; and many of the very circumstances which at the time seemed most unbearable brought forth in later years rich fruit.

And so, living under her father's watchful eye and relentless rule—with long days of drudgery and out-ward acquiescence in his scheme of life that she devote herself, mind, body, and soul, to the service of himself, his wife, and their children, and in return to be poorly fed and scantily clad—Tillie nevertheless grew up in a world apart, hidden to the sealed vision of those about her; as unknown to them in her real life as though they had never looked upon her face; and while her father never for an instant doubted the girl's entire submission to him, she was day by day waxing stronger in her resolve to heed Miss Margaret's constant advice and make a fight for her right to the education her father had denied her, and for a life other than that to which his will would consign her.

There were dark times when her steadfast purpose seemed impossible of fulfilment. But Tillie felt she would rather die in the struggle than become the sort of apathetic household drudge she beheld in her stepmother—a condition into which it would be so easy to sink, once she loosed her wagon from its star.

It was when Tillie was seventeen years old—a slight, frail girl, with a look in her eyes as of one who lives in two worlds—that Absalom Puntz, one Sunday evening in the fall of the year, saw her safe home from meeting and asked permission to "keep comp'ny" with her.

Now that morning Tillie had received a letter from Miss Margaret (sent to her, as always, under cover to the doctor), and Absalom's company on the way from church was a most unwelcome interruption to her happy brooding over the precious messages of love and helpfulness which those letters always brought her.

A request for permission to "keep comp'ny" with a young lady meant a very definite thing in Canaan Township. "Let's try each other," was what it signified; and acceptance of the proposition involved on each side an exclusion of all association with others of the opposite sex. Tillie of course understood this.

"But you're of the World's people, Absalom," her soft, sweet voice answered him. They were walking along in the dim evening on the high dusty pike toward the Getz farm. "And I'm a member of meeting. I can't marry out of the meeting."

"This long time a'ready, Tillie, I was thinkin' about givin' myself up and turnin' plain," he assured her. "To be sure, I know I'd have to, to git you. You've took notice, ain't you, how reg'lar I 'tend meeting? Well, oncet me and you kin settle this here question of gittin' married, I'm turnin' plain as soon as I otherwise [possibly] kin."

"I have never thought about keeping company, Absalom."

"Nearly all the girls around here as old as you has their friend a'ready."

Absalom was twenty years old, stoutly built and coarse-featured, a deeply ingrained obstinacy being the only characteristic his heavy countenance suggested. He still attended the district school for a few months of the winter term. His father was one of the richest farmers of the neighborhood, and Absalom, being his only child, was considered a matrimonial prize.

"Is there nobody left for you but me?" Tillie inquired in a matter-of-fact tone. The conjugal relation, as she saw it in her father's home and in the neighborhood, with its entirely practical basis and utter absence of sentiment, had no attraction or interest for her, and she had long since made up her mind that she would none of it.

"There ain't much choice," granted Absalom. "But I anyways would pick out you, Tillie."

"Why me?"

"I dunno. I take to you. And I seen a'ready how handy you was at the work still. Mom says, too, you'd make me a good housekeeper."

Tillie never dreamed of resenting this practical approval of her qualifications for the post with which Absalom designed to honor her. It was because of her familiarity with such matrimonial standards as these that from her childhood up she had determined never to marry. From what she gathered of Miss Margaret's married life, through her letters, and from what she learned from the books and magazines which she read, she knew that out in the great unknown world there existed another basis of marriage. But she did not understand it and she never thought about it. The strongly emotional tide of her girlhood, up to this time, had been absorbed by her remarkable love for Miss Margaret and by her earnest religiousness.

"There's no use in your wasting your time keeping company with me, Absalom. I never intend to marry. I've made up my mind."

"Is it that your pop won't leave you, or whatever?"

"I never asked him. I don't know what he would say."

"Mom spoke somepin about mebbe your pop he'd want to keep you at home, you bein' so useful to him and your mom. But I sayed when you come eighteen, you're your own boss. Ain't, Tillie?"

"Father probably would object to my marrying because I'm needed at home," Tillie agreed. "That's why they wouldn't leave me go to school after I was eleven. But I don't want to marry."

"You leave me be your steady friend, Tillie, and I'll soon get you over them views," urged Absalom, confidently.

But Tillie shook her head. "It would just waste your time, Absalom."

In Canaan Township it would have been considered highly dishonorable for a girl to allow a young man to "sit up with her Sundays" if she definitely knew she would never marry him. Time meant money, and even the time spent in courting must be judiciously used.

"I don't mind if I do waste my time settin' up with you Sundays, Tillie. I take to you that much, it's something surprising, now! Will you give me the dare to come next Sunday?"

"If you don't mind wasting your time—" Tillie reluctantly granted.

"It won't be wasted. I'll soon get you to think different to what you think now. You just leave me set up with you a couple Sundays and see!"

"I know I'll never think any different, Absalom. You must not suppose that I will."

"Is it somepin you're got ag'in' me?" he asked incredulously, for he knew he was considered a prize. "I'm well-fixed enough, ain't I? I'd make you a good purvider, Tillie. And I don't addict to no bad habits. I don't chew. Nor I don't drink. Nor I don't swear any. The most I ever sayed when I was spited was 'confound it.'"

"It isn't that I have anything against you, Absalom, especially. But—look here, Absalom, if you were a woman, would *you* marry? What does a woman gain?"

Absalom stared at her in the dusky evening light of the high road. To ask of his slow-moving brain that it question the foundations of the universe and wrestle with a social and psychological problem like this made the poor youth dumb with bewilderment.

"Why *should* a woman get married?" Tillie repeated.

"That's what a woman's *fur,*" Absalom found his tongue to say.

"She loses everything and gains nothing."

"She gets kep'," Absalom argued.

"Like the horses. Only not so carefully. No, thank you, Absalom. I can keep myself."

"I'd keep you better'n your pop keeps you, anyways, Tillie. I'd make you a good purvider."

"I won't ever marry," Tillie repeated.

"I didn't know you was so funny," Absalom sullenly answered. "You might be glad I want to be your reg'lar friend."

"No," said Tillie, "I don't care about it."

They walked on in silence for a few minutes. Tillie looked away into the starlit night and thought of Miss Margaret and wished she were alone, that her thoughts might be uninterrupted. Absalom, at her side, kicked up the dust with his heavy shoes, as he sulkily hung his head.

Presently he spoke again.

"Will you leave me come to see you Sundays, still, if I take my chancet that I'm wastin' my time?"

"If you'll leave it that way," Tillie acquiesced, "and not hold me to anything."

"All right. Only you won't leave no one else set up with you, ain't not?"

"There isn't anyone else."

"But some chance time another feller might turn up oncet that wants to keep comp'ny with you too."

"I won't promise anything, Absalom. If you want to come Sundays to see me and the folks, you can. That's all I'll say."

"I never seen such a funny girl as what you are!" growled Absalom.

Tillie made no reply, and again they went on in silence.

"Say!" It was Absalom who finally spoke.

Tillie's absent, dreamy gaze came down from the stars and rested upon his heavy, dull face.

"Ezra Herr he's resigned William Penn. He's gettin' more pay at Abra'm Lincoln in Janewille. It comes unhandy, his leavin', now the term's just started and most all the applicants took a'ready. Pop he got a letter from in there at Lancaster off of Superintendent Reingruber and he's sendin' us a applicant out till next Saturday three weeks—fur the directors to see oncet if he'll do."

Absalom's father was secretary of the Board, and Mr. Getz was the treasurer.

"Pop he's goin' over to see your pop about it till tomorrow evenin' a'ready if he can make it suit."

"When does Ezra go?" Tillie inquired. The New Mennonite rule which forbade the use of all titles had led to the custom in this neighborhood, so populated with Mennonites, of calling each one by his Christian name.

"Till next Friday three weeks," Absalom replied. "Pop says he don't know what to think about this here man Superintendent Reingruber's sendin' out. He ain't no Millersville Normal. The superintendent says he's a 'Harvard gradyate'—whatever that is, pop says! Pop he sayed it ain't familiar with him what that there is. And I guess the other directors don't know neither. Pop he sayed when we're payin' as much as forty dollars a month we had ought, now, to have a Millersville Normal, and nothin' less. Who wants to pay forty dollars a month fur such a Harvard gradyate that we don't know right what it is."

"What pay will Ezra get at Janeville?" Tillie asked. Her heart beat fast as she thought how *she* might, perhaps, in another year be the applicant for a vacancy at William Penn.

"Around forty-five dollars," Absalom answered.

"Oh!" Tillie said; "it seems so much, don't it?"

"Fur settin' and doin' nothin' but hearin' off spellin' and readin' and whatever, it's too much! Pop says he's goin' to ast your pop and the rest of the Board if they hadn't ought to ast this here Harvard gradyate to take a couple dollars less, seein' he ain't no Millersville Normal."

They had by this time reached the farm, and Tillie, not very warmly, asked Absalom whether he would "come in and sit awhile." She almost sighed audibly as he eagerly consented.

When he had left at twelve o'clock that night, she softly climbed the stairs to her room, careful not to disturb the sleeping household. Tillie wondered why it was that every girl of her acquaintance exulted in being asked to keep company with a gentleman friend. She had found "sitting up" a more fatiguing task than even the dreaded Monday's washing which would confront her on the morrow.

"Seein' it's the first time me and you set up together, I mebbe better not stay just so late," Absalom had explained when, after three hours' courting, he had reluctantly risen to take his leave, under the firm conviction, as Tillie plainly saw, that she felt as sorry to have him go as evidently he was to part from her!

"How late," thought Tillie, "will he stay the *second* time he sits up with me? And what," she wondered, "do other girls see in it?"

The following Sunday night, Absalom came again, and this time he stayed until one o'clock, with the result that on the following Monday morning Tillie overslept herself and was one hour late in starting the washing.

It was that evening, after supper, while Mrs. Getz was helping her husband make his toilet for a meeting of the School Board—at which the application of that suspicious character, the Harvard graduate, was to be considered—that the husband and wife discussed these significant Sunday night visits. Mrs. Getz opened up the subject while she performed the wifely office of washing her husband's neck, his increasing bulk making that duty a rather difficult one for him. Standing over him as he sat in a chair in the kitchen, holding on his knees a tin basin full of soapy water, she scrubbed his fat, sunburned neck with all the vigor and enthusiasm that she would have applied to the cleaning of the kitchen porch or the scouring of an iron skillet.

A custom prevailed in the county of leaving one's parlor plainly furnished, or entirely empty, until the eldest daughter should come of age; it was then fitted up in style, as a place to which she and her "regular friend" could retire from the eyes of the girl's folks of a Sunday night to do their "setting up." The occasion of a girl's "furnishing" was a notable one, usually celebrated by a party; and it was this fact that led her stepmother to remark presently:

"Say, pop, are you furnishin' fur Tillie, now she's comin' eighteen years old?"

"I ain't thought about it," Mr. Getz answered shortly. "That front room's furnished good enough a'ready. No—I ain't spendin' any!"

"Seein' she's a member and wears plain, it wouldn't cost wery expensive to furnish fur her, fur she hasn't the dare to have nothin' stylish like a organ or gilt-framed landscapes or sich stuffed furniture that way."

"The room's good enough the way it is," repeated Mr. Getz. "I don't see no use spendin' on it."

"She scrubbed his fat, sunburned neck"

"It needs new paper and carpet. Pop, it'll get put out if you don't furnish fur her. The neighbors'll talk how you're so close with your own child after she worked fur you so good still. I don't like it so well, pop, havin' the neighbors talk."

"Leave 'em talk. Their talkin' don't cost *me* nothin'. I *ain't* furnishin'!" His tone was obstinate and angry.

His wife rubbed him down with a crash towel as vigorously as she had washed him, then fastened his shirt, dipped the family comb in the soapy water and began with artistic care to part and comb his hair.

"Absalom Puntz he's a nice party, pop. He'll be well-fixed till his pop's passed away a'ready."

"You think! Well, now look here, mom!" Mr. Getz spoke with stern decision. "Tillie ain't got the dare to keep comp'ny Sundays! It made her a whole hour late with the washin' this mornin'. I'm tellin' her she's got to tell Absalom Puntz he can't come no more."

Mrs. Getz paused with comb poised in air, and her feeble jaw dropped in astonishment.

"Why, pop!" she said. "Ain't you leavin' Tillie keep comp'ny?"

"No," affirmed Mr. Getz. "I ain't. What does a body go to the bother of raisin' childern *fur?* Just to lose 'em as soon as they are growed enough to help earn a little? I ain't *leavin'* Tillie get married! She's stayin' at home to help her pop and mom—except in winter when they ain't so much work, and mebbe then I'm hirin' her out to Aunty Em at the *hotel* where she can earn a little, too, to help along. She can easy earn enough to buy the childern's winter clo'es and gums and schoolbooks."

"When she comes eighteen, pop, she'll have the right to get married whether or no you'd conceited you wouldn't give her the dare."

"If I say I ain't buyin' her her aus styer, Absalom Puntz nor no other feller would take her."

An "aus styer" is the household outfit always given to a bride by her father.

"Well, to be sure," granted Mrs. Getz, "I'd like keepin' Tillie home to help me out with the work still. I didn't see how I was ever goin' to get through without her. But I thought when Absalom Puntz begin to come Sundays, certainly you'd be fur her havin' him. I was sayin' to her only this mornin' that if she didn't want to dishearten Absalom from comin' to set up with her, she'd have to take more notice to him and not act so dopplig with him—like as if she didn't care whether or no he made up to her. I tole her I'd think, now, she'd be wonderful pleased at his wantin' her, and him so well-fixed. Certainly I never conceited you'd be ag'in' it. Tillie she didn't answer nothin'. Sometimes I do now think Tillie's some different to what other girls is."

"I'd be glad," said Jacob Getz in a milder tone, "if she ain't set on havin' him. I was some oneasy she might take it a little hard when I tole her she darsent get married."

"Och, Tillie she never takes nothin' hard," Mrs. Getz answered easily. "She ain't never ast me was you goin' to furnish fur her. She don't take no interest.

She's so funny that way. I think to myself, still, Tillie is, now, a little dumm!"

It happened that while this dialogue was taking place, Tillie was in the room above the kitchen, putting the two most recently arrived Getz babies to bed; and as she sat near the open register with a baby on her lap, every word that passed between her father and step-mother was perfectly audible to her.

With growing bitterness she listened to her father's frank avowal of his selfish designs. At the same time she felt a thrill of exultation, as she thought of the cherished secret locked in her breast—hidden the more securely from those with whom she seemed to live nearest. How amazed they would be, her stolid, unsuspicious parents, when they discovered that she had been secretly study-ing and, with Miss Margaret's help, preparing herself for the high calling of a teacher! One more year, now, and she would be ready, Miss Margaret assured her, to take the county superintendent's examination for a cer-tificate to teach. Then good-by to household drudgery and the perpetual self-sacrifice that robbed her of all that was worthwhile in life.

With a serene mind, Tillie rose, with the youngest baby in her arms, and tenderly tucked it in its little bed.

CHAPTER THIRTEEN

Ezra Herr, Pedagogue

It was a few days later, at the supper table, that Tillie's father made an announcement for which she was not wholly unprepared.

"I'm hirin' you out this winter, Tillie, at the *hotel*. Aunty Em says she's leavin' both the girls go to school again this winter and she'll need hired help. She'll pay me two dollars a week fur you. She'll pay it to me and I'll buy you what you need, still, out of it. You're goin' till next Monday."

Tillie's heart leaped high with pleasure at this news. She was fond of her Aunty Em; she knew that life at the country hotel would be varied and interesting in comparison with the dull, grubbing existence of her own home; she would have to work very hard, of course, but not so hard, so unceasingly, as under her father's eye; and she would have absolute freedom to devote her spare time to her books. The thought of escaping from her father's watchfulness, and the prospect of hours of safe and uninterrupted study, filled her with secret joy.

"I tole Aunty Em she's not to leave you waste no time readin'; when she don't need you, you're to come home and help mom still. Mom she says she can't get through the winter sewin' without you. Well, Aunty Em she says you can sew evenin's over there at the *hotel*, on the childern's clo'es. Mom she can easy get through the other work without you, now Sallie's goin' on thirteen. Till December a'ready Sally'll be thirteen. And the winter work's easy to what the summer is. In summer, to be sure, you'll have to come home and help me and mom. But in winter I'm hirin' you out."

"But Sally ain't as handy as what Tillie is," said Mrs. Getz, plaintively. "And I don't see how I'm goin' to get through oncet without Tillie."

"Sally's got to *learn* to be handier, that's all. She's got to get learnt like what I always learnt Tillie fur you."

Fire flashed in Tillie's soft eyes—a momentary flame of shame and aversion; if her blinded father had seen and understood, he would have realized how little, after all, he had ever succeeded in "learning" her the subservience he demanded of his children.

As for the warning to her aunt, she knew that it would be ignored; that Aunty Em would never interfere with the use she made of the free time allowed her, no matter what her father's orders were to the contrary.

"And you ain't to have Absalom Puntz comin' over there Sundays neither," her father added. "I tole Aunty Em like I tole you the other day, I ain't leavin' you keep comp'ny. I raised you, now you have the right to work and help along a little. It's little enough a girl can earn anyways."

Tillie made no comment. Her silence was of course understood by her father to mean submission; while her stepmother felt in her heart a contempt for a meekness that would bear, without a word of protest, the loss of a steady friend so well-fixed and so altogether desirable as Absalom Puntz.

In Absalom's two visits Tillie had been sufficiently impressed with the steadiness of purpose and obstinacy of the young man's character to feel appalled at the fearful task of resisting his dogged determination to marry her. So confident he evidently was of ultimately winning her that at times Tillie found herself quite sharing his confidence in the success of his courting, which her father's interdict she knew would not interfere with in the least. She always shuddered at the thought of being Absalom's wife; and a feeling she could not always fling off, as of some impending doom, at times buried all the high hopes which for the past seven years had been the very breath of her life.

Tillie had one especially strong reason for rejoicing in the prospect of going to the village for the winter. The Harvard graduate, if elected, would no doubt board at the hotel, or necessarily near by, and she could get him to lend her books and perhaps to give her some help with her studies.

The village of New Canaan and all the township were curious to see this stranger. The school directors had felt that they were conceding a good deal in consenting to consider the application of such an unknown quantity, when they could, at forty dollars a month, easily secure the services of a Millersville Normal. But the stress that had been brought to bear upon them by the county superintendent, whose son had been a classmate of the candidate, had been rather too strong to be resisted; and so the "Harvard gradyate man" was coming.

That afternoon Tillie had walked over in a pouring rain to William Penn to carry "gums" and umbrellas to her four younger brothers and sisters, and she had realized, with deep exultation, while listening to Ezra Herr's teaching, that she was already far better equipped than was Ezra to do the work he was doing—and *he* was a Millersville Normal!

It happened that Ezra was receiving a visit from a committee of Janeville school directors, and he had departed from his everyday mechanical style of teaching in favor of some fancy methods which he had imbibed at the Normal School during his attendance at the spring term, and which he reserved for use on occasions like the present. Tillie watched him with profound attention, but hardly with profound respect.

"Childern," Ezra said, with a look of deep thought, as he impressively paced up and down before the class of small boys and girls ranged on the platform, "now, childern, what's this reading lesson *about?*"

"'Bout a apple tree!" answered several eager little voices.

"Yes," said Ezra. "About an apple tree. Correct. Now, childern—er—what grows on apple trees, heh?"

"Apples!" answered the intelligent class.

"Correct. Apples. And—now—what was it that came to the apple tree?"

"A little bird."

"Yes. A bird came to the apple tree. Well—er," he floundered for a moment, then, by a sudden inspiration, "what can a bird do?"

"Fly! And sing!"

"A bird can fly and sing," Ezra nodded. "Very good. Now, Sadie, you dare begin. I'll leave each one read a werse."

The next recitation was a Fourth Reader lesson consisting of a speech of Daniel Webster's, the import of which not one of the children, if indeed the teacher himself, had the faintest suspicion. And so the class was permitted to proceed, without interruption, in its labored conning of the massive eloquence of that great statesman; and the directors presently took their departure in the firm conviction that in Ezra Herr they had made a good investment of the forty-five dollars a month appropriated to their town out of the State treasury, and they agreed, on their way back to Janeville, that New Canaan was to be pitied for having to put up with anything so unheard-of as "a Harvard gradyate or whatever," after having had the advantages of an educator like Ezra Herr.

And Tillie, as she walked home with her four brothers and sisters, hoped, for the sake of her own advancement, that a Harvard graduate was at least not *less* intelligent than a Millersville Normal.

CHAPTER FOURTEEN

THE HARVARD GRADUATE

THAT A MAN HOLDING A HARVARD DEGREE SHOULD consider so humble an educational post as that of New Canaan needs a word of explanation.

Walter Fairchilds was the protégé of his uncle, the High Church bishop of a New England State, who had practically, though not legally, adopted him, upon the death of his father, when the boy was fourteen years old, his mother having died at his birth.

It was tacitly understood by Walter that his uncle was educating him for the priesthood. His life, from the time the bishop took charge of him until he was ready for college, was spent in Church boarding schools.

A spiritually minded, thoughtful boy, of an emotional temperament which responded to every appeal of beauty, whether of form, color, sound, or ethics, Walter easily fell in with his uncle's designs for him, and rivaled him in the fervor of his devotion to the esthetic ritual of his Church.

His summer vacations were spent at Bar Harbor with the bishop's family, which consisted of his wife and two anemic daughters. They were people of limited interests, who built up barriers about their lives on all sides; social hedges which excluded all humanity but a select and very dull, uninteresting circle; intellectual walls which never admitted a stray unconventional idea; moral demarcations which nourished within them the Mammon of self-righteousness, and theological barriers which shut out the sunlight of a broad charity.

Therefore, when in the course of his career at Harvard, Walter Fairchilds discovered that intellectually he had outgrown not only the social creed of the divine right of the well-born, in which these people had educated him, but their theological creed as well, the necessity of breaking the fact to them, of wounding their affection for him, of disappointing the fond and cherished hope with which for years his uncle had spent money upon his education—the ordeal which he had to face was a fiery one.

When, in deepest sorrow, and with all the delicacy of his sensitive nature, he told the bishop of his changed mental attitude toward the problem of religion, it seemed to him that in his uncle's reception of it the spirit of the Spanish Inquisitors was revived, so mad appeared to him his horror of this heresy and his conviction that he, Walter, was a poison in the moral atmosphere, which must be exterminated at any cost.

In this interview between them, the bishop stood revealed to him in a new character, and yet Walter seemed to realize that in his deeper consciousness he had always known him for what he really was, though all the circumstances of his conventional life had conduced to hide his real self. He saw, now, how the submissiveness of his own dreamy boyhood had never called into active force his guardian's native love of domineering; his intolerance of opposition; the pride of his exacting will. But on the first provocation of circumstances, these traits stood boldly forth.

"Is it for this that I have spent my time and money upon you—to bring up an *infidel?*" Bishop Fairchilds demanded, when he had in part recovered from the first shock of amazement the news had given him.

"I am not an infidel even if I have outgrown High Church dogmas. I have a Faith—I have a Religion; and I assure you that I never so fully realized the vital truth of my religion as I do now—now that I see things, not in the dim cathedral light, but out under the broad heavens!"

"How can you dare to question the authority of our Holy Mother, the Church, whose teachings have come down to us through all these centuries, bearing the sacred sanction of the most ancient authority?"

"Old things can rot!" Walter answered.

"And you fancy," the bishop indignantly demanded, "that I will give one dollar for your support while you are adhering to this blasphemy? That I will ever again even so much as break bread with you, until, in humble contrition, you return to your allegiance to the Church?"

Walter lifted his earnest eyes and met squarely his uncle's frowning stare. Then the boy rose.

"Nothing, then, is left for me," he said steadily, "but to leave your home, give up the course of study I had hoped to continue at Harvard, and get to work."

"You fully realize all that this step must mean?" his uncle coldly asked him. "You are absolutely penniless."

"In a matter of this kind, uncle, you must realize that such a consideration could not possibly enter in."

"You have not a penny of your own. The few thousands that your father left were long ago used up in your school bills."

"And I am much in your debt; I know it all."

"So you choose poverty and hardship for the sake of this perversity?"

"Others have suffered harder things for principle."

Thus they parted.

And thus it was, through the suddenness and unexpectedness of the loss of his home and livelihood, that Walter Fairchilds came to apply for the position at William Penn.

"HERE, Tillie, you take and go up to Sister Jennie Hershey's and get some mush. I'm makin' fried mush fur supper," said Aunty Em, bustling into the hotel kitchen where her niece was paring potatoes, one Saturday afternoon. "Here's a quarter. Get two pound."

"Oh, Tillie," called her cousin Rebecca from the adjoining dining room, which served also as the family sitting room, "hurry on and you'll mebbe be in time to see the stage come in with the new teacher in. Mebbe you'll see him to speak to yet up at Hershey's."

"Lizzie Hershey's that wonderful tickled that the teacher's going to board at their place!" said Amanda, the second daughter, a girl of Tillie's age, as she stood in the kitchen doorway and watched Tillie put on her black hood over the white Mennonite cap. Stout Aunty Em also wore the Mennonite dress, which lent a certain dignity to her round face with its alert but kindly eyes; but her two daughters were still "of the world's people."

"When Lizzie she tole me about it, comin' out from Lancaster after market this morning," continued Amanda, "she was now that tickled! She sayed he's such a good-looker! Och, I wisht he was stoppin' here; ain't, Tillie? Lizzie'll think herself much, havin' a town fellah stoppin' at their place."

"If he's stoppin' at Hershey's," said Rebecca, appearing suddenly, "that ain't sayin' he has to get in with Lizzie so wonderful thick! I hope he's a *jolly* fellah."

Amanda and Rebecca were now girls of seventeen and eighteen years—buxom, rosy, absolutely unideal country lasses. Beside them, frail little Tillie seemed a creature of another clay.

"Lizzie tole me: she sayed how he come up to their market-stall in there at Lancaster this morning," Amanda related, "and tole her he'd heard Jonas Hershey's pork-stall at market was where he could mebbe find out a place he could board at in New Canaan with a private family—he'd sooner live with a private family that way than at the *hotel*. Well, Lizzie she coaxed her pop right there in front of the teacher to say *they'd* take him, and Jonas Hershey he sayed *he* didn't care any. So Lizzie she tole him then he could come to their place, and he sayed he'd be out this after in the four-o'clock stage."

"Well, and I wonder what her mother has to say to her and Jonas fixin' it up between 'em to take a boarder and not waitin' to ast *her!*" Aunty Em said. "I guess mebbe Sister Jennie's spited!"

The appellation of "sister" indicated no other relation than that of the Mennonite church membership, Mrs. Jonas Hershey being also a New Mennonite.

"Now don't think you have to run all the way there and back, Tillie," was her aunt's parting injunction. "*I* don't time you like what your pop does! Well, I guess not! I take notice you're always out of breath when you come back from an urrand. It's early yet—you dare stop awhile and talk to Lizzie."

Tillie gave her aunt a look of grateful affection as she left the house. Often when she longed to thank her for her many little acts of kindness, the words would not come. It was the habit of her life to repress every emotion of her mind, whether of bitterness or pleasure, and an unconquerable shyness seized upon her in any least attempt to reveal herself to those who were good to her.

It was four o'clock on a beautiful October afternoon as she walked up the village street, and while she enjoyed, through all her sensitive maiden soul, the sweet sunshine and soft autumn coloring, her thought dwelt with a pleasant expectancy on her almost inevitable meeting with "the Teacher," if he did indeed arrive in the stage now due at New Canaan.

Unlike her cousins Amanda and Rebecca, and their neighbor Lizzie Hershey, Tillie's eagerness to meet the young man was not born of a feminine hunger for romance. Life as yet had not revealed those emotions to her except as she had known them in her love for Miss Margaret—which love was indeed full of a sacred sentiment. It was only because the teacher meant an aid to the realization of her ambition to become "educated" that she was interested in his coming.

It was but a few minutes' walk to the home of Jonas Hershey, the country pork butcher. As Tillie turned in at the gate, she heard, with a leap of her heart, the distant rumble of the approaching stage coach.

Jonas Hershey's home was probably the cleanest, neatest-looking red brick house in all the county. The boardwalk from the gate to the door fairly glistened from the effects of soap and water. The flowerbeds, almost painfully neat and free from weeds, were laid out on a strictly mathematical plan. A border of white-washed clamshells, laid side by side with military precision, set off the brilliant reds and yellows of the flowers, and a glance at them was like gazing into the face of the midday sun. Tillie shaded her dazzled eyes as she walked across the garden to the side door which opened into the kitchen. It stood open and she stepped in without ceremony. For a moment she could see nothing but red and yellow flowers and whitewashed clamshells. But as her vision cleared, she perceived her neighbor, Lizzie Hershey, a well-built, healthy-looking country lass of eighteen years, cutting bread at a table, and her mother, a large fat woman wearing the Mennonite dress, standing before a huge kitchen range, stirring "ponhaus" in a caldron.

The immaculate neatness of the large kitchen gave evidence, as did garden, boardwalk, and front porch, of that morbid passion for "cleaning up" characteristic of the Dutch housewife.

Jonas Hershey did a very large and lucrative business, and the work of his establishment was heavy. But he hired no "help" and his wife and daughter worked early and late to aid him in earning the dollars which he hoarded.

"Sister Jennie!" Tillie accosted Mrs. Hershey with the New Mennonite formal greeting, "I wish you the grace and peace of the Lord."

"The same to you, sister," Mrs. Hershey replied, bending to receive Tillie's kiss as the girl came up to her at the stove—the Mennonite interpretation of the command, "Salute the brethren with a holy kiss."

"Well, Lizzie," was Tillie's only greeting to the girl at the table. Lizzie was not a member of meeting and the rules forbade the members to kiss those who were still in the world.

"Well, Tillie," answered Lizzie, not looking up from the bread she was cutting.

Tillie instantly perceived a lack of cordiality. Something was wrong. Lizzie's face was sullen and her mother's countenance looked grim and determined. Tillie wondered whether their evident ill-humor were in any way connected with herself, or whether her Aunty Em's surmise were correct, and Sister Jennie was really "spited."

"I've come to get two pound of mush," she said, remembering her errand.

"It's all," Mrs. Hershey returned. "We solt every cake at market, and no more's made yet. It was all a'ready till market was only half over."

"Aunty Em'll be disappointed. She thought she'd make fried mush for supper," said Tillie.

"Have you strangers?" inquired Mrs. Hershey.

"No, we haven't anybody for supper, unless some come on the stage this after. We had four for dinner."

"Were they such agents, or what?" asked Lizzie.

Tillie turned to her. "Whether they were agents? No, they were just pleasure-seekers. They were out for a drive and stopped off to eat."

At this instant the rattling old stage coach drew up at the gate.

The mother and daughter, paying no heed whatever to the sound, went on with their work, Mrs. Hershey looking a shade more grimly determined as she stirred her ponhaus and Lizzie more sulky.

Tillie had just time to wonder whether she had better slip out before the stranger came in, when a knock on the open kitchen door checked her.

Neither mother nor daughter glanced up in answer to the knock. Mrs. Hershey resolutely kept her eyes on her caldron as she turned her big spoon about in it, and Lizzie, with sullen, averted face, industriously cut her loaf.

A second knock, followed by the appearance of a good-looking, well-dressed young man on the threshold, met with the same reception. Tillie, in the background, and hidden by the stove, looked on wonderingly.

The young man glanced, in evident mystification, at the woman by the stove and at the girl at the table, and a third time rapped loudly.

"Good afternoon!" he said pleasantly, an inquiring note in his voice.

Mrs. Hershey and Lizzie went on with their work as though they had not heard him.

He took a step into the room, removing his hat. "You were expecting me this afternoon, weren't you?" he asked.

"This is the place," Lizzie remarked at last.

"You were looking for me?" he repeated.

Mrs. Hershey suddenly turned upon Lizzie. "Why don't you speak?" she inquired half-tauntingly. "You spoke *before.*"

Tillie realized that Sister Jennie must be referring to Lizzie's readiness at market that morning to "speak," in making her agreement with the young man for board.

"You spoke this morning," the mother repeated. "Why can't you speak now?"

"Och, why don't you speak yourself?" retorted Lizzie. "It ain't fur *me* to speak!"

The stranger appeared to recognize that he was the subject of a domestic unpleasantness.

"You find it inconvenient to take me to board?" he hesitatingly inquired of Mrs. Hershey. "I shouldn't think of wishing to intrude. There is a hotel in the place, I suppose?"

"Yes. There *is* a *hotel* in New Canaan."

"I can get board there, no doubt?"

"Well," Mrs. Hershey replied argumentatively, "that's a public house and this ain't. We never made no practice of takin' boarders. To be sure, Jonas he always was *fur* boarders. But I *ain't* fur!"

"Oh, yes," gravely nodded the young man. "Yes. I see."

He picked up the dress-suit case which he had set on the sill. "Where is the hotel, may I ask?"

"Just up the road a piece. You can see the sign out," said Mrs. Hershey, while Lizzie banged the bread-box shut with an energy forcibly expressive of her feelings.

"Thank you," responded the gentleman, a pair of keen, bright eyes sweeping Lizzie's gloomy face.

He bowed, put his hat on his head and stepped out of the house.

There was a back door at the other side of the kitchen. Not stopping for the ceremony of leave-taking, Tillie slipped out of it to hurry home before the stranger should reach the hotel.

Her heart beat fast as she hurried across fields by a shortcut, and there was a sparkle of excitement in her eyes. Her ears were tingling with sounds to which they were unaccustomed, and which thrilled them exquisitely—the speech, accent, and tones of one who belonged to that world unknown to her except through books—out of which Miss Margaret had come and to which this new teacher, she at once recognized, belonged. Undoubtedly he was what was called, by magazine- and novel-writers, a "gentleman." And it was suddenly revealed to Tillie that in real life the phenomenon thus named was even more interesting than in literature. The clean cut of the young man's thin face, his pale forehead, the fineness of the white hand he had lifted to his hat, his modulated voice and speech, all these things had, in her few minutes' observation of him, impressed themselves instantly and deeply upon the girl's fresh imagination.

Out of breath from her hurried walk, she reached the back door of the hotel several minutes before the teacher's arrival. She had just time to report to her aunt that Sister Jennie's mush was "all," and to reply in the affirmative to the eager questions of Amanda and Rebecca as to whether she had seen the teacher, when the sound of the knocker on the front door arrested their further catechism.

"The stage didn't leave out whoever it is—it drove right apast," said Aunty Em. "You go, Tillie, and see oncet who is it."

Tillie was sure that she had not been seen by the evicted applicant for board, as she had been hidden behind the stove. This impression was confirmed when she now opened the door to him, for there was no recognition in his eyes as he lifted his hat. It was the first time in Tillie's life that a man had taken off his hat to her, and it almost palsied her tongue as she tried to ask him to come in.

In reply to his inquiry as to whether he could get board here, she led him into the darkened parlor at the right of a long hall. Groping her way across the floor to the window she drew up the blind.

"Just sit down," she said timidly. "I'll call Aunty Em."

"Thank you," he bowed with a little air of ceremony that for an instant held her spellbound. She stood staring at him—only recalled to herself and to a sense of shame for her rudeness by the sudden entrance of her aunt.

"How d' do?" said Mrs. Wackernagel in her brisk, businesslike tone. "D'you want supper?"

"I am the applicant for the New Canaan school. I want to get board for the winter here, if I can—and in case I'm elected."

"Well, I say! Tillie! D'you hear that? Why us we all heard you was goin' to Jonas Hershey's."

"They decided it wasn't convenient to take me and sent me here."

"Now think! If that wasn't like Sister Jennie yet! All right!" she announced conclusively. "We can accommodate you to satisfaction, I guess."

"Have you any other boarders?" the young man inquired.

"No reg'lar boarders—except, to be sure, the Doc; and he's lived with us it's comin' fifteen years, I think, or how long, till November a'ready. It's just our own fam'ly here and my niece where helps with the work, and the Doc. We have a many to meals though, just passing through that way, you know. We don't often have more'n one reg'lar boarder at oncet, so we just make 'em at home still, like as if they was one of us. Now *you*," she hospitably concluded, "we'll lay in our best bed. We don't lay 'em in the best bed unless they're some clean-lookin'."

Tillie noticed as her aunt talked that while the young man listened with evident interest, his eyes moved about the room, taking in every detail of it. To Tillie's mind, this hotel parlor was so "pleasing to the eye" as to constitute one of those Temptations of the Enemy against which her New Mennonite faith prescribed most rigid discipline. She wondered whether the stranger did not think it very handsome.

The arrangement of the room was evidently, like Jonas Hershey's flowerbeds, the work of a mathematical genius. The chairs all stood with their stiff backs squarely against the wall, the same number facing each other from the four sides of the apartment. Photographs in narrow oval frames, six or eight, formed another oval, all equidistant from the largest, which occupied the dead center, not only of this group, but of the wall from which it depended. The books on the square oak table, which stood in the exact middle of the floor, were arranged in cubical piles in the same rigid order. Tillie saw the new teacher's glance sweep their titles: *Touching Incidents, and Remarkable Answers to Prayer*; *From Tannery to White House*; *Gems of Religious*

Thought, by Talmage; *History of the Galveston Horror; Illustrated*; *Platform Echoes, or Living Truths for Heart and Head,* by John B. Gough.

"Lemme see—your name's Fairchilds, ain't?" the landlady abruptly asked.

"Yes," bowed the young man.

"Will you, now, take it all right if I call you by your Christian name? Us Mennonites daresent call folks Mr. and Mrs. because us we don't favor titles. What's your first name now?"

Mr. Fairchilds considered the question with the appearance of trying to remember. "You'd better call me Pestalozzi," he answered, with a look and tone of solemnity.

"Pesky Louzy!" Mrs. Wackernagel exclaimed. "Well, now think! That's a name where ain't familiar 'round here. Is it after some of your folks?"

"It was a name I think I bore in a previous incarnation as a teacher of youth," Fairchilds gravely replied.

Mrs. Wackernagel looked blank. "Tillie!" she appealed to her niece, who had shyly stepped half behind her, "do you know right what he means?"

Tillie dumbly shook her head.

"Pesky Louzy!" Mrs. Wackernagel experimented with the unfamiliar name. "Don't it, now, beat all! It'll take me awhile till I'm used to that a'ready. Mebbe I'll just call you Teacher; ain't?"

She looked at him inquiringly, expecting an answer. "Ain't?" she repeated in her vigorous, whole-souled way.

"Eh—ain't *what?*" Fairchilds asked, puzzled.

"Och, I just mean, *say not?* Can't you mebbe talk English wery good? We had such a foreigners at this *hotel* a'ready. We had oncet one, he was from Phil'delphy and he didn't know what we meant right when we sayed, 'The butter's all anymore.' He'd ast like you, 'All what?' Yes, he was that dumm! Och, well," she added consolingly, "people can't help fur their dispositions, that way!"

"And what must I call you?" the young man inquired.

"My name's Wackernagel."

"Miss or Mrs.?"

"Well, I guess not *Miss* anyhow! I'm the mother of four!"

"Oh, excuse me!"

"Oh, that's all right!" responded Mrs. Wackernagel, amiably. "Well, I must go make supper now. You just make yourself at home that way."

"May I go to my room?"

"Now?" asked Mrs. Wackernagel, incredulously. "Before night?"

"To unpack my dress-suit case," the young man explained. "My trunk will be brought out tomorrow on the stage."

"All right. If you want. But we ain't used to goin' upstairs in the daytime. Tillie, you take his satchel and show him up. This is my niece, Tillie Getz."

Again Mr. Fairchilds bowed to the girl as his eyes rested on the fair face looking out from her white cap. Tillie bent her head in response, then stooped to pick up the suit case. But he interposed and took it from her hands—and the touch of chivalry in the act went to her head like wine.

She led the way upstairs to the close, musty, best spare bedroom.

"He interposed and took it from her"

CHAPTER FIFTEEN

The Wackernagels at Home

At the supper table, the apparently inexhaustible topic of talk was the refusal of the Hersheys to receive the new teacher into the bosom of their family. A return to this theme again and again, on the part of the various members of the Wackernagel household, did not seem to lessen its interest for them, though the teacher himself did not take a very animated part in its discussion. Tillie realized, as with an absorbing interest she watched his fine face, that all he saw and heard here was as novel to him as the world whence he had come would be to her and her kindred and neighbors, could they be suddenly transplanted into it. Tillie had never looked upon any human countenance which seemed to express so much of that ideal world in which she lived her real life.

"To turn him off after he got there!" Mrs. Wackernagel exclaimed, reverting for the third time to the episode which had so excited the family. "And after Lizzie and Jonas they'd sayed he could come yet!"

"Well, I say!" Mr. Wackernagel shook his head, as though the story, even at its third recital, were full of surprises.

Mr. Wackernagel was a tall, raw-boned man with conspicuously large feet and hands. He wore his hair plastered back from his face in a unique, not to say distinguished style, which he privately considered highly becoming his position as the proprietor of the New Canaan Hotel. Mr. Wackernagel's self-satisfaction did indeed cover every detail of his life—from the elegant fashion of his hair to the quality of the whisky which he sold over the bar, and of which he never tired of boasting. Not only was he entirely pleased with himself, but his good-natured satisfaction included all his possessions—his horse first, then his wife, his two daughters, his permanent boarder, "the Doc," and his wife's niece Tillie. For people outside his own horizon, he had a tolerant but contemptuous pity.

Mr. Wackernagel and the doctor both sat at table in their shirt-sleeves, the proprietor wearing a clean white shirt (his extravagance and vanity in using two white shirts a week being one of the chief historical facts of the village), while the doctor was wont to appear in a brown cotton shirt, the appearance of which suggested the hostler rather than the physician.

That Fairchilds should "eat in his coat" placed him, in the eyes of the Wackernagels, on the high social plane of the drummers from the city, many of whom yearly visited the town with their wares.

"And Teacher he didn't press 'em none, up at Jonas Hershey's, to take him in, neither, he says," Mrs. Wackernagel pursued.

"He says?" repeated Mr. Wackernagel, inquiringly.

"Well, that's like what I was, too, when I was a young man," he boasted. "If I thought I ain't wanted when I went to see a young lady—if she passed any insinyations—she never wasn't worried with *me* ag'in!"

"I guess Lizzie's spited that Teacher's stoppin' at our place," giggled Rebecca, her pretty face rosy with pleasurable excitement in the turn affairs had taken. She sat directly opposite Mr. Fairchilds, while Amanda had the chair at his side.

Tillie could see that the young man's eyes rested occasionally upon the handsome, womanly form of her very good-looking cousin Amanda. Men always looked at Amanda a great deal, Tillie had often observed. The fact had never before had any special significance for her.

"Are you from Lancaster, or wherever?" the doctor inquired of Mr. Fairchilds.

"From Connecticut," he replied in a tone that indefinably, but unmistakably checked further questioning.

"Now think! So fur off as that!"

"Yes, ain't!" exclaimed Mrs. Wackernagel. "It's a wonder a body'd ever be contented to live that fur off."

"We're had strangers here in this *hotel*," Mr. Wackernagel began to brag, while he industriously ate of his fried sausage and fried potatoes, "from as fur away as Illinois yet! And from as fur south as down in Maine! Yes, indeed! Ain't, mom?" he demanded of his wife.

"Och, yes, many's the strange meals I cooked a'ready in this house. One week I cooked forty strange meals; say not, Abe?" she returned.

"Yes, I mind of that week. It was Mrs. Johnson and her daughter we had from Illinois and Mrs. Snyder from Maine," Abe explained to Mr. Fairchilds. "And them Johnsons stayed the whole week."

"They stopped here while Mr. Johnson went over the county sellin' milk-separators," added Mrs. Wackernagel. "And Abe he was in Lancaster that week, and the Doc he was over to East Donegal, and there was no man here except only us ladies! Do you mind, Rebecca?"

Rebecca nodded, her mouth too full for utterance.

"Mrs. Johnson she looked younger than her own daughter yet," Mrs. Wackernagel related, with animation, innocent of any suspicion that the teacher might not find the subject of Mrs. Johnson as absorbing as she found it.

"There is nothing like good health as a preserver of youth," responded Fairchilds.

"*Hotel*-keepin' didn't pay till we got the license," Mr. Wackernagel chatted confidentially to the stranger. "Mom, to be sure, she didn't favor my havin' a bar, because she belonged to meetin'. But I seen I couldn't make nothin' if I didn't. It was never no temptation to me—I was always among the whisky and I never got tight oncet. And it ain't the hard work farmin' was. I had to give up followin' farmin'. I got it so in my leg. Why, sometimes I can't hardly walk no more."

"And can't your doctor cure you?" Fairchilds asked, with a curious glance at the unkempt little man across the table.

"Och, yes, he's helped me a heap a'ready. Him he's as good a doctor as any they're got in Lancaster even!" was the loyal response. "Here a couple months back, a lady over in East Donegal Township she had wrote him a letter over here, how the five different kinds of doses where he give her daughter done her so much good, and she was that grateful, she sayed she just felt indebted fur a letter to him! Ain't, Doc? She sayed now her daughter's engaged to be married and her mind's more settled—and to be sure, that made somepin too. Yes, she sayed her gettin' engaged done her near as much good as the five different kind of doses done her."

"Are you an Allopath?" Fairchilds asked the doctor.

"I'm a Eclectic," he responded glibly. "And do you know, Teacher, I'd been practisin' that there style of medicine fur near twelve years before I knowed it was just to say the Eclectic School, you understand."

"Like Molière's prose-writer!" remarked the teacher, then smiled at himself for making such an allusion in such a place.

"Won't you have some more sliced radishes, Teacher?" urged the hostess. "I made a-plenty."

"No, I thank you," Fairchilds replied, with his little air of courtesy that so impressed the whole family. "I can't eat radishes in the evening with impunity."

"But these is with *winegar*," Mrs. Wackernagel corrected him.

Before Mr. Fairchilds could explain, Mr. Wackernagel broke in, confirming the doctor's proud claim.

"Yes, Doc he's a Eclectic," he repeated, evidently feeling that the fact reflected credit on the hotel. "You can see his sign on the side door."

"I was always *interested* in science," explained the doctor, under the manifest impression that he was continuing the subject. "Phe-non-e-ma. That's what I like. Odd things. I'm stuck on 'em! Now this here wireless *telegraphy*. I'm stuck on that, you bet! To me that there's a phe-non-e-ma."

"Teacher," interrupted Mrs. Wackernagel, "you ain't eatin' hearty. Leave me give you some more sausage."

"If you please," Mr. Fairchilds bowed as he handed his plate to her.

"Why don't you leave him help hisself," protested Mr. Wackernagel. "He won't feel to make hisself at home if he can't help hisself like as if he was one of us that way."

"Och, well," confessed Mrs. Wackernagel, "I just keep astin' him will he have more, so I can hear him speak his manners so nice." She laughed aloud at her own vanity. "You took notice of it too, Tillie, ain't? You can't eat fur lookin' at him!"

A tide of color swept Tillie's face as the teacher, with a look of amusement, turned his eyes toward her end of the table. Her glance fell upon her plate, and she applied herself to cutting up her untouched sausage.

"Now, there's Doc," remarked Amanda, critically, "he's *got* good manners, but he don't use 'em."

"Och," said the doctor, "it ain't worthwhile to trouble."

"I think it would be wonderful nice, Teacher," said Mrs. Wackernagel, "if you learnt them manners you got to your scholars this winter. I wisht 'Manda and Rebecca knowed such manners. *They're* to be your scholars this winter."

"Indeed?" said Fairchilds; "are they?"

"'Manda there," said her father, "she's so much fur actin' up you'll have to keep her right by you to keep her straight, still."

"That's where I shall be delighted to keep her," returned Fairchilds, gallantly, and Amanda laughed boisterously and grew several shades rosier as she looked boldly up into the young man's eyes.

"Ain't you fresh though!" she exclaimed coquettishly.

How dared they all make so free with this wonderful young man, marveled Tillie. Why didn't they realize, as she did, how far above them he was? She felt almost glad that in his little attentions to Amanda and Rebecca he had scarcely noticed her at all; for the bare thought of talking to him overwhelmed her with shyness.

"Mind Tillie!" laughed Mr. Wackernagel, suddenly, "lookin' scared at the way yous are all talkin' up to Teacher! Tillie she's afraid of you," he explained to Mr. Fairchilds. "She ain't never got her tongue with her when there's strangers. Ain't, Tillie?"

Tillie's burning face was bent over her plate, and she did not attempt to answer. Mr. Fairchilds' eyes rested for an instant on the delicate, sensitive countenance of the girl. But his attention was diverted by an abrupt exclamation from Mrs. Wackernagel.

"Oh, Abe!" she suddenly cried, "you ain't tole Teacher yet about the Albright sisters astin' you, on market, what might your name be!"

The tone in which this serious omission was mentioned indicated that it was an anecdote treasured among the family archives.

"Now, I would mebbe of forgot that!" almost in consternation said Mr. Wackernagel. "Well," he began, concentrating his attention upon the teacher, "it was this here way. The two Miss Albrights they had bought butter off of us, on market, for twenty years back a'ready, and all that time we didn't know what was their name, and they didn't know ourn; fur all, I often says to mom, 'Now I wonder what's the name of them two thin little women.' Well, you see, I was always a wonderful man fur my jokes. Yes, I was wery fond of makin' a joke, still. So here one day the two sisters come along and bought their butter, and then one of 'em she says, 'Excuse me, but here I've been buyin' butter off of yous fur this twenty years back a'ready and I ain't never heard your name. What might your name *be?*' Now I was such a man fur my jokes, still, so I says to her"—Mr. Wackernagel's whole face twinkled with amusement, and his shoulders shook with laughter as he contemplated the joke he had perpetrated—"I says, 'Well, it *might* be Gener'l Jackson'"—laughter again choked his utterance, and the stout form of Mrs. Wackernagel also was convulsed with amusement, while Amanda and Rebecca giggled appreciatively. Tillie and the doctor alone remained unaffected. "'It might be Gener'l Jackson,' I says. 'But it ain't. It's Abe Wackernagel,' I says. You see," he explained, "she ast me what *might* my name be. See? And I says 'It might be Jackson'—*might* be, you know, because she put it that way, what might it be. 'But it ain't,' I says. 'It's Wackernagel.'"

Mr. and Mrs. Wackernagel and their daughters leaned back in their chairs and gave themselves up to prolonged and exuberant laughter, in which the teacher obligingly joined as well as he was able.

When this hilarity had subsided, Mr. Wackernagel turned to Mr. Fairchilds with a question. "Are you mebbe feelin' oneasy, Teacher, about meetin' the school directors tonight? You know they meet here in the *hotel* parlor at seven o'clock to take a look at you; and if you suit, then you and them signs the agreement."

"And if I don't suit?"

"They'll turn you down and send you back home!" promptly answered the doctor. "That there Board ain't conferrin' William Penn on no one where don't suit 'em pretty good! They're a wonderful partic'lar Board!"

After supper the comely Amanda agreed eagerly to the teacher's suggestion that she go with him for a walk, before the convening of the School Board at seven o'clock, and show him the schoolhouse, as he would like to behold, he said, "the seat of learning" which, if the Board elected him, was to be the scene of his winter's campaign.

Amanda improved this opportunity to add her word of warning to that of the doctor.

"That there Board's awful hard to suit, still. Oncet they got a Millersville Normal out here, and when she come to sign they seen she was near-sighted that way, and Nathaniel Puntz—he's a director—he up and says that wouldn't suit just so well, and they sent her back home. And here oncet a lady come out to apply and she should have sayed [she is reported to have said] she was afraid New Canaan hadn't no accommodations good enough fur her, and the directors ast her, 'Didn't most of our Presidents come out of log cabins?' So they wouldn't elect her. Now," concluded Amanda, "you see!"

"Thanks for your warning. Can you give me some pointers?"

"What's them again?"

"Well, I must not be near-sighted, for one thing, and I must not demand 'all the modern improvements.' Tell me what manner of man this School Board loves and admires. To be in the dark as to their tastes, you know—"

"You must make yourself nice and common," Amanda instructed him. "You haven't dare to put on no city airs. To be sure, I guess they come a good bit natural to you, and, as mom says still, a body can't help fur their dispositions; but our directors is all plain that way and they don't like tony people that wants to come out here and think they're much!"

"Yes? I see. Anything else?"

"Well, they'll be partic'lar about your bein' a perfessor."

"How do you mean?"

Amanda looked at him in astonishment. "If you're a perfessor or no. They'll be sure to ast you."

Mr. Fairchilds thoughtfully considered it.

"You mean," he said, light coming to him, "they will ask me whether I am a professor of religion, don't you?"

"Why, to be sure!"

"Oh!"

"And you better have your answer ready."

"What, in your judgment, may I ask, would be a suitable answer to that?"

"Well, *are* you a perfessor?"

"Oh, I'm anything at all that will get me this 'job.' I've got to have it as a makeshift until I can get hold of something better. Let me see—will a Baptist do?"

"Are you a Baptist?" the girl stolidly asked.

"When circumstances are pressing. Will they be satisfied with a Baptist?"

"That's one of the fashionable churches of the world," Amanda replied gravely. "And the directors is most all Mennonites and Amish and Dunkards. All them is *plain* churches and loosed of the world, you know."

"Oh, well, I'll wriggle out somehow! Trust to luck!" Fairchilds dismissed the subject, realizing the injudiciousness of being too confidential with this girl on so short an acquaintance.

At the momentous hour of seven, the directors promptly assembled. When Tillie, at her aunt's request, carried two kerosene lamps into the parlor, a sudden determination came to the girl to remain and witness the reception of the new teacher by the School Board.

She was almost sick with apprehension lest the Board should realize, as she did, that this Harvard graduate was too fine for such as they. It was an austere Board, hard to satisfy, and there was nothing they would so quickly resent and reject as evident superiority in an applicant. The Normal School students, their usual candidates, were for the most part, though not always, what was called in the neighborhood "nice and common." The New Canaan Board was certainly not accustomed to sitting in judgment upon an applicant such as this Pestalozzi Fairchilds. (Tillie's religion forbade her to call him by the vain and worldly form of Mr.)

No one noticed the pale-faced girl as, after placing one lamp on the marble-topped table about which the directors sat and another on the mantelpiece, she moved quietly away to the farthest corner of the long, narrow parlor and seated herself back of the stove.

The applicant, too, when he came into the room, was too much taken up with what he realized to be the perils of his case to observe the little watcher in the corner, though he walked past her so close that his coat brushed her shoulder, sending along her nerves, like a faint electric shock, a sensation so novel and so exquisite that it made her suddenly close her eyes to steady her throbbing head.

There were present six members of the Board—two Amishmen, one Old Mennonite, one patriarchal-looking Dunkard, one New Mennonite, and one Evangelical, the difference in their religious creeds being attested by their various costumes and the various cuts of beard and hair. The Evangelical, the New Mennonite, and the Amishmen were farmers, the Dunkard kept the store and the post office, and the Old Mennonite was the stage-driver. Jacob Getz was the Evangelical; and Nathaniel Puntz, Absalom's father, the New Mennonite.

The investigation of the applicant was opened up by the president of the Board, a long-haired Amishman, whose clothes were fastened by hooks and eyes instead of buttons and buttonholes, these latter being considered by his sect as a worldly vanity.

"What was your experience a'ready as a teacher?"

Fairchilds replied that he had never had any.

Tillie's heart sank as, from her post in the corner, she heard this answer. Would the members think for one moment of paying forty dollars a month to a teacher without experience? She was sure they had never before done so. They were shaking their heads gravely over it, she could see.

But the investigation proceeded.

"What was your Persuasion then?"

Tillie saw, in the teacher's hesitation, that he did not understand the question.

"My 'Persuasion?' Oh! I see. You mean my Church?"

"Yes, what's your conwictions?"

He considered a moment. Tillie hung breathlessly upon his answer. She knew how much depended upon it with this Board of "plain" people. Could he assure them that he was "a Bible Christian?" Otherwise, they would never elect him to the New Canaan school.

He gave his reply, presently, in a tone suggesting his having at that moment recalled to memory just what his "Persuasion" was. "Let me see—yes—I'm a Truth-Seeker."

"What's that again?" inquired the president, with interest. "I have not heard yet of that Persuasion."

"A Truth-Seeker," he gravely explained, "is one who believes in—eh—in a progress from an indefinite, incoherent homogeneity to a definite, coherent heterogeneity."

The members looked at each other cautiously.

"Is that the English you're speakin', or whatever?" asked the Dunkard member. "Some of them words ain't familiar with me till now, and I don't know right what they mean."

"Yes, I'm talking English," nodded the applicant. "We also believe," he added, growing bolder, "in the fundamental, biogenetic law that ontogenesis is an abridged repetition of philogenesis."

"He says they believe in Genesis," remarked the Old Mennonite, appealing for aid, with bewildered eyes, to the other members.

"Maybe he's a Jew yet!" put in Nathaniel Puntz.

"We also believe," Mr. Fairchilds continued, beginning to enjoy himself, "in the revelations of science."

"He believes in Genesis and in Revelations," explained the president to the others.

"Maybe he's a Cat'lic!" suggested the suspicious Mr. Puntz.

"No," said Fairchilds, "I am, as I said, a Truth-Seeker. A Truth-Seeker can no more be a Catholic or a Jew in faith than an Amishman can, or a Mennonite, or a Brennivinarian."

Tillie knew he was trying to say "Winebrennarian," the name of one of the many religious sects of the county, and she wondered at his not knowing better.

"You ain't a gradyate, neither, are you?" was the president's next question, the inscrutable mystery of the applicant's creed being for the moment dropped.

"Why, yes, I thought you knew that. Of Harvard."

"Och, that!" contemptuously; "I mean you ain't a gradyate of Millersville Normal?"

"No," humbly acknowledged Fairchilds.

"When I was young," Mr. Getz irrelevantly remarked, "we didn't have no gradyate teachers like what they have now, still. But we anyhow learnt more *according.*"

"How long does it take you to get 'em from a, b, c's to the Testament?" inquired the patriarchal Dunkard.

"That depends upon the capacity of the pupil," was Mr. Fairchilds' profound reply.

"Can you learn 'em 'rithmetic good?" asked Nathaniel Puntz. "I got a son his last teacher couldn't learn 'rithmetic to. He's wonderful dumm in 'rithmetic, that there boy is. Absalom by name. After the grandfather. His teacher tried every way to learn him to count and figger good. He even took and spread toothpicks out yet—but that didn't learn him neither. I just says, he ain't *appointed* to learn 'rithmetic. Then the teacher he tried him with such a Algebry. But Absalom he'd get so mixed up! He couldn't keep them x's spotted."

"I have a method," Mr. Fairchilds began, "which I trust—"

To Tillie's distress, her aunt's voice, at this instant calling her to "come stir the sots [yeast] in," summoned her to the kitchen.

It was very hard to have to obey. She longed so to stay till Fairchilds should come safely through his fiery ordeal. For a moment she was tempted to ignore the summons, but her conscience, no less than her grateful affection for her aunt, made such behavior impossible. Softly she stole out of the room and noiselessly closed the door behind her.

A half-hour later, when her aunt and cousins had gone to bed, and while the august School Board still occupied the parlor, Tillie sat sewing in the sitting room, while the doctor, at the other side of the table, nodded over his newspaper.

Since Tillie had come to live at the hotel, she and the doctor were often together in the evening; the Doc was fond of a chat over his pipe with the child whom he so helped and befriended in her secret struggles to educate herself. There was, of course, a strong bond of sympathy and friendship between them in their common conspiracy with Miss Margaret, whom the doctor had never ceased to hold in tender memory.

Just now Tillie's ears were strained to catch the sounds of the adjourning of the Board. When at last she heard their shuffling footsteps in the hall, her heart beat fast with suspense. A moment more and the door leading from the parlor opened and Fairchilds came out into the sitting room.

Tillie did not lift her eyes from her sewing, but the room seemed suddenly filled with his presence.

"Well!" the doctor roused himself to greet the young man; "were you 'lected?"

Breathlessly, Tillie waited to hear his answer.

"Oh, yes; I've escaped alive!" Fairchilds leaned against the table in an attitude of utter relaxation. "They roasted me brown, though! Galileo at Rome, and Martin Luther at Worms, had a dead easy time compared to what I've been through!"

"I guess!" the doctor laughed. "Ain't!"

"I'm going to bed," the teacher announced in a tone of collapse. "Good night!"

"*Good* night!" answered the doctor, cordially.

Fairchilds drew himself up from the table and took a step toward the stairway; this brought him to Tillie's side of the table, and he paused a moment and looked down upon her as she sewed.

Her fingers trembled, and the pulse in her throat beat suffocatingly; but she did not look up.

"Good night, Miss—Tillie, isn't it?"

"Matilda Maria," Tillie's soft, shy voice replied as her eyes, full of light, were raised, for an instant, to the face above her.

The man smiled and bowed his acknowledgment; then, after an instant's hesitation, he said, "Pardon me: the uniform you and Mrs. Wackernagel wear—may I ask what it is?"

"'Uniform?'" breathed Tillie, wonderingly. "Oh, you mean the garb? We are members of meeting. The world calls us New Mennonites."

"And this is the uni—the garb of the New Mennonites?"

"Yes, sir."

"It is a very becoming garb, certainly," Fairchilds smiled, gazing down upon the fair young girl with a puzzled look in his own face, for he recognized, not only in her delicate features, and in the light of her beautiful eyes, but also in her speech, a something that set her apart from the rest of this household.

Tillie colored deeply at his words, and the doctor laughed outright.

"By gum! They wear the garb to make 'em look *unbecomin'*! And he ups and tells her it's becomin' yet! That's a choke, Teacher! One on you, ain't? That there cap's to hide the hair which is a pride to the sek! And that cape over the bust is to hide woman's allurin' figger. See? And you ups and tells her it's a becomin' *unyform!* Unyforms is what New Mennonites don't uphold to! Them's fur Cat'lics and 'Piscopals—and fur warriors— and the Mennonites don't favor war! Unyforms yet!" he laughed. "I'm swanged if that don't tickle me!"

"I stand corrected. I beg pardon if I've offended," Fairchilds said hastily. "Miss—Matilda—I hope I've not hurt your feelings? Believe me, I did not mean to."

"Och!" the doctor answered for her, "Tillie she ain't so easy hurt to her feelin's, are you, Tillie? Gosh, Teacher, them manners you got must keep you busy! Well, sometimes I think I'm better off if I stay common. Then I don't have to bother."

The door leading from the barroom opened suddenly and Jacob Getz stood on the threshold.

"Well, Tillie," he said by way of greeting. "Uncle Abe sayed you wasn't went to bed yet, so I stopped to see you a minute."

"Well, father," Tillie answered as she put down her sewing and came up to him.

Awkwardly he bent to kiss her, and Tillie, even in her emotional excitement, realized, with a passing wonder, that he appeared glad to see her after a week of separation.

"It's been some lonesome, havin' you away," he told her.

"Is everybody well?" she asked.

"Yes, middlin'. You was sewin', was you?" he inquired, glancing at the work on the table.

"Yes, sir."

"All right. Don't waste your time. Next Saturday I'll stop off after market on my way out from Lancaster and see you oncet, and get your wages off of Aunty Em."

"Yes, sir."

A vague idea of something unusual in the light of Tillie's eyes arrested him. He glanced suspiciously at the doctor, who was speaking in a low tone to the teacher.

"Look-ahere, Tillie. If Teacher there wants to keep comp'ny with one of yous girls, it ain't to be you, mind. He ain't to be makin' up to you! I don't want you to waste your time that there way."

Apprehensively, Tillie darted a sidelong glance at the teacher to see if he had heard—for though no tender sentiment was associated in her mind with the idea of "keeping company," yet intuitively she felt the unseemliness of her father's warning and its absurdity in the eyes of such as this stranger.

Mr. Fairchilds was leaning against the table, his arms folded, his lips compressed and his face flushed. She was sure that he had overheard her father. Was he angry, or—almost worse—did that compressed mouth mean concealed amusement?

"Well, now, I must be goin'," said Mr. Getz. "Be a good girl, mind. Och, I 'most forgot to tell you. Me and your mom's conceited we'd drive up to Puntz's Sunday afternoon after the dinner work's through a'ready. And if Aunty Em don't want you partic'lar, you're to come home and mind the childern, do you hear?"

"Yes, sir."

"Now, don't forget. Well, good-by, then."

Again he bent to kiss her, and Tillie felt Fairchilds' eyes upon her, as unresponsively she submitted to the caress.

"Good night to you, Teacher." Mr. Getz gruffly raised his voice to speak to the pair by the table. "And to you, Doc."

They answered him and he went away. When Tillie slowly turned back to the table, the teacher hastily took his leave and moved away to the stairway at the other end of the room. As she took up her sewing, she heard him mount the steps and presently close and lock the door of his room at the head of the stairs.

"He was, now, wonderful surprised, Tillie," the doctor confided to her, "when I tole him Jake Getz was your pop. He don't think your pop takes after you any. I says to him, 'Tillie's pop, there, bein' one of your bosses, you better make up to Tillie,' I says, and he sayed, 'You don't mean to tell me that that Mr. Getz of the School Board is the father of this girl?' 'That's what,' I says. 'He's that much her father,' I says, 'that you'd better keep on the right side of him by makin' up to Tillie,' I says, just to plague him. And just then your pop up and sayed if Teacher wanted to keep comp'ny he must pick out 'Manda or Rebecca—and I seen Teacher wanted to laugh, but his manners wouldn't leave him. He certainly has, now, a lot of manners, ain't, Tillie?"

Tillie's head was bent over her sewing and she did not answer.

The doctor yawned, stretched himself, and guessed he would step into the barroom.

Tillie bent over her sewing for a long time after she was left alone. The music of the young man's grave voice as he had spoken her name and called her "Miss

Matilda" sang in her brain. The fascination of his smile as he had looked down into her eyes, and the charm of his chivalrous courtesy, so novel to her experience, haunted and intoxicated her. And tonight, Tillie felt her soul flooded with a life and light so new and strange that she trembled as before a miracle.

Meanwhile, Walter Fairchilds, alone in his room, his mind too full of the events and characters to which the past day had introduced him to admit of sleep, was picturing, with mingled amusement and regret, the genuine horror of his fastidious relatives could they know of his present environment, among people for whom their vocabulary had but one word—a word which would have consigned them all, even that sweet-voiced, clear-eyed little Puritan, Matilda Maria, to outer darkness; and that he, their adopted son and brother, should be breaking bread and living on a footing of perfect equality with these villagers he knew would have been, in their eyes, an offense only second in heinousness to that of his apostasy.

CHAPTER SIXTEEN

THE WACKERNAGELS "CONWERSE"

THE NEXT DAY, BEING THE SABBATH, BROUGHT TO Tillie two of the keenest temptations she had ever known. In the first place, she did not want to obey her father and go home after dinner to take care of the children. All in a day the hotel had become to her the one haven where she would be, outside of which the sun did not shine.

True, by going home she might hope to escape the objectionable Sunday evening sitting-up with Absalom; for in spite of the note she had sent him, telling him of her father's wish that he must not come to see her at the hotel, she was unhappily sure that he would appear as usual. Indeed, with his characteristic dogged persistency, he was pretty certain to follow her, whithersoever she went. And even if he did not, it would be easier to endure the slow torture of his endless visit under this roof, which sheltered also that other presence, than to lose one hour away from its wonderful and mysterious charm.

"Now, look here, Tillie," said Aunty Em, at the breakfast table, "you worked hard this week, and this after

you're restin'—leastways, unless you *want* to go home
and take care of all them litter of childern. If you don't
want to go, you just stay—and *I'll* take the blame! I'll say
I needed you."

"Let Jake Getz come 'round *here* tryin' to bully you,
Tillie," exclaimed Mr. Wackernagel, "and it won't take
me a week to tell him what I think of *him!* I don't owe
him nothin'!"

"No," agreed Jake Getz's sister, "we don't live off
of him!"

"And I don't care who fetches him neither!" added
Mr. Wackernagel—which expression of contempt
was one of the most scathing known to the tongue of
a Pennsylvania Dutchman.

"What are you goin' to do, Tillie?" Amanda asked.
"Are you goin' or stayin'?"

Tillie wavered a moment between duty and inclination; between the habit of servility to her father and the
magic power that held her in its fascinating spell here
under her uncle's roof.

"I'm staying," she faltered.

"Good fur you, Tillie!" laughed her uncle. "You're
gettin' learnt here to take your own head a little fur
things. Well, I'd like to get you spoilt good fur your
pop—that's what I'd like to do!"

"We darsent go too fur," warned Aunty Em, "or he
won't leave her stay with us at all."

"Now there's you, Abe," remarked the doctor, dryly;
"from the time your childern could walk and talk a'ready
all you had to say was 'Go'—and they stayed. Ain't?"

Mr. Wackernagel joined in the loud laughter of his wife and daughters.

Tillie realized that the teacher, as he sipped his coffee, was listening to the dialogue with astonishment and curiosity, and she hungered to know all that was passing through his mind.

Her second temptation came to her upon hearing Fairchilds, as they rose from the breakfast table, suggest a walk in the woods with Amanda and Rebecca.

"And won't Miss Tillie go too?" he inquired.

Her aunt answered for her. "Och, she wouldn't have dare, her bein' a member, you know. It would be breakin' the Sabbath. And anyways, even if it wasn't Sunday, us New Mennonites don't take walks or do anything just fur pleasure when they ain't nothin' useful in it. If Tillie went, I'd have to report her to the meetin', even if it did go ag'in' me to do it."

"And then what would happen?" Mr. Fairchilds inquired curiously.

"She'd be set back."

"'Set back?'"

"She wouldn't have dare to greet the sisters with a kiss, and she couldn't speak with me or eat with me or any of the brothers and sisters till she gave herself up ag'in and obeyed to the rules."

"This is very interesting," commented Fairchilds, his contemplative gaze moving from the face of Mrs. Wackernagel to Tillie. "But," he questioned, "Mrs. Wackernagel, why are your daughters allowed to do what you think wrong and would not do?"

"Well," began Aunty Em, entering with relish into the discussion, for she was strong in theology, "we don't hold to forcin' our childern or interferin' with the free work of the Holy Spirit in bringin' souls to the truth. We don't do like them fashionable churches of the world where teaches their childern to say their prayers and makes 'em read the Bible and go to Sunday school. We don't uphold to Sunday schools. You can't read nothin' in the Scripture about Sunday schools. We hold everybody must come by their free will, and learnt only of the Holy Spirit, into the light of the One True Way."

Fairchilds gravely thanked her for her explanation and pursued the subject no further.

When Tillie presently saw him start out with her cousins, an unregenerate longing filled her soul to stay away from meeting and go with them, to spend this holy Sabbath day in worshiping, not her God, but this most god-like being who had come like the opening up of heaven into her simple, uneventful life. In her struggle with her conscience to crush such sinful desires, Tillie felt that now, for the first time, she understood how Jacob of old had wrestled with the Angel.

Her spiritual struggle was not ended by her going dutifully to meeting with her aunt. During all the long services of the morning she fought with her wandering attention to keep it upon the sacred words that were spoken and sung. But her thoughts would not be controlled. Straying like a wicked imp into forbidden paths, her fancy followed the envied ones into the soft, cool shadows of the autumn woods and along the banks of the beautiful Conestoga, and mingling with the gentle murmuring of the leaves and the rippling of the water, she heard that resonant voice, so unlike any voice she had ever heard before, and that little abrupt laugh with its odd falsetto note, which haunted her like a strain of music; and she saw, in the sunlight of the lovely October morning, against a background of gold and brown leaves and silver water, the finely chiseled face, the thoughtful, pale forehead, the kind eyes, the capable white hands, of this most wonderful young man.

Tillie well understood that could the brethren and sisters know in what a worldly frame of mind she sat in the house of God this day, undoubtedly they would present her case for "discipline," and even, perhaps, "set her back." But all the while that she tried to fight back the enemy of her soul, who thus subtly beset her with temptation to sin, she felt the utter uselessness of her struggle with herself. For even when she did succeed in forcing her attention upon some of the hymns, it was in whimsical and persistent terms of the teacher that she considered them. How was it possible, she wondered, for him, or any unconverted soul, to hear, without being moved to "give himself up," such lines as these:

> He washed them all to make them clean,
> But Judas still was full of sin.
> May none of us, like Judas, sell
> Our Lord for gold, and go to hell!

And these:

> O man, remember, thou must die;
> The sentence is for you and I.
> Where shall we be, or will we go,
> When we must leave this world below?

In the same moment that Tillie was wondering how a "Truth-Seeker" would feel under these searching words, she felt herself condemned by them for her wandering attention.

The young girl's feelings toward the stranger at this present stage of their evolution were not, like those of Amanda and Rebecca, the mere instinctive feminine craving for masculine admiration. She did not think of herself in relation to him at all. A great hunger possessed her to know him—all his thoughts, his emotions, the depths and the heights of him; she did not long, or even wish, that he might know and admire *her*.

The three-mile drive home from church seemed to Tillie, sitting in the high, old-fashioned buggy at her aunt's side, an endless journey. Never had old Dolly traveled so deliberately or with more frequent dead stops in the road to meditate upon her long-past youth. Mrs. Wackernagel's ineffectual slaps of the reins upon the back of the decrepit animal inspired in Tillie an inhuman longing to seize the whip and lash the feeble beast into a swift pace. The girl felt appalled at her own feelings, so novel and inexplicable they seemed to her. Whether there was more of ecstasy, or torture in them, she hardly knew.

Immediately after dinner the teacher went out and did not turn up again until evening, when he retired immediately to the seclusion of his own room.

The mystification of the family at this unaccountably unsocial behavior, their curiosity as to where he had been, their suspense as to what he did when alone so long in his bedroom, reached a tension that was painful.

Promptly at half-past six, Absalom, clad in his Sunday suit, appeared at the hotel, to perform his weekly stint of sitting-up.

As Rebecca always occupied the parlor on Sunday evening with her gentleman friend, there was only left to Absalom and Tillie to sit either in the kitchen or with the assembled family in the sitting room. Tillie preferred the latter. Of course she knew that such respite as the presence of the family gave her was only temporary, for in friendly consideration of what were supposed to be her feelings in the matter, they would all retire early. Absalom also knowing this, accepted the brief inconvenience of their presence without any marked restiveness.

"Say, Absalom," inquired the doctor, as the young man took up his post on the settee beside Tillie, sitting as close to her as he could without pushing her off, "how did your pop pass his opinion about the new teacher after the Board meeting Saturday, heh?"

The doctor was lounging in his own special chair by the table, his fat legs crossed and his thumbs thrust into his vest arms. Amanda idly rocked back and forth in a large luridly painted rocking chair by the window, and Mrs. Wackernagel sat by the table before an open Bible in which she was not too much absorbed to join occasionally in the general conversation.

"He sayed he was afraid he was some tony," answered Absalom. "And," he added, a reflection in his tone of his father's suspicious attitude on Saturday night toward Fairchilds, "pop sayed *he* couldn't make out what was his conwictions. He couldn't even tell right was he a Bible Christian or no."

"He certainly does, now, have pecooliar views," agreed the doctor. "I was talkin' to him this after—"

"You *was!*" exclaimed Amanda, a note of chagrin in her voice. "Well, I'd like to know where at? Where had he took himself to?"

"Up to the woods there by the old mill. I come on him there at five o'clock—layin' readin' and musin'— when I was takin' a short cut home through the woods comin' from Adam Oberholzer's."

"Well I never!" cried Amanda. "And was he out there all by hisself the whole afternoon?" she asked incredulously.

"So much as I know. *Ain't* he, now, a queer feller not to want a girl along when one was so handy?" teased the doctor.

"Well," retorted Amanda, "I think he's hard up—to be spendin' a whole afternoon *readin'!*"

"Oh, Doc!" Tillie leaned forward and whispered, "he's up in his room and perhaps he can hear us through the register!"

"I wisht he *kin,*" declared Amanda, "if it would learn him how dumm us folks thinks a feller where spends a whole Sunday afternoon by hisself *readin'!*"

"Why, yes," put in Mrs. Wackernagel; "what would a body be wantin' to waste time like that fur? When he could of spent his nice afternoon settin' there on the porch with us all, conwersin'."

"And he's at it ag'in this evenin', up there in his room," the doctor informed them. "I went up to give him my lamp, and I'm swanged if he ain't got a many books and such pamp'lets in his room! As many as ten, I guess! I tole him: I says, 'It does, now, beat all the way you take to them books and pamp'lets and things!'"

"It's a pity of him!" said motherly Mrs. Wackernagel.

"And I says to him," added the doctor, "I says, 'You ain't much fur sociability, are you?' I says."

"Well, I did think, too, Amanda," sympathized her mother, "he'd set up with you mebbe tonight, seein' Rebecca and Tillie's each got their gent'man comp'ny— even if he didn't mean it fur really, but only to pass the time."

"Och, he needn't think I'm dyin' to set up with *him!* There's a plenty others would be glad to set up with me, if I was one of them that was fur keepin' comp'ny with just *anybody!* But I did think when I heard he was goin' to stop here that mebbe he'd be a *jolly* feller that way. Well," Amanda concluded scathingly, "I'm goin' to tell Lizzie Hershey she ain't missin' much!"

"What's them pecooliar views of hisn you was goin' to speak to us, Doc?" said Absalom.

"Och, yes, I was goin' to tell you them. Well, here this after we got to talkin' about the subject of prayer, and I ast him his opinion. And if I understood right what he meant, why, prayin' is no different to him than musin'. Leastways, that's the thought I got out of his words."

"Musin'," repeated Absalom. "What's musin'?"

"Yes, what's that ag'in?" asked Mrs. Wackernagel alert with curiosity, theological discussions being always of deep interest to her.

"Musin' is settin' by yourself and thinkin' of your learnin'," explained the doctor. "I've took notice, this long time back, *educated* persons they like to set by theirselves, still, and muse."

"And do you say," demanded Absalom, indignantly, "that Teacher he says it's the same to him as prayin'— this here musin'?"

"So much as I know, that's what he sayed."

"Well," declared Absalom, "that there ain't in the Bible! He'd better watch out! If he ain't a Bible Christian, pop and Jake Getz and the other directors'll soon put him off William Penn!"

"Och, Absalom, go sass your gran'mom!" was the doctor's elegant retort. "What's ailin' *you,* anyways, that you want to be so spunky about Teacher? I guess you're mebbe thinkin' he'll cut you out with Tillie, ain't?"

"I'd like to see him try it oncet!" growled Absalom.

Tillie grew cold with fear that the teacher might hear them; but she knew there was no use in protesting.

"Are you goin' to keep on at William Penn all winter, Absalom?" Mrs. Wackernagel asked.

"Just long enough to see if he kin learn 'rithmetic to me. Ezra Herr, he was too dumm to learn me."

"Mebbe," said the doctor, astutely, "you was too dumm to *get* learnt!"

"I *am* wonderful dumm in 'rithmetic," Absalom acknowledged shamelessly. "But pop says this here teacher is smart and kin mebbe learn me. I've not saw him yet myself."

Much as Tillie disliked being alone with her suitor, she was rather relieved this evening when the family, *en masse,* significantly took its departure to the second floor; for she hoped that with no one but Absalom to deal with, she could induce him to lower his voice so their talk would not be audible to the teacher in the room above.

Had she been able but faintly to guess what was to ensue on her being left alone with him, she would have fled upstairs with the rest of the family and left Absalom to keep company with the chairs.

CHAPTER SEVENTEEN

THE TEACHER MEETS ABSALOM

ONLY A SHORT TIME HAD THE SITTING ROOM BEEN abandoned to them when Tillie was forced to put a check upon her lover's ardor.

"Now, Absalom," she firmly said, moving away from his encircling arm, "unless you leave me be, I'm not sitting on the settee alongside you at all. You *must not* kiss me or hold my hand—or even touch me. Never again. I told you so last Sunday night."

"But why?" Absalom asked, genuinely puzzled. "Is it that I kreistle you, Tillie?"

"N—no," she hesitated. An affirmative reply, she knew, would be regarded as a cold-blooded insult. In fact, Tillie herself did not understand her own repugnance to Absalom's caresses.

"You act like as if I made you feel repulsive to me, Tillie," he complained.

"N—no. I don't want to be touched. That's all."

"Well, I'd like to know what fun you think there is in settin' up with a girl that won't leave a feller kiss her or hug her!"

"'Unless you leave me be, I'm not sitting on the settee alongside you at all'"

"I'm sure I don't know what you do see in it, Absalom. I told you not to come."

"If I ain't to hold your hand or kiss you, what are we to do to pass the time?" he reasoned.

"I'll tell you, Absalom. Let me read to you. Then we wouldn't be wasting the evening."

"I ain't much fur readin'. I ain't like Teacher." He frowned and looked at her darkly. "I've took notice how much fur books you are that way. Last Sunday night, too, you sayed, 'Let me read somepin to you.' Mebbe you and Teacher will be settin' up readin' together. And mebbe the Doc wasn't just jokin' when he sayed Teacher might cut me out!"

"Please, Absalom," Tillie implored him, "don't talk so loud!"

"I don't care! I hope he hears me sayin' that if he ever comes tryin' to get my girl off me, I'll get pop to have him put off his job!"

"None of you know what you are talking about," Tillie indignantly whispered. "You can't understand. The teacher is a man that wouldn't any more keep company with one of us country girls than you would keep company, Absalom, with a gipsy. He's *above* us!"

"Well, I guess if you're good enough fur me, Tillie Getz, you're good enough fur anybody else—leastways fur a man that gets his job off the wotes of your pop and mine!"

"The teacher is a—a gentleman, Absalom."

Absalom did not understand. "Well, I guess I know he ain't a *lady*. I guess I know what his sek is!"

Tillie sighed in despair, and sank back on the settee. For a few minutes they sat in strained silence.

"I never seen a girl like what you are! You're wonderful different to the other girls I've knew a'ready."

Tillie did not reply.

"Where d'you come by them books you read?"

"The Doc gets them for me."

"Well, Tillie, look-ahere. I spoke somepin to the Doc how I wanted to fetch you somepin along when I come over sometime, and I ast him what, now, he thought you would mebbe like. And he sayed a book. So I got Cousin Sally Puntz to fetch one along fur me from the Methodist Sunday school li-bry, and here I brung it over to you."

He produced a small volume from his coat pocket.

"I was 'most ashamed to bring it, it's so wonderful little. I tole Cousin Sally, 'Why didn't you bring me a bigger book?' And she sayed she did try to get a bigger one, but they was all. There's one in that li-bry with four hunderd pages. I tole her, now, she's to try to get me that there one next Sunday before it's took by somebody. This one's 'most too little."

Tillie smiled as she took it from him. "Thank you, Absalom. I don't care if it's *little*, so long as it's interesting—and instructive," she spoke primly.

"The Bible's such a big book, I thought the bigger the book was, the nearer it was like the Bible," said Absalom.

"But there's the dictionary, Absalom. It's as big as the Bible."

"Don't the size make nothin'?" Absalom asked.

Tillie shook her head, still smiling. She glanced down and read aloud the title of the book she held: *What a Young Husband Ought to Know.*

"But, Absalom!" she faltered.

"Well? What?"

She looked up into his heavy, blank face, and suddenly a faint sense of humor seemed born in her—and she laughed.

The laugh illumined her face, and it was too much for Absalom. He seized her and kissed her, with resounding emphasis, squarely on the mouth.

Instantly Tillie wrenched herself away from him and stood up. Her face was flushed and her eyes sparkled. And yet, she was not indignant with him in the sense that a less unsophisticated girl would have been. Absalom, according to New Canaan standards, was not exceeding his rights under the circumstances. But an instinct, subtle, undefined, incomprehensible to herself, contradicted, indeed, by every convention of the neighborhood in which she had been reared, made Tillie feel that in yielding her lips to this man for whom she did not care, and whom, if she could hold out against him, she did not intend to marry, she was desecrating her womanhood. Vague and obscure as her feeling was, it was strong enough to control her.

"I meant what I said, Absalom. If you won't leave me be, I won't stay here with you. You'll have to go home, for now I'm going right upstairs."

She spoke with a firmness that made the dull youth suddenly realize a thing of which he had never dreamed, that however slightly Tillie resembled her father in other respects, she did have a bit of his determination.

She took a step toward the stairs, but Absalom seized her skirts and pulled her back. "You needn't think I'm leavin' you act like that to me, Tillie!" he muttered, his ardor whetted by the difficulties of his courting. "Now I'll learn you!" and holding her slight form in his burly grasp he kissed her again and again.

"Leave me go!" she cried. "I'll call out if you don't! Stop it, Absalom!"

Absalom laughed aloud, his eyes glittering as he felt her womanly helplessness in his strong clasp.

"What you goin' to do about it, Tillie? You can't help yourself—you got to get kissed if you want to or no!" And again his articulate caresses sounded upon her shrinking lips, and he roared with laughter in his own satisfaction and in his enjoyment of her predicament. "You can't help yourself," he said, crushing her against him in a bearish hug.

"Absalom!" the girl's voice rang out sharply in pain and fear.

Then of a sudden Absalom's wrists were seized in a strong grip, and the young giant found his arms pinned behind him.

"Now, then, Absalom, you let this little girl alone. Do you understand?" said Fairchilds, coolly, as he let go his hold on the youth and stepped round to his side.

Absalom's face turned white with fury as he realized who had dared to interfere. He opened his lips, but speech would not come to him. Clenching his fingers, he drew back his arm, but his heavy fist, coming swiftly forward, was caught easily in Fairchilds' palm—and held there.

"Come, come," he said soothingly, "it isn't worthwhile to row, you know. And in the presence of the lady!"

"You mind to your *own* business!" spluttered Absalom, struggling to free his hand, and, to his own surprise, failing. Quickly he drew back his left fist and again tried to strike, only to find it too caught and held, with no apparent effort on the part of the teacher. Tillie, at first pale with fright at what had promised to be so unequal a contest in view of the teacher's slight frame and the brawny, muscular strength of Absalom, felt her pulses bound with a thrill of admiration for this cool, quiet force which could render the other's fury so helpless; while at the same time she felt sick with shame.

"Blame you!" cried Absalom, wildly. "Le' me be! It don't make nothin' to you if I kiss my girl! I don't owe *you* nothin'! You le' me be!"

"Certainly," returned Fairchilds, cheerfully. "Just stop annoying Miss Tillie, that's all I want."

He dropped the fellow's hands and deliberately drew out his handkerchief to wipe his own.

A third time Absalom made a furious dash at him, to find his two wrists caught in the vise-like grip of his antagonist.

"Tut, tut, Absalom, this is quite enough. Behave yourself, or I shall be obliged to hurt you."

"*You*—you white-faced, woman-faced mackerel! *You* think you kin hurt me! You—"

"Now then," Fairchilds again dropped Absalom's hands and picked up from the settee the book which the youth had presented to Tillie. "Here, Absalom, take your *What a Young Husband Ought to Know* and go home."

Something in the teacher's quiet, confident tone cowed Absalom completely—for the time being, at least. He was conquered. It was very bewildering. The man before him was not half his weight and was not in the least ruffled. How had he so easily "licked" him? Absalom, by reason of his stalwart physique and the fact that his father was a director, had, during most of his school life, found pleasing diversion in keeping the various teachers of William Penn cowed before him. He now saw his supremacy in that quarter at an end—physically speaking at least. There might be a moral point of attack.

"Look-ahere!" he blustered. "Do you know my pop's Nathaniel Puntz, the director?"

"You are a credit to him, Absalom. By the way, will you take a message to him from me? Tell him, please, that the lock on the schoolroom door is broken, and I'd be greatly obliged if he would send up a locksmith to mend it."

Absalom looked discouraged. A Harvard graduate was, manifestly, a freak of nature—invulnerable at all points.

"If pop gets down on you, you won't be long at William Penn!" he bullied. "You'll soon get chased off your job!"

"My job at breaking you in? Well, well, I might be spending my time more profitably, that's so."

"You go on out of here and le' me alone with my girl!" quavered Absalom, blinking away tears of rage.

"That will be as she says. How is it, Miss Tillie? Do you want him to go?"

Now Tillie knew that if she allowed Absalom Puntz to leave her in his present state of baffled anger, Fairchilds would not remain in New Canaan a month. Absalom was his father's only child, and Nathaniel Puntz was known to be both suspicious and vindictive. "Clothed in a little brief authority," as school director, he never missed an opportunity to wield his precious power.

With quick insight, Tillie realized that the teacher would think meanly of her if, after her outcry at Absalom's amorous behavior, she now inconsistently ask that he remain with her for the rest of the evening. But what the teacher might think about *her* did not matter so much as that he should be saved from the wrath of Absalom.

"Please leave him stay," she answered in a low voice.

Fairchilds gazed in surprise upon the girl's sweet, troubled face. "Let him stay?"

"Yes."

"Then perhaps my interference was unwelcome?"

"I thank you, but—I want him to stay."

"Yes? I beg pardon for my intrusion. Good night."

He turned away somewhat abruptly and left the room.
And Tillie was again alone with Absalom.

In his chamber, getting ready for bed, Fairchilds'
thoughts idly dwelt upon the strange contradictions he
seemed to see in the character of the little Mennonite
maiden. He had thought that he recognized in her a
difference from the rest of this household—a difference in speech, in feature, in countenance, in her
whole personality. And yet she could allow the amorous
attentions of that coarse, stupid cub; and her protestations against the fellow's liberties with her had been
mere coquetry. Well, he would be careful, another
time, how he played the part of a Don Quixote.

Meantime Tillie, with suddenly developed histri-
onic skill, was, by a Spartan self-sacrifice in submitting
to Absalom's lovemaking, overcoming his wrath against
the teacher. Absalom never suspected how he was
being played upon, or what a mere tool he was in the
hands of this gentle little girl, when, somewhat to his
own surprise, he found himself half promising that the
teacher should not be complained of to his father.
The infinite tact and scheming it required on Tillie's
part to elicit this assurance without further arousing
his jealousy left her, at the end of his prolonged sitting-
up, utterly exhausted.

Yet when at last her weary head found her pillow, it
was not to rest or sleep. A haunting, fearful certainty
possessed her. "Dumm" as he was, Absalom, in his
invulnerable persistency, had become to the tired,

tortured girl simply an irresistible force of Nature. And Tillie felt that, struggle as she might against him, there would come a day when she could fight no longer, and so at last she must fall a victim to this incarnation of Dutch determination.

CHAPTER EIGHTEEN

TILLIE REVEALS HERSELF

IN THE NEXT FEW DAYS, TILLIE TRIED IN VAIN TO summon courage to appeal to the teacher for assistance in her winter's study. Day after day she resolved to speak to him, and as often postponed it, unable to conquer her shyness. Meantime, however, under the stimulus of his constant presence, she applied herself in every spare moment to the schoolbooks used by her two cousins, and in this unaided work she succeeded, as usual, in making headway.

Fairchilds' attention was arrested by the frequent picture of the little Mennonite maiden conning schoolbooks by lamplight.

One evening he happened to be alone with her for a few minutes in the sitting room. It was Hallowe'en, and he was waiting for Amanda to come down from her room, where she was arraying herself for conquest at a party in the village, to which he had been invited to escort her.

"Studying all alone?" he inquired sociably, coming to the table where Tillie sat, and looking down upon her.

"Yes," said Tillie, raising her eyes for an instant.

"May I see?"

He bent to look at her book, pressing it open with his palm, and the movement brought his hand in contact with hers. Tillie felt for an instant as if she were going to swoon, so strangely delicious was the shock.

"*Hiawatha*," he, said, all unconscious of the tempest in the little soul apparently so close to him, yet in reality so immeasurably far away. "Do you enjoy it?" he inquired curiously.

"Oh, yes"; then quickly she added, "I am parsing it."

"Oh!" There was a faint disappointment in his tone.

"But," she confessed, "I read it all through the first day I began to parse it, and—and I wish I was parsing something else, because I keep reading this instead of parsing it, and—"

"You enjoy the story and the poetry?" he questioned.

"But a body mustn't read just for pleasure," she said timidly; "but for instruction; and this *Hiawatha* is a temptation to me."

"What makes you think you ought not to read 'just for pleasure'?"

"That would be a vanity. And we Mennonites are loosed from the things of the world."

"Do you never do anything just for the pleasure of it?"

"When pleasure and duty go hand in hand, then pleasure is not displeasing to God. But Christ, you

know, did not go about seeking pleasure. And we try to
follow him in all things."

"But, child, has not God made the world beautiful for
our pleasure? Has he not given us appetites and pas-
sions for our pleasure? Minds and hearts and bodies
constructed for pleasure?"

"Has he made anything for pleasure apart from use-
fulness?" Tillie asked earnestly, suddenly forgetting
her shyness.

"But when a thing gives pleasure it is serving the
highest possible use," he insisted. "It is blasphemous to
close your nature to the pleasures God has created for
you. Blasphemous!"

"Those thoughts have come to me still," said Tillie.
"But I know they were sent to me by the Enemy."

"'The Enemy'?"

"The Enemy of our souls."

"Oh!" he nodded; then abruptly added, "Now do
you know, little girl, I wouldn't let *him* bother me at
this stage of the game, if I were you! He's a back number, really!" He checked himself, remembering how
dangerous such heresies were in New Canaan. "Don't
you find it dull working alone?" he asked hastily, "and
rather uphill?"

"It is often very hard."

"Often? Then you have been doing it for some time?"

"Yes," Tillie answered hesitatingly. No one except
the doctor shared her secret with Miss Margaret. Self-
concealment had come to be the habit of her life—her
instinct for self-preservation. And yet, the teacher's

evident interest, his presence so close to her, brought all her soul to her lips. She had a feeling that if she could overcome her shyness, she would be able to speak to him as unrestrainedly, as truly, as she talked in her letters to Miss Margaret.

"Do you have no help at all?" he pursued.

Could she trust him with the secret of Miss Margaret's letters? The habit of secretiveness was too strong upon her. "There is no one here to help me—unless *you* would sometimes," she timidly answered.

"I am at your service always. Nothing could give me greater pleasure."

"Thank you." Her face flushed with delight.

"You have, of course, been a pupil at William Penn?" he asked.

"Yes, but father took me out of school when I was twelve. Ever since then I've been trying to educate myself, but—" she lifted troubled eyes to his face, "no one here knows it but the doctor. No one must know it."

"Trust me," he nodded. "But why must they not know it?"

"Father would stop it if he found it out."

"Why?"

"He wouldn't leave me waste the time."

"You have had courage—to have struggled against such odds."

"It has not been easy. But—it seems to me the things that are worth having are never easy to get."

Fairchilds looked at her keenly.

"'The things that are worth having'? What do you count as such things?"

"Knowledge and truth; and personal freedom to be true to one's self."

He concealed the shock of surprise he felt at her words. "What have we here?" he wondered, his pulse quickening as he looked into the shining upraised eyes of the girl and saw the tumultuous heaving of her bosom. He had been right after all, then, in feeling that she was different from the rest of them! He could see that it was under the stress of unusual emotion that she gave expression to thoughts which of necessity she must seldom or never utter to those about her.

"'Personal freedom to be true to one's self?'" he repeated. "What would it mean to you if you had it?"

"Life!" she answered. "I am only a dead machine, except when I am living out my true self."

He deliberately placed his hand on hers as it lay on the table. "You make me want to clasp hands with you. Do you realize what a big truth you have gotten hold of—and all that it involves?"

"I only know what it means to me."

"You are not free to be yourself?"

"I have never drawn a natural breath except in secret."

Tillie's face was glowing. Scarcely did she know herself in this wonderful experience of speaking freely, face to face, with one who understood.

"My own recent experiences of life," he said gravely, "have brought me, too, to realize that it is death in life not to be true to one's self. But if you wait for the *freedom* to be so—" he shrugged his shoulders. "One always has that freedom if he will take it—at its fearful cost. To be uncompromisingly and always true to one's self simply means martyrdom in one form or another."

He, too, marveled that he should have found anyone in this household to whom he could speak in such a vein as this.

"I always thought," Tillie said, "that when I was enough educated to be a teacher and be independent of father, I would be free to live truly. But I see that *you* cannot. You, too, have to hide your real self. Else you could not stay here in New Canaan."

"Or anywhere else, child," he smiled. "It is only with the rare few whom one finds on one's own line of march that one can be absolutely one's self. Your secret life, Miss Tillie, is not unique."

A fascinating little brown curl had escaped from Tillie's cap and lay on her cheek, and she raised her hand to push it back where it belonged, under its snowy Mennonite covering.

"Don't!" said Fairchilds. "Let it be. It's pretty!"

Tillie stared up at him, a new wonder in her eyes.

"In that Mennonite cap, you look like—like a Madonna!" Almost unwittingly the words had leaped from his lips; he could not hold them back. And in uttering them, it came to him that in the freedom permissible to him with an unsophisticated but interesting and gifted girl like this—freedom from the conventional restraints which had always limited his intercourse with the girls of his own social world—there might be

"*Tillie stared up at him, a new wonder in her eyes*"

possible a friendship such as he had never known except with those of his own sex—and with them but rarely. The thought cheered him mightily; for his life in New Canaan was heavy with loneliness.

With the selfishness natural to man, he did not stop to consider what such companionship might come to mean to this inexperienced girl steeped in a life of sordid labor and unbroken monotony.

There came the rustle of Amanda's skirts on the stairs.

Fairchilds clasped Tillie's passive hand. "I feel that I have found a friend tonight."

Amanda, brilliant in a scarlet frock and pink ribbons, appeared in the doorway. The vague, almost unseeing look with which the teacher turned to her was interpreted by the vanity of this buxom damsel to be the dazzled vision of eyes half blinded by her radiance.

For a long time after they had gone away together, Tillie sat with her face bowed upon her book, happiness surging through her with every great throb of her heart.

At last she rose, picked up the lamp and carried it into the kitchen to the little mirror before which the family combed their hair. Holding the lamp high, she surveyed her features. As long as her arm would bear the weight of the uplifted lamp, she gazed at her reflected image.

When presently with trembling arm she set it on the dresser, Tillie, like Mother Eve of old, had tasted of the Tree of Knowledge. Tillie knew that she was very fair.

*"Amanda, brilliant in a scarlet
frock and pink ribbons"*

That evening marked another crisis in the girl's inner life. Far into the night she lay with her eyes wide open, staring into the darkness, seeing there strange new visions of her own soul, gazing into its hitherto unsounded depths and seeing there the heaven or the hell—she scarcely knew which—that possessed all her being.

"Blasphemous to close your nature to the pleasures God has created for you!" His words burned themselves into her brain. Was it to an abyss of degradation that her nature was bearing her in a swift and fatal tide—or to a holy height of blessedness? Alternately her fired imagination and awakened passion exalted her adoration of him into an almost religious joy, making her yearn to give herself to him, soul and body, as to a god; then plunged her into an agony of remorse and terror at her own idolatry and lawlessness.

A new universe was opened up to her, and all of life appeared changed. All the poetry and the stories which she had ever read held new and wonderful meanings. The beauty in Nature, which, even as a child, she had felt in a way she knew those about her could never have understood, now spoke to her in a language of infinite significance. The mystery, the wonder, the power of love were revealed to her, and her soul was athirst to drink deep at this magic fountain of living water.

"You look like a Madonna!" Oh, surely, thought Tillie, in the long hours of that wakeful night, this bliss which filled her heart *was* a temptation of the Evil One, who did not scruple to use even such as the teacher for an instrument to work her undoing! Was not his satanic hand clearly shown in these vain and wicked thoughts which crowded upon her—thoughts of how fair *she* would look in a red gown like Amanda's, or in a blue hat like Rebecca's, instead of in her white cap and black hood? She crushed her face in her pillow in an agony of remorse for her own faithlessness, as she felt how hideous was that black Mennonite hood and all the plain garb which hitherto had stood to her for the peace, the comfort, the happiness, of her life! With all her mind, she tried to force back such wayward, sinful thoughts, but the more she wrestled with them, the more persistently did they obtrude themselves.

On her knees she passionately prayed to be delivered from the temptation of such unfaithfulness to her Lord, even in secret thought. Yet even while in the very act of pleading for mercy, forgiveness, help, to her own unutterable horror she found herself wondering whether she would dare brave her father's wrath and ask her aunt, in the morning, to keep back from her father a portion of her week's wages that she might buy some new white caps, her old ones being of poor material and very worn.

It was a tenet of her church that "wearing apparel was instituted by God as a necessity for the sake of propriety and also for healthful warmth, but when used for purposes of adornment it becomes the evidence of an un-Christlike spirit." Now Tillie knew that her present yearning for new caps was prompted, not by the praiseworthy and simple desire to be merely neat, but wholly by her vain longing to appear more fair in the eyes of the teacher.

Thus until the small hours of the morning did the young girl wrestle with the conflicting forces in her soul.

But the Enemy had it all his own way; for when Tillie went downstairs next morning to help her aunt get breakfast, she knew that she intended this day to buy those new caps in spite of the inevitable penalty she would have to suffer for daring to use her own money without her father's leave.

And when she walked into the kitchen, her aunt was amazed to see the girl's fair face looking out from a halo of tender little brown curls, which, with a tortured conscience, and an apprehension of retribution at the hands of the meeting, Tillie had brushed from under her cap and arranged with artful care.

CHAPTER NINETEEN

TILLIE TELLS A LIE

IT WAS ELEVEN O'CLOCK ON THE FOLLOWING SATURDAY morning, a busy hour at the hotel, and Mrs. Wackernagel and Tillie were both hard at work in the kitchen, while Rebecca and Amanda were vigorously applying their young strength to "the upstairs work."

The teacher was lounging on the settee in the sitting room, trying to read his Boston *Transcript* and divert his mind from its irritation and discontent under a condition of things which made it impossible for him to command Tillie's time whenever he wanted a companion for a walk in the woods, or for a talk in which he might unburden himself of his pent-up thoughts and feelings. The only freedom she had was in the evening; and even then she was not always at liberty. There was Amanda always ready and at hand—it kept him busy dodging her. Why was Fate so perverse in her dealings with him? Why couldn't it be Tillie instead of Amanda? Fairchilds chafed under this untoward condition of things like a fretful child—or, rather, just like a man who can't have what he wants.

Both Tillie and her aunt went about their tasks this morning with a nervousness of movement and an anxiety of countenance that told of something unwonted in the air. Fairchilds was vaguely conscious of this as he sat in the adjoining room, with the door ajar.

"Tillie!" said her aunt, with a sharpness unusual to her, as she closed the oven door with a spasmodic bang, "you put on your shawl and bonnet and go right up to Sister Jennie Hershey's for some bacon."

"Why, Aunty Em!" said Tillie, in surprise, looking up from the table where she was rolling out paste; "I can't let these pies."

"I'll finish them pies. You just go now."

"But we've got plenty of bacon."

"If we've got bacon a-plenty, then get some ponhaus. Or some mush. Hurry up and go, Tillie!"

She came to the girl's side and took the rolling-pin from her hands. "And don't hurry back. Set awhile. Now get your things on quick."

"But, Aunty Em—"

"Are you mindin' me, Tillie, or ain't you?" her aunt sharply demanded.

"But in about ten minutes father will be stopping on his way from Lancaster market," Tillie said, though obediently going toward the corner where hung her shawl and bonnet, "to get my wages and see me, Aunty Em— like what he does every Saturday still."

"Well, don't be so dumm, Tillie! That's why I'm sendin' you off!"

"Oh, Aunty Em, I don't want to go away and leave you to take all the blame for those new caps! And, anyhow, father will stop at Sister Jennie Hershey's if he don't find me here."

"I won't tell him you're there. And push them curls under your cap, or Sister Jennie'll be tellin' the meeting, and you'll be set back yet! I don't know what's come over you, Tillie, to act that wain and unregenerate!"

"Father will guess I'm at Sister Jennie's, and he'll stop to see."

"That's so, too." Aunty Em thoughtfully considered the situation. "Go out and hide in the stable, Tillie."

Tillie hesitated as she nervously twisted the strings of her bonnet. "What's the use of hiding, Aunty Em? I'd have to see him *next* Saturday."

"He won't be so mad about it till next Saturday."

Tillie shook her head. "He'll keep getting angrier—until he has satisfied himself by punishing me in some way for spending that money without leave."

The girl's face was pale, but she spoke very quietly, and her aunt looked at her curiously.

"Tillie, ain't you afraid of your pop no more?"

"Oh, Aunty Em! *Yes,* I am afraid of him."

"I'm all fidgety myself, thinkin' about how mad he'll be. Dear knows what *you* must feel yet, Tillie—and what all your little life you've been feelin', with his fear always hangin' over you still. Sometimes when I think how my brother Jake trains up his childern!"

indignation choked her—"I have feelin's that are un-Christlike, Tillie!"

"And yet, Aunty Em," the girl said earnestly, "father does care for me too—even though he always did think I ought to want nothing else but to work for him. But he does care for me. The couple of times I was sick already, he was concerned. I can't forget it."

"To be sure, he'd have to be a funny man if he wasn't concerned when his own child's sick, Tillie. I don't give him much for *that.*"

"But it always puzzled me, Aunty Em—if father's concerned to see me sick or suffering, why will he himself deliberately make me suffer more than I ever suffered in any sickness? I never could understand that."

"He always thinks he's doin' his duty by you. That we must give him. Och, my! There's his wagon stoppin' *now!* Go on out to the stable, Tillie! Quick!"

"Aunty Em!" Tillie faltered, "I'd sooner stay and have it done with now, than wait and have it hanging over me all the week till next Saturday."

There was another reason for her standing her ground and facing it out. Ever since she had yielded to the temptation to buy the caps and let her hair curl about her face, her conscience had troubled her for her vanity; and a vague feeling that in suffering her father's displeasure she would be expiating her sin made her almost welcome his coming this morning.

There was the familiar heavy tread in the barroom which adjoined the kitchen. Tillie flushed and paled by turns as it drew near, and her aunt rolled out the paste with a vigor and an emphasis that expressed her inward agitation. Even Fairchilds, in the next room, felt himself infected with the prevailing suspense.

"Well!" was Jake Getz's greeting as he entered the kitchen. "Em!" he nodded to his sister. "Well, Tillie!"

There was a note of affection in his greeting of his daughter. Tillie realized that her father missed her presence at home almost as much as he missed the work that she did. The nature of his regard for her was a mystery that had always puzzled the girl. How could one be constantly hurting and thwarting a person whom one cared for?

Tillie went up to him dutifully and held out her hand. He took it and bent to kiss her.

"Are you well? You're lookin' some pale. And your hair's strubbly [untidy]."

"She's been sewin' too steady on them clo'es fur your childern," said Aunty Em, quickly. "It gives her such a pain in her side still to set and sew. I ain't leavin' her set up every night to sew no more! You can just take them clo'es home, Jake. They ain't done, and they won't get done here."

"Do you mebbe leave her set up readin' books or such pamp'lets, ain't?" Mr. Getz inquired.

"I make her go to bed early still," Mrs. Wackernagel said evasively, though her Mennonite conscience reproached her for such want of strict candor.

"That dude teacher you got stayin' here mebbe gives her things to read, ain't?" Mr. Getz pursued his suspicions.

"He's never gave her nothin' that I seen him," Mrs. Wackernagel affirmed.

"Well, mind you don't leave her waste time readin'. She ain't to."

"You needn't trouble, Jake!"

"Well," said Jake, "I'll leave them clo'es another week, and mebbe Tillie'll feel some better and can get 'em done. Mom won't like it when I come without 'em this mornin'. She's needin' 'em fur the childern, and she thought they'd be done till this morning a'ready."

"Why don't you hire your washin' or buy her a washin'-machine? Then she'd have time to do her own sewin'."

"Work don't hurt a body," Mr. Getz maintained. "It's healthy. What's Tillie doin' this morning?"

"She was bakin' these pies, but I want her now to redd up. Take all them pans to the dresser, Tillie."

Tillie went to the table to do as she was bid.

"Well, I must be goin' home now," said Mr. Getz. "I'll take Tillie's wages, Em."

Mrs. Wackernagel set her lips as she wiped her hands on the roller-towel and opened the dresser drawer to get her purse.

"How's *her?*" she inquired, referring to Mrs. Getz to gain time, as she counted out the money.

"She's old-fashioned."

"Is the childern all well?"

"Yes, they're all middlin' well. Hurry up, Em; I'm in a hurry, and you're takin' wonderful long to count out them two dollars."

"It's only one and a half this week, Jake. Tillie she had to have some new caps, and they come to fifty cents. And I took notice her underclo'es was too thin fur this cold spell, and I wanted her to buy herself a warm petticoat, but she wouldn't take the money."

An angry red dyed the swarthy neck and forehead of the man, as his keen eyes, very like his sister's, only lacking their expression of kindness, flashed from her face to the countenance of his daughter at the dresser.

"What business have you lettin' her buy anything?" he sternly demanded. "You was to give me her wages, and *I* was to buy her what she couldn't do without. You're not keepin' your bargain!"

"She needed them caps right away. I couldn't wait till Saturday to ast you oncet. And," she boldly added, "you ought to leave her have another fifty cents to buy herself a warm petticoat!"

"Tillie!" commanded her father, "you come here!"

The girl was very white as she obeyed him. But her eyes, as they met his, were not afraid.

"It's easy seen why you're pale! I guess it ain't no pain in your side took from settin' up sewin' fur mom that's made you pale! Now see here," he sternly said, "what did you do somepin like this fur? Spendin' fifty cents without astin' me!"

"I needed the caps," she quietly answered. "And I knew you would not let me buy them if I asked you, father."

"You're standin' up here in front of me and sayin' to my face you done somepin you knowed I wouldn't give you darst to do! And you have no business, anyhow, wearin' them New Mennonite caps! I never wanted you to take up with that blamed foolishness! Well, I'll learn you! If I had you home I'd whip you!"

"You ain't touchin' her 'round *here!*" exclaimed his sister. "You just try it, Jake, and I'll call Abe out!"

"Is she my own child or ain't she, Em Wackernagel? And can I do with my own what I please, or must I ast you and Abe Wackernagel?"

"She's too growed up fur to be punished, Jake, and you know it."

"Till she's too growed up to obey her pop, she'll *get* punished," he affirmed. "Where's the good of your religion, I'd like to know, Em—settin' a child on to defy her parent? And you, Tillie, you *stole* that money off of me! Your earnin's ain't yourn till you're twenty-one. Is them New Mennonite principles to take what ain't yourn? It ain't only the fifty cents I mind—it's your disobedience and your stealin'."

"Oh, father! it wasn't *stealing!*"

"Of course it wasn't stealin'—takin' what you earnt yourself—whether you *are* seventeen instead of twenty-one!" her aunt warmly assured her.

"Now look-ahere, Em! If yous are goin' to get her so spoilt fur me, over here, she ain't stayin' here. I'll take her home!"

"Well, take her!" diplomatically answered his sister. "I can get Abe's niece over to East Donegal fur one-seventy-five. She'd be glad to come!"

Mr. Getz at this drew in his sails a bit. "I'll give her one more chancet," he compromised. "But I ain't givin' her no second chancet if she does somepin again where she ain't got darst to do. Next time I hear of her disobeyin' me, home she comes. I'd sooner lose the money than have her spoilt fur me. Now look-ahere, Tillie, you go get them new caps and bring 'em here."

Tillie turned away to obey.

"Now, Jake, what are you up to?" his sister demanded as the girl left the room.

"Do you suppose I'd leave her *keep* them caps she stole the money off of me to buy?" Getz retorted.

"She earnt the money!" maintained Mrs. Wackernagel.

"The money wasn't hern, and I'd sooner throw them caps in the rag-bag than leave her wear 'em when she disobeyed me to buy 'em."

"Jake Getz, you're a reg'lar tyrant! You mind me of Herod yet—and of Punshus Palate!"

"Ain't I followin' Scripture when I train up my child to obey to her parent?" he wanted to know.

"Now look-ahere, Jake; I'll give you them fifty cents and make a present to Tillie of them caps if you'll leave her keep 'em."

But in spite of his yearning for the fifty cents, Mr. Getz firmly refused this offer. Paternal discipline must be maintained even at a financial loss. Then, too, penurious and saving as he was, he was strictly honest, and he would not have thought it right to let his sister pay for his child's necessary wearing apparel.

"No, Tillie's got to be punished. When I want her to have new caps, I'll buy 'em fur her."

Tillie reëntered the room with the precious bits of linen tenderly wrapped up in tissue paper. Her pallor was now gone, and her eyes were red with crying. She came to her father's side and handed him the soft bundle.

"These here caps," he said to her, "mom can use fur nightcaps, or what. When you buy somepin unknownst to me, Tillie, I ain't leavin' you *keep* it! Now go 'long back to your dishes. And next Saturday, when I come, I want to find them clo'es done, do you understand?"

Tillie's eyes followed the parcel as it was crushed ruthlessly into her father's coat pocket—and she did not heed his question.

"Do you hear me, Tillie?" he demanded.

"Yes," she answered, looking up at him with brimming eyes.

His sister, watching them from across the room, saw in the man's face the working of conflicting feelings—his stern displeasure warring with his affection. Mrs. Wackernagel had realized, ever since Tillie had come to live with her, that Jake's brief weekly visits to his daughter were a pleasure to the hard man; and not only because of the two dollars which he came to collect. Just now, she could see how he hated to part from her in anger. Justice having been meted out in the form of the crushed and forfeited caps in his pocket, he would fain take leave of the girl with some expression of his kindlier feelings toward her.

"Now are you behavin' yourself—like a good girl—till I come again?" he asked, laying his hand upon her shoulder.

"Yes," she said dully.

"Then give me good-by." She held up her face and submitted to his kiss.

"Good-by, Em. And mind you stop spoilin' my girl fur me!"

He opened the door and went away.

And Fairchilds, an unwilling witness to the father's brutality, felt every nerve in his body tingle with a longing first to break the head of that brutal Dutchman, and then to go and take little Tillie in his arms and kiss her. To work off his feelings, he sprang up from the settee, put on his hat, and flung out of the house to walk down to "the krik."

"Never you mind, Tillie," her aunt consoled her. "I'm goin' in town next Wednesday, and I'm buyin' you some caps myself fur a present."

"Oh, Aunty Em, but maybe you'd better not be so good to me!" Tillie said, dashing away the tears as she industriously rubbed her pans. "It was my vanity made me want new caps. And father's taking them was maybe the Lord punishing my vanity."

"You needed new caps—your old ones was wore out. *And don't you be judgin' the Lord by your pop!* Don't try to stop me—I'm buyin' you some caps."

Now Tillie knew how becoming the new caps were to her, and her soul yearned for them even as (she told herself) Israel of old yearned after the flesh-pots of Egypt. To lose them was really a bitter disappointment to her.

But Aunty Em would spare her that grief! A sudden passionate impulse of gratitude and love toward her aunt made her do a most unwonted thing. Taking her hands from her dishwater, she dried them hastily, went over to Mrs. Wackernagel, threw her arms about her neck, and kissed her.

"Oh, Aunty Em, I love you like I've never loved anyone—except Miss Margaret and—"

She stopped short as she buried her face in her aunt's motherly bosom and clung to her.

"And who else, Tillie?" Mrs. Wackernagel asked, patting the girl's shoulder, her face beaming with pleasure at her niece's affectionate demonstration.

"No one else, Aunty Em."

Tillie drew herself away and again returned to her work at the dresser.

But all the rest of that day her conscience tortured her that she should have told this lie.

For there was someone else.

"Oh, Aunty Em, I love you like I've never loved anyone—except Miss Margaret and—'"

CHAPTER TWENTY

TILLIE IS "SET BACK"

ON SUNDAY MORNING, IN SPITE OF HER AUNT'S protestations, Tillie went to meeting with her curls outside her cap.

"They'll set you back!" protested Mrs. Wackernagel, in great trouble of spirit.

"It would be worse to be deceitful than to be vain," Tillie answered. "If I am going to let my hair curl weekdays, I won't be a coward and deceive the meeting about myself."

"But whatever made you take it into your head to act so wain, Tillie?" her bewildered aunt inquired for the hundredth time. "It can't be fur Absalom, fur you don't take to him. And, anyways, he says he wants to be led of the Spirit to give hisself up. To be sure, I hope he ain't tempted to use religion as a means of gettin' the girl he wants!"

"I know I'm doing wrong, Aunty Em," Tillie replied sorrowfully. "Maybe the meeting today will help me to conquer the Enemy."

She and her aunt realized during the course of the morning that the curls were creating a sensation. An explanation would certainly be demanded of Tillie before the week was out.

After the service, they did not stop long for "sociability"—the situation was too strained—but hurried out to their buggy as soon as they could escape.

Tillie marveled at herself as, on the way home, she found how small was her concern about the disapproval of the meeting, and even about her sin itself, before the fact that the teacher thought her curls adorable.

Aunty Em, too, marveled as she perceived the girl's strange indifference to the inevitable public disgrace at the hands of the brethren and sisters. Whatever was the matter with Tillie?

At the dinner table, to spare Tillie's evident embarrassment (perhaps because of the teacher's presence), Mrs. Wackernagel diverted the curiosity of the family as to how the meeting had received the curls.

"What did yous do all while we was to meeting?" she asked of her two daughters.

"Me and Amanda and Teacher walked to Buckarts Station," Rebecca answered.

"Did yous, now?"

"Up the pike a piece was all the fu'ther I felt fur goin'," continued Rebecca, in a rather injured tone; "but Amanda she was so fur seein' oncet if that fellah with those black *mustache* was at the blacksmith's shop yet, at Buckarts! I tole her she needn't be makin' up to *him,* fur he's keepin' comp'ny with Lizzie Hershey!"

"Say, mom," announced Amanda, ignoring her sister's rebuke, "I stopped in this morning to see Lizzie Hershey, and she's that spited about Teacher's comin' here instead of to their place that she never so much as ast me would I spare my hat!"

"Now look!" exclaimed Mrs. Wackernagel.

"And when I said, after while, 'Now I must go,' she was that unneighborly she never ast me, 'What's your hurry?'"

"Was she that spited!" said Mrs. Wackernagel, half pityingly. "Well, it was just like Sister Jennie Hershey, if she didn't want Teacher stayin' there, to tell him right out. Some ain't as honest. Some talks to please the people."

"What fur sermont did yous have this morning?" asked Mr. Wackernagel, his mouth full of chicken.

"We had Levi Harnish. He preached good," said Mrs. Wackernagel. "Ain't he did, Tillie?"

"Yes," replied Tillie, coloring with the guilty consciousness that scarcely a word of that sermon had she heard.

"I like to hear a sermont, like hisn, that does me good to my heart," said Mrs. Wackernagel.

"Levi Harnish, he's a learnt preacher," said her husband, turning to Fairchilds. "He reads wonderful much. And he's always thinkin' so earnest about his learnin' that I've saw him walk along the street in Lancaster a'ready and a'most walk into people!"

"He certainly can stand on the pulpit elegant!" agreed Mrs. Wackernagel. "Why, he can preach his whole sermont with the Bible shut, yet! And he can put out elocution that it's something turrible!"

"You are not a Mennonite, are you?" Fairchilds asked of the landlord.

"No," responded Mr. Wackernagel, with a shrug. "I bothered a whole lot at one time about religion. Now I never bother."

"We had Silas Trout to lead the singin' this morning," continued Mrs. Wackernagel. "I wisht I could sing by note, like him. I don't know notes; I just sing by random."

"Where's Doc, anyhow?" suddenly inquired Amanda, for the doctor's place at the table was vacant.

"He was fetched away. Mary Holzapple's mister come fur him!" Mr. Wackernagel explained, with a meaning nod.

"I say!" cried Mrs. Wackernagel. "So soon a'ready! And last week it was Sue Hess! Doc's always gettin' fetched! Nothin' but babies and babies!"

Tillie, whose eyes were always on the teacher, except when he chanced to glance her way, noted wonderingly the blush that suddenly covered his face and neck at this exclamation of her aunt's. In the primitive simplicity of her mind, she could see nothing embarrassing in the mere statement of any fact of natural history.

"Here comes Doc now!" cried Rebecca, at the opening of the kitchen door. "Hello, Doc!" she cried as he came into the dining room. "What *is* it?"

"Twin girls!" the doctor proudly announced, going over to the stove to warm his hands after his long drive.

"My lands!" exclaimed Amanda.

"Now what do you think!" ejaculated Mrs. Wackernagel.

"How's missus?" Rebecca inquired.

"Doin' fine! But mister he ain't feelin' so well. He wanted a boy—*or* boys, as the case might be. It's gettin' some cold out," he added, rubbing his hands and holding them to the fire.

That evening, when again Fairchilds was unable to have a chat alone with Tillie, because of Absalom Puntz's unfailing appearance at the hotel, he began to think, in his chagrin, that he must have exaggerated the girl's superiority, since week after week she could endure the attentions of "that lout."

He could not know that it was for *his* sake—to keep him in his place at William Penn—that poor Tillie bore the hated caresses of Absalom.

That next week was one never to be forgotten by Tillie. It stood out, in all the years that followed, as a week of wonder—in which were revealed to her the depths and the heights of ecstatic bliss—a bliss which so filled her being that she scarcely gave a thought to the disgrace hanging over her—her suspension from meeting.

The fact that Tillie and the teacher sat together, now, every evening, called forth no surmises or suspicions from the Wackernagels, for the teacher was merely helping Tillie with some studies. The family was charged to guard the fact from Mr. Getz.

The lessons seldom lasted beyond the early bedtime of the family, for as soon as Tillie and Fairchilds found the sitting room abandoned to their private use, the schoolbooks were put aside. They had somewhat to say to each other.

Tillie's story of her long friendship with Miss Margaret, which she related to Fairchilds, made him better understand much about the girl that had seemed inexplicable in view of her environment; while her wonder at and sympathetic interest in his own story of how he had come to apply for the school at New Canaan both amused and touched him.

"Do *you* never have any doubts, Tillie, of the truth of your creed?" he asked curiously, as they sat one evening at the sitting-room table, the schoolbooks and the lamp pushed to one end.

He had several times, in this week of intimacy, found it hard to reconcile the girl's fine intelligence and clear thought in some directions with her religious superstition. He hesitated to say a word to disturb her in her apparently unquestioning faith, though he felt she was worthy of a better creed than this impossibly narrow one of the New Mennonites. "She isn't ready yet," he had thought, "to take hold of a larger idea of religion."

"I have sometimes thought," she said earnestly, "that if the events which are related in the Bible should happen now, we would not credit them. An infant born of a virgin, a star leading three travelers, a man who raised the dead and claimed to be God—we would think the folks who believed these things were ignorant and superstitious. And because they happened so long ago, and are in the Book which we are told came from God, we believe. It is very strange! Sometimes my thoughts trouble me. I try hard not to leave such thoughts come to me."

"*Let*, Tillie, not 'leave.'"

"Will I ever learn not to get my 'leaves' and 'lets' mixed!" sighed Tillie, despairingly.

"Use 'let' whenever you find 'leave' on the end of your tongue, and vice versa," he advised, with a smile.

She looked at him doubtfully. "Are you joking?"

"Indeed, no! I couldn't give you a better rule."

"There's another thing I wish you would tell me, please," she said, her eyes downcast.

"Well?"

"I can't call you 'Mr.' Fairchilds, because such complimentary speech is forbidden to us New Mennonites. It would come natural to me to call you 'Teacher,' but you would think that what you call 'provincial.'"

"But you say 'Miss' Margaret."

"I could not get out of the way of it, because I had called her that so many years before I gave myself up. That makes it seem different. But you—what must I call you?"

"I don't see what's left—unless you call me 'Say'!"

"I must have something to call you," she pleaded. "Would you mind if I called you by your Christian name?"

"I should like nothing better."

He drew forward a volume of Mrs. Browning's poems which lay among his books on the table, opened it at the fly-leaf, and pointed to his name.

"'Walter'?" read Tillie. "But I thought—"

"It was Pestalozzi? That was only my little joke. My name's Walter."

On the approach of Sunday, Fairchilds questioned her one evening about Absalom.

"Will that lad be taking up your whole Sunday evening again?" he demanded.

She told him, then, why she suffered Absalom's unwelcome attentions. It was in order that she might use her influence over him to keep the teacher in his place.

"But I can't permit such a thing!" he vehemently protested. "Tillie, I am touched by your kindness and self-sacrifice! But, dear child, I trust I am man enough to hold my own here without *your* suffering for me! You must not do it."

"You don't know Nathaniel Puntz!" She shook her head. "Absalom will never forgive you, and, at a word from him, his father would never rest until he had got rid of you. You see, none of the directors like you— they don't understand you—they say you are 'too tony.' And then your methods of teaching—they aren't like those of the Millersville Normal teachers we've had, and therefore are unsound! I discovered last week, when I was out home, that my father is very much opposed to you. They all felt just so to Miss Margaret."

"I see. Nevertheless, *you* shall not bear my burdens. And don't you see it's not just to poor Absalom? You can't marry him, so you ought not to encourage him."

"If I refused to le—*let* Absalom come, you would not remain a month at New Canaan," was her answer.

"But it isn't a matter of life and death to me to stay at New Canaan! I need not starve if I lose my position here. There are better places."

Tillie gazed down upon the chenille table-cover, and did not speak. She could not tell him that it did seem to *her* a matter of life and death to have him stay.

"It seems to me, Tillie, you could shake off Absalom through your father's objections to his attentions. The fellow could not blame you for that."

"But don't you see I must keep him by me, in order to protect you."

"My dear little girl, that's rough on Absalom; and I'm not sure it's worthy of you."

"But you don't understand. You think Absalom will be hurt in his feelings if I refuse to marry him. But I've told him all along I won't marry him. And it isn't his feelings that are concerned. He only wants a good housekeeper."

Fairchilds' eyes rested on the girl as she sat before him in the fresh bloom of her maidenhood, and he realized what he knew she did not—that unsentimental, hardheaded, and practical as Absalom might be, if she allowed him the close intimacy of "setting-up" with her, the fellow must suffer in the end in not winning her. But the teacher thought it wise to make no further comment, as he saw, at any rate, that he could not move her in her resolution to defend him.

And there was another thing that he saw. The extraneous differences between himself and Tillie, and even the radical differences of breeding and heredity which, he had assumed from the first, made any least romance or sentiment on the part of either of them unthinkable, however much they might enjoy a good comradeship—all these differences had strangely sunk out of sight as he had, from day to day, grown in touch with the girl's real self, and he found himself unable to think of her and himself except in that deeper sense in which her soul met his. Any other consideration of their relation seemed almost grotesque. This was his feeling—but his reason struggled with his feeling and bade him beware. Suppose that she too should come to feel that with the meeting of their spirits the difference in their conditions melted away like ice in the sunshine. Would not the result be fraught with tragedy for her? For himself, he was willing, for the sake of his present pleasure, to risk a future wrestling with his impracticable sentiments; but what must be the cost of such a struggle to a frail, sensitive girl, with no compensations whatever in any single phase of her life? Clearly, he was treading on dangerous ground. He must curb himself.

Before another Sunday came around, the ax had fallen—the brethren came to reason with Tillie, and finding her unable to say she was sincerely repentant and would amend her vain and carnal deportment, she was, in the course of the next week, "set back."

"The brethren came to reason with Tillie"

"I would be willing to put back the curls," she said to her aunt, who also reasoned with her in private; "but it would avail nothing. For my heart is still vain and carnal. 'Man looketh upon the outward appearance, but God looketh on the heart.'"

"Then, Tillie," said her aunt, her kindly face pale with distress in the resolution she had taken, "you'll have to go home and stay. You can't stay here as long as you're not holding out in your professions."

Tillie's face went white, and she gazed into her aunt's resolute countenance with anguish in her own.

"I'd not do it to send you away, Tillie, if I could otherwise help it. But look how inconwenient it would be havin' you here to help work, and me not havin' dare to talk or eat with you. I'm not obeyin' to the 'Rules' *now* in talkin' to you. But I tole the brethren I'd only speak to you long enough to reason with you some—and then, if that didn't make nothin', I'd send you home."

The Rules forbade the members to sit at table or hold any unnecessary word of communication with one who had failed to "hold out," and who had in consequence been "set back." Tillie, in her strange indifference to the disgrace of being set back, had not foreseen her inevitable dismissal from her aunt's employ. She recognized, now, with despair in her soul, that Aunty Em could not do otherwise than send her home.

"When must I go, Aunty Em?"

"As soon as you make your mind up you *ain't* goin' to repent of your carnal deportment."

"I *can't* repent, Aunty Em!" Tillie's voice sounded hollow to herself as she spoke.

"Then, Tillie, you're got to go tomorrow. I'll have to get my niece from East Donegal over."

It sounded to Tillie like the crack of doom.

The doctor, who was loath to have her leave, who held her interests at heart, and who knew what she would forfeit in losing the help which the teacher was giving her daily in her studies, undertook to add his expostulations to that of the brethern and sisters.

"By gum, Tillie, slick them swanged curls *back,* if they don't suit the taste of the meeting! Are you willin' to leave go your nice education, where you're gettin', fur a couple of damned curls? I don't know what's got *into* you to act so blamed stubborn about keepin' your hair strubbled 'round your face!"

"But the vanity would still be in my heart even if I did brush them back. And I don't want to be deceitful."

"Och, come now," urged the doctor, "just till you're got your certificate a'ready to teach! That wouldn't be long. Then, after that, you can be as undeceitful as you want."

But Tillie could not be brought to view the matter in this light.

She did not sit at table with the family that day, for that would have forced her aunt to stay away from the table. Mrs. Wackernagel could break bread without reproach with all her unconverted household; but not with a backslider—for the prohibition was intended as a discipline, imposed in all love, to bring the recalcitrant member back into the fold.

That afternoon, Tillie and the teacher took a walk together in the snow-covered woods.

"It all seems so extraordinary, so inexplicable!" Fairchilds repeated over and over. Like all the rest of the household, he could not be reconciled to her going. His regret was, indeed, greater than that of any of the rest, and rather surprised himself. The pallor of Tillie's face and the anguish in her eyes he attributed to the church discipline she was suffering. He never dreamed how wholly and absolutely it was for him.

"Is it any stranger," Tillie asked, her low voice full of pain, "than that your uncle should send you away because of your *unbelief*?" This word, "*unbelief*," stood for a very definite thing in New Canaan—a lost and hopeless condition of the soul. "It seems to me, the idea is the same," said Tillie.

"Yes," acknowledged Fairchilds, "of course you are right. Intolerance, bigotry, narrowness—they are the same the world over—and stand for ignorance always."

Tillie silently considered his words. It had not occurred to her to question the perfect justice of the meeting's action.

Suddenly she saw in the path before her a half-frozen, fluttering sparrow. They both paused, and Tillie stooped, gently took it up, and folded it in her warm shawl. As she felt its throbbing little body against her hand, she thought of herself in the hand of God. She turned and spoke her thought to Fairchilds.

"Could I possibly hurt this little bird, which is so entirely at my mercy? Could I judge it, condemn and punish it, for some mistake or wrong or weakness it had committed in its little world? And could God be less kind, less merciful to me than I could be to this little bird? Could he hold my soul in the hollow of his hand and vivisect it to judge whether its errors were worthy of his divine anger? He knows how weak and ignorant I am. I will not fear him," she said, her eyes shining. "I will trust myself in his power—and believe in his love."

"The New Mennonite creed won't hold her long," thought Fairchilds.

"Our highest religious moments, Tillie," he said, "come to us, not through churches, nor even through Bibles. They are the moments when we are most receptive of the message Nature is always patiently waiting to speak to us—if we will only hear. It is she alone that can lead us to see God face to face, instead of 'through another man's dim thought of him.'"

"Yes," agreed Tillie, "I have often felt more—more *religious,*" she said, after an instant's hesitation, "when I've been walking here alone in the woods, or down by the creek, or up on Chestnut Hill—than I could feel in church. In church we hear *about* God, as you say, through other men's dim thoughts of him. Here, alone, we are *with* him."

They walked in silence for a space, Tillie feeling with mingled bliss and despair the fascination of this parting hour. But it did not occur to Fairchilds that her departure from the hotel meant the end of their intercourse.

"I shall come out to the farm to see you, Tillie, as often as you will let me. You know, I've no one else to talk to, about here, as I talk with you. What a pleasure it has been!"

"Oh, but father will never le—let me spend my time with you as I did at the hotel! He will be angry at my being sent home, and he will keep me constantly at work to make up for the loss it is to him. This is our last talk together!"

"I'll risk your father's wrath, Tillie. You don't suppose I'd let a small matter like that stand in the way of our friendship?"

"But father will not l—*let*—me spend time with you. And if you come when he told you not to he would put you out of William Penn!"

"I'm coming, all the same, Tillie."

"Father will blame *me,* if you do."

"Can't you take your own part, Tillie?" he gravely asked. "No, no," he hastily added, for he did not forget the talk he had overheard about the new caps, in which Mr. Getz had threatened personal violence to his daughter. "I know you must not suffer for my sake. But you cannot mean that we are not to meet at all after this?"

"Only at chance times," faltered Tillie; "that is all."

Very simply and somewhat constrainedly they said good-by the next morning, Fairchilds to go to his work at William Penn and Tillie to drive out with her Uncle Abe to meet her father's displeasure.

CHAPTER TWENTY-ONE

"I'LL MARRY HIM TOMORROW!"

MR. GETZ HAD PLAINLY GIVEN ABSALOM TO understand that he did not want him to sit up with Tillie, as he "wasn't leaving her marry." Absalom had answered that he guessed Tillie would have something to say to that when she was "eighteen a'ready." And on the first Sunday evening after her return home he had boldly presented himself at the farm.

"That's where you'll get fooled, Absalom, fur she's been raised to mind her pop!" Mr. Getz had responded. "If she disobeyed to my word, I wouldn't give her no aus styer. I guess you wouldn't marry a girl where wouldn't bring you no aus styer!"

Absalom, who was frugal, had felt rather baffled at this threat. Nevertheless, here he was again on Sunday evening at the farm to assure Tillie that *he* would stand by her, and that if she was not restored to membership in the meeting, he wouldn't give himself up, either.

Mr. Getz dared not go to the length of forbidding Absalom his house, for that would have meant a family feud between all the Getzes and all the Puntzes of the county. He could only insist that Tillie "dishearten him," and that she dismiss him not later than ten o'clock. To almost any other youth in the neighborhood, such opposition would have proved effectual. But every new obstacle seemed only to increase Absalom's determination to have what he had set out to get.

Tonight he produced another book, which he said he had bought at the second-hand bookstore in Lancaster.

Cupid and Psyche, Tillie read the title. "Oh, Absalom, thank you. This is lovely. It's a story from Greek mythology—I've been hearing some of these stories from the teacher"—she checked herself, suddenly, at Absalom's look of jealous suspicion.

"I'm wonderful glad you ain't in there at the *hotel* no more," he said. "I hadn't no fair chancet, with Teacher right there on the *grounds.*"

"Absalom," said Tillie, gravely, with a little air of dignity that did not wholly fail to impress him, "I insist on it that you never speak of the teacher in that way in connection with me. You might as well speak of my marrying the county superintendent! He'd be just as likely to ask me!"

The county superintendent of public instruction was held in such awe that his name was scarcely mentioned in an ordinary tone of voice.

"As if there's no difference from a teacher at William Penn to the county superintendent! You ain't that dumm, Tillie!"

"The difference is that the teacher at William Penn is superior in every way to the county superintendent!"

She spoke impulsively, and she regretted her words the moment they were uttered. But Absalom only half comprehended her meaning.

"You think you ain't good enough fur him, and you think I ain't good enough fur *you!*" he grumbled. "I have never saw such a funny girl! Well," he nodded confidently, "you'll think different one of these here days!"

"You must not cherish any false hopes, Absalom," Tillie insisted in some distress.

"Well, fur why don't you want to have me?" he demanded for the hundredth time.

"Absalom," Tillie tried a new mode of discouragement, "I don't want to get married because I don't want to be a farmer's wife—they have to work too hard!"

It was enough to drive away any lover in the countryside, and for a moment Absalom was staggered.

"Well!" he exclaimed, "a woman that's afraid of work ain't no wife fur me, anyways!"

Tillie's heart leaped high for an instant in the hope that now she had effectually cooled his ardor. But it sank again as she recalled the necessity of retaining at least his goodwill and friendship, that she might protect the teacher.

"Now, Absalom," she feebly protested, "did you ever see me afraid of work?"

"Well, then, if you ain't afraid of workin', what makes you talk so *contrary?*"

"I don't know. Come, let me read this nice book you've brought me," she urged, much as she might have tried to divert one of her little sisters or brothers.

"I'd ruther just set. I ain't much fur readin'. Jake Getz he says he's goin' to chase you to bed at ten—and ten comes wonderful soon Sundays. Leave us just set."

Tillie well understood that this was to endure Absalom's clownish wooing. But for the sake of the cause, she said to herself, she would conquer her repugnance and bear it.

For two weeks after Tillie's return home, she did not once have a word alone with Fairchilds. He came several times, ostensibly on errands from her aunt; but on each occasion he found her hard at work in her father's presence. At his first visit, Tillie, as he was leaving, rose from her corn-husking in the barn to go with him to the gate, but her father interfered.

"You stay where you're at!"

With burning face, she turned to her work. And Fairchilds, carefully suppressing an impulse to shake Jake Getz till his teeth rattled, walked quietly out of the gate and up the road.

Her father was more than usually stern and exacting with her in these days of her suspension from meeting, inasmuch as it involved her dismissal from the hotel and the consequent loss to him of two dollars a week.

As for Tillie, she found a faint consolation in the fact of the teacher's evident chagrin and indignation at the tyrannical rule which forbade intercourse between them.

At stated intervals, the brethren came to reason with her, but while she expressed her willingness to put her curls back, she would not acknowledge that her heart was no longer "carnal and vain," and so they found it impossible to restore her to favor.

A few weeks before Christmas, Absalom, deciding that he had imbibed all the arithmetical erudition he could hold, stopped school. On the evening that he took his books home, he gave the teacher a parting blow, which he felt sure quite avenged the outrageous defeat he had suffered at his hands on that Sunday night at the hotel.

"Me and Tillie's promised. It ain't put out yet, but I conceited I'd better tell you, so's you wouldn't be wastin' your time tryin' to make up to her."

"You and Tillie are engaged to be married?" Fairchilds incredulously asked.

"That's what! As good as, anyways. I always get somepin I want when I make up my mind oncet." And he grinned maliciously.

Fairchilds pondered the matter as, with depressed spirits, he walked home over the frozen road.

"No wonder the poor girl yielded to the pressure of such an environment," he mused. "I suppose she thinks Absalom's rule will not be so bad as her father's. But that a girl like Tillie should be pushed to the wall like that—it is horrible! And yet—if she were worthy a better fate would she not have held out? It is too bad, it is unjust to her 'Miss Margaret' that she should give up now! I feel," he sadly told himself, "disappointed in Tillie!"

WHEN the notable "Columbus Celebration" came off in New Canaan, in which event several schools of the township united to participate, and which was attended by the entire countryside, as if it were a funeral, Tillie hoped that here would be an opportunity for seeing and speaking with Walter Fairchilds. But in this she was bitterly disappointed.

It was not until a week later, at the township Institute, which met at New Canaan, and which was also attended by the entire population, that her deep desire was gratified.

It was during the reading of an address, before the Institute, by Miss Spooner, the teacher at East Donegal, that Fairchilds deliberately came and sat by Tillie in the back of the schoolroom.

Tillie's heart beat fast, and she found herself doubting the reality of his precious nearness after the long, dreary days of hungering for him.

She dared not speak to him while Miss Spooner held forth, and, indeed, she feared even to look at him, lest curious eyes read in her face what consciously she strove to conceal.

She realized his restless impatience under Miss Spooner's eloquence.

"It was a week back already, we had our Columbus Celebration," read this educator of Lancaster County, genteelly curving the little finger of each hand, as she held her address, which was esthetically tied with blue ribbon. "It was an inspiring sight to see those one hundred enthusiastic and paterotic children marching two by two, led by their equally enthusiastic and paterotic teachers! Forming a semicircle in the open air, the exercises were opened by a song, 'O my Country,' sung by clear—r-r-ringing—childish voices. . . ."

It was the last item on the program, and by mutual and silent consent, Tillie and Fairchilds, at the first stir of the audience, slipped out of the schoolhouse together. Tillie's father was in the audience, and so was Absalom. But they had sat far forward, and Tillie hoped they had not seen her go out with the teacher.

"Let us hurry over to the woods, where we can be alone and undisturbed, and have a good talk!" proposed Fairchilds, his face showing the pleasure he felt in the meeting.

After a few minutes' hurried walking, they were able to slacken their pace and stroll leisurely through the bleak winter forest.

"Tillie, Tillie!" he said, "why won't you abandon this 'carnal' life you are leading, be restored to the approbation of the brethren, and come back to the hotel? I am very lonely without you."

Tillie could scarcely find her voice to answer, for the joy that filled her at his words—a joy so full that she felt but a very faint pang at his reference to the ban under which she suffered. She had thought his failure to speak to her at the "Celebration" had indicated indifference or forgetfulness. But now that was all forgotten; every nerve in her body quivered with happiness.

He, however, at once interpreted her silence to mean that he had wounded her. "Forgive me for speaking so lightly of what to you must be a sacred and serious matter. God knows, my own experience—which, as you say, was not unlike your own—was sufficiently serious to me. But somehow, I can't take *this* seriously—this matter of your pretty curls!"

"Sometimes I wonder whether you take any person or any thing, here, seriously," she half smiled. "You seem to me to be always mocking at us a little."

"Mocking? Not so bad as that. And never at *you*, Tillie."

"You were sneering at Miss Spooner, weren't you?"

"Not at her; at Christopher Columbus—though, up to the time of that celebration, I was always rather fond of the discoverer of America. But now let us talk of *you*, Tillie. Allow me to congratulate you!"

"What for?"

"True enough. I stand corrected. Then accept my sincere sympathy." He smiled whimsically.

Tillie lifted her eyes to his face, and their pretty look of bewilderment made him long to stoop and snatch a kiss from her lips. But he resisted the temptation.

"I refer to your engagement to Absalom. That's one reason why I wanted you to come out here with me this afternoon—so that you could tell me about it—and explain to me what made you give up all your plans. What will your Miss Margaret say?"

Tillie stopped short, her cheeks reddening.

"What makes you think I am promised to Absalom?"

"The fact is, I've only his word for it."

"He told you that?"

"Certainly. Isn't it true?"

"Do *you* think so poorly of me?" Tillie asked in a low voice.

He looked at her quickly. "Tillie, I'm sorry; I ought not to have believed it for an instant!"

"I have a higher ambition in life than to settle down to take care of Absalom Puntz!" said Tillie, fire in her soft eyes, and an unwonted vibration in her gentle voice.

"My credulity was an insult to you!"

"Absalom did not mean to tell you a lie. He has made up his mind to have me, so he thinks it is all as good as settled. Sometimes I am almost afraid he will win me just by thinking he is going to."

"Send him about his business! Don't keep up this folly, dear child!"

"I would rather stand Absalom," she faltered, "than stand having you go away."

"But, Tillie," he turned almost fiercely upon her— "Tillie, I would rather see you dead at my feet than to see your soul tied to that clod of earth!"

A wild thrill of rapture shot through Tillie's heart at his words. For an instant she looked up at him, her soul shining in her eyes. "Does he—does *he*—care that much what happens to me?" throbbed in her brain.

For the first time Fairchilds fully realized, with shame at his blind selfishness, the danger and the cruelty of his intimate friendship with this little Mennonite maid. For her it could but end in a heartbreak; for him—"I have been a cad, a despicable cad!" he told himself in bitter self-reproach. "If I had only known!

But now it's too late—unless—" In his mind he rapidly went over the simple history of their friendship as they walked along; and, busy with her own thought, Tillie did not notice his abstraction.

"Tillie," he said suddenly. "Next Saturday there is an examination of applicants for certificates at East Donegal. You must take that examination. You are perfectly well prepared to pass it."

"Oh, do you really, *really* think I am?" the girl cried breathlessly.

"I know it. The only question is, How are you going to get off to attend the examination?"

"Father will be at the Lancaster market on Saturday morning!"

"Then I'll hire a buggy, come out to the farm, and carry you off!"

"No—oh, no, you must not do that. Father would be so angry with you!"

"You can't walk to East Donegal. It's six miles away."

"Let me think. Uncle Abe would do anything I asked him—but he wouldn't have time to leave the hotel Saturday morning. And I couldn't make him or Aunty Em understand that I was educated enough to take the examination. But there's the Doc!"

"Of course!" cried Fairchilds. "The Doc isn't afraid of the whole county! Shall I tell him you'll go if he'll come for you?"

"Yes!"

"Good! I'll undertake to promise for him that he'll be there!"

"When father comes home from market and finds me gone!" Tillie said—but there was exultation, rather than fear, in her voice.

"When you show him your certificate, won't that appease him? When he realizes how much more you can earn by teaching than by working for your aunt, especially as he bore none of the expense of giving you your education? It was your own hard labor, and none of his money, that did it! And now I suppose he'll get all the profit of it!" Fairchilds could not quite keep down the rising indignation in his voice.

"No," said Tillie, quietly, though the color burned in her face. "Walter! I'm going to refuse to give father my salary if I am elected to a school. I mean to save my money to go to the Normal—where Miss Margaret is."

"So long as you are under age, he can take it from you, Tillie."

"If the school I teach is near enough for me to live at home, I'll pay my board. More than that I won't do."

"But how are you going to help yourself?"

"I haven't made up my mind, yet, how I'm going to do it. It will be the hardest struggle I've ever had—to stand out against him in such a thing," Tillie continued; "but I will not be weak, I will not! I have studied and worked all these years in the hope of a year at the Normal—with Miss Margaret. And I won't falter now!"

Before he could reply to her almost impassioned earnestness, they were startled by the sound of footsteps behind them in the woods—the heavy steps of men. Involuntarily, they both stopped short, Tillie with the feeling of one caught in a stolen delight; and Fairchilds with mingled annoyance at the interruption, and curiosity as to who might be wandering in this unfrequented patch of woods.

"I seen 'em go out up in here!"

It was the voice of Absalom. The answer came in the harsh, indignant tones of Mr. Getz. "Next time I leave her go to a Instytoot or such a Columbus Sallybration, she'll stay at *home!* Wastin' time walkin' 'round in the woods with that dude teacher! And on a week-day, too!"

Tillie looked up at Fairchilds with an appeal that went to his heart. Grimly he waited for the two.

"So here's where you are!" cried Mr. Getz, striding up to them, and, before Fairchilds could prevent it, he had seized Tillie by the shoulder. "What you mean, runnin' off up here, heh? What you mean?" he demanded, shaking her with all his cruel strength.

"Stop that, you brute!" Fairchilds, unable to control his fury, drew back and struck the big man squarely on the chest. Getz staggered back, amazement at this unlooked-for attack for a moment getting the better of his indignation. He had expected to find the teacher cowed with fear at being discovered by a director and a director's son in a situation displeasing to them.

"Let the child alone, you great coward—or I'll horsewhip you!"

Getz recovered himself. His face was black with passion. He lifted the horsewhip which he carried.

"You'll horsewhip me—me, Jake Getz, that can put you off William Penn *tomorrow* if I want! Will you do it

"Stop that, you brute!"

with this here?" he demanded, grasping the whip more tightly and lifting it to strike—but before it could descend, Fairchilds wrenched it out of his hand.

"Yes," he responded, "if you dare to touch that child again, you shameless dog!"

Tillie, with anguished eyes, stood motionless as marble, while Absalom, with clenched fists, awaited his opportunity.

"If I dare!" roared Getz. "If I have dare to touch my own child!" He turned to Tillie. "Come along," he exclaimed, giving her a cuff with his great paw; and instantly the whip came down with stinging swiftness on his wrist. With a bellow of pain, Getz turned on Fairchilds, and at the same moment, Absalom sprang on him from behind, and with one blow of his brawny arm brought the teacher to the ground. Getz sprawled over his fallen antagonist and snatched his whip from him.

"Come on, Absalom—we'll learn him oncet!" he cried fiercely. "We'll learn him what horsewhippin' is! We'll give him a lickin' he won't forget!"

Absalom laughed aloud in his delight at this chance to avenge his own defeat at the hands of the teacher, and with clumsy speed the two men set about binding the feet of the half-senseless Fairchilds with Absalom's suspenders.

Tillie felt herself spellbound, powerless to move or to cry out.

"Now!" cried Getz to Absalom, "git back, and I'll give it to him!"

The teacher, stripped of his two coats and bound hand and foot, was rolled over on his face. He uttered no word of protest, though they all saw that he had recovered consciousness. The truth was, he simply recognized the uselessness of demurring.

"Warm him up, so he don't take cold!" shouted Absalom—and even as he spoke, Jake Getz's heavy arm brought the lash down upon Fairchilds' back.

At the spiteful sound, life came back to Tillie. Like a wild thing, she sprang between them, seized her father's arm and hung upon it. "Listen to me! Listen! Father! If you strike him again, *I'll marry Absalom tomorrow!*"

By inspiration she had hit upon the one argument that would move him.

Her father tried to shake her off, but she clung to his arm with the strength of madness, knowing that if she could make him grasp, even in his passionate anger, the real import of her threat, he would yield to her.

"I'll marry Absalom! I'll marry him tomorrow!" she repeated.

"You darsent—you ain't of age! Let go my arm, or I'll slap you ag'in!"

"I shall be of age in three months! I'll marry Absalom if you go on with this!"

"That suits me!" cried Absalom. "Keep on with it, Jake!"

"If you do, I'll marry him tomorrow!"

There was a look in Tillie's eyes and a ring in her voice that her father had learned to know. Tillie would do what she said.

And here was Absalom "siding along with her" in her unfilial defiance! Jacob Getz wavered. He saw no graceful escape from his difficulty.

"Look-ahere, Tillie! If I don't lick this here feller, I'll punish *you* when I get you home!"

Tillie saw that she had conquered him, and that the teacher was safe. She loosed her hold of her father's arm and, dropping on her knees beside Fairchilds, began quickly to loosen his bonds. Her father did not check her.

"Jake Getz, you ain't givin' in *that* easy?" demanded Absalom, angrily.

"She'd up and do what she says! I know her! And I ain't leavin' her marry! You just wait"—he turned threateningly to Tillie as she knelt on the ground—"till I get you home oncet!"

Fairchilds staggered to his feet, and drawing Tillie up from the ground, he held her two hands in his as he turned to confront his enemies.

"You call yourselves men—you cowards and bullies! And you!" he turned his blazing eyes upon Getz, "you would work off your miserable spite on a weak girl— who can't defend herself! Dare to touch a hair of her head and I'll break *your* damned head and every bone in your body! Now take yourselves off, both of you, you curs, and leave us alone!"

"My girl goes home along with me!" retorted the furious Getz. "And *you*—you'll lose your job at next Board Meetin', Saturday night! So you might as well pack your trunk! Here!" He laid his hand on Tillie's arm, but Fairchilds drew her to him and held his arm about her waist, while Absalom, darkly scowling, stood uncertainly by.

"Leave her with me. I must talk with her. *Must,* I say. Do you hear me? She—"

His words died on his lips, as Tillie's head suddenly fell forward on his shoulder, and, looking down, Fairchilds saw that she had fainted.

CHAPTER TWENTY-TWO

THE DOC CONCOCTS A PLOT

"SO YOU SEE I'M THROUGH WITH THIS PLACE!" Fairchilds concluded as, late that night, he and the doctor sat alone in the sitting room, discussing the afternoon's happenings.

"I was forced to believe," he went on, "when I saw Jake Getz's fearful anxiety and real distress while Tillie remained unconscious, that the fellow, after all, does have a heart of flesh under all his brutality. He had never seen a woman faint, and he thought at first that Tillie was dead. We almost had *him* on our hands unconscious!"

"Well, the faintin' saved Tillie a row with him till he got her home oncet a'ready," the doctor said, as he puffed away at his pipe, his hands in his vest arms, his feet on the table, and a newspaper under them to spare the chenille table-cover.

"Yes. Otherwise I don't know how I could have borne to see her taken home by that ruffian—to be punished for so heroically defending *me!*"

"You bet! That took cheek, ain't? Fur that little girl to stand there and jaw Jake Getz—and make him quit lickin' you! By gum, that minds me of sceneries I've saw a'ready in the theayter! They most gener'ly faints away in a swoond that way, too. Well, Tillie she come round all right, ain't? Till a little while?"

"Yes. But she was very pale and weak, poor child!" Fairchilds answered, resting his head wearily upon his palm. "When she became conscious, Getz carried her out of the woods to his buggy that he had left near the schoolhouse."

"How did Absalom take it, anyhow?"

"He's rather dazed, I think! He doesn't quite know how to make it all out. He is a man of one idea—one at a time and far apart. His idea at present is that he is going to marry Tillie."

"Yes, and I never seen a Puntz yet where didn't come by what he set his stubborn head to!" the doctor commented. "It wonders me sometimes, how Tillie's goin' to keep from marryin' him, now he's made up his mind so firm!"

"Tillie knows her own worth too well to throw herself away like that."

"Well, now I don't know," said the doctor, doubtfully. "To be sure, I never liked them Puntzes, they're so damned thickheaded. Dummness runs in that family so, it's somepin' surprisin'! Dummness and stubbornness is all they got to 'em. But Absalom he's so well fixed—Tillie she might go furder and do worse. Now there's you, Teacher. If she took up with you and yous two got married, you'd have to rent. Absalom he'd own his own farm."

"Now, come, Doc," protested Fairchilds, disgusted, "you know better—you know that to almost any sort of a woman marriage means something more than getting herself 'well fixed,' as you put it. And to a woman like Tillie!"

"Yes—yes—I guess," answered the doctor, pulling briskly at his pipe. "It's the same with a male—he mostly looks to somepin besides a good housekeeper. There's me, now—I'd have took Miss Margaret—and she couldn't work nothin'. I tole her I don't mind if my wife *is* smart, so she don't bother me any."

"You did, did you?" smiled Fairchilds. "And what did the lady say to that?"

"Och, she was sorry!"

"Sorry to turn you down, do you mean?"

"It was because I didn't speak soon enough," the doctor assured him. "She was promised a'ready to one of these here tony perfessers at the Normal. She was sorry I hadn't spoke sooner. To be sure, after she had gave her word, she had to stick to it." He thoughtfully knocked the ashes from his pipe, while his eyes grew almost tender. "She was certainly, now, an allurin' female!

"So now," he added, after a moment's thoughtful pause, "you think your game's played out here, heh?"

"Getz and Absalom left me with the assurance that at the Saturday-night meeting of the Board I'd be voted out. If it depends on them—and I suppose it does—I'm done for. They'd like to roast me over a slow fire!"

"You bet they would!"

"I suppose I haven't the least chance?"

"Well, I don' know—I don' know. It would suit me wonderful to get ahead of Jake Getz and them Puntzes in this here thing—if I anyways could! Le' me see." He thoughtfully considered the situation. "The Board meets day after tomorrow. There's six directors. Nathaniel Puntz and Jake can easy get 'em all to wote to put you out, fur they ain't anyways stuck on you—you bein' so tony that way. Now me, I don't mind it—them things don't never bother me any—manners and cleanness and them."

"Cleanness?"

"Och, yes; us we never seen any person where wasted so much time washin' theirself—except Miss Margaret. I mind missus used to say a clean towel didn't last Miss Margaret a week, and no one else usin' it! You see, what the directors don't like is your *always* havin' your hands so clean. Now they reason this here way—a person that never has dirty hands is lazy and too tony."

"Yes?"

"But me, I don't mind. And I'm swanged if I wouldn't like to beat out Jake and Nathaniel on this here deal! Say! I'll tell you what. This here game's got fun in it fur me! I believe I got a way of *doin'* them fellers. I ain't tellin' you what it is!" he said, with a chuckle. "But it's a way that's goin' to *work!* I'm swanged if it ain't! You'll see oncet! You just let this here thing to me and you won't be chased off your job! I'm doin' it fur the sake of the fun I'll get out of seein' Jake Getz surprised! Mebbe that old Dutchman won't be wonderful spited!"

"I shall be very much indebted to you, doctor, if you can help me, as it suits me to stay here for the present."

"That's all right. Fur one, there's Adam Oberholzer; he'll be an easy guy when it comes to his wote. Fur if I want, I can bring a bill ag'in' the estate of his pop, disceased, and make it 'most anything. His pop he died last month. Now that there was a man"—the doctor settled himself comfortably, preparatory to the relation of a tale—"that there was a man that was so wonderful set on speculatin' and savin' and layin' by, that when he come to die a pecooliar thing happened. You might call that there thing phe-non-e-ma. It was this here way. When ole Adam Oberholzer (he was named after his son, Adam Oberholzer, the school directer) come to die, his wife she thought she'd better send fur the Evangelical preacher over, seein' as Adam he hadn't been inside a church fur twenty years back, and, to be sure, he wasn't just so well prepared. Oh, well, he was deef fur three years back, and churches don't do much good to deef people. But then he never did go when he did have his sound hearin'. Many's the time he sayed to me, he sayed, 'I don't believe in the churches,' he sayed, 'and blamed if it don't keep me busy believin' in a Gawd!' he sayed. So you see, he wasn't just what you might call a pillar of the church. One time he had such a cough and he come to me and sayed whether I could do somepin. 'You're to leave tobacco be,' I sayed. Ole Adam he looked serious. 'If you sayed it was caused by goin' to church,' he answered to me, 'I might mebbe break off. But tobacco—that's some serious,' he says. Adam he used to have some notions about the Bible and religion that I did think, now, was damned unushal. Here one day when he was first took sick, before he got so deef yet, I went to see him, and the Evangelical preacher was there, readin' to him that there piece of Scripture where, you know, them that worked a short time was paid the same as them that worked all day. The preacher he sayed he thought that par'ble might fetch him 'round oncet to a deathbed conwersion. But I'm swanged if Adam didn't just up and say, when the preacher got through, he says, 'That wasn't a square deal accordin' to *my* way of lookin' at things.' Yes, that's the way that there feller talked. Why, here oncet—" the doctor paused to chuckle at the recollection—"when I got there, Reverend was wrestlin' with Adam to get hisself conwerted, and it was one of Adam's days when he was at his deefest. Reverend he shouted in his ear, 'You must experience religion—and get a change of heart—and be conwerted before you die!' 'What d'you say?' Adam he ast. Then Reverend, he seen that wouldn't work, so he cut it short, and he says wery loud, 'Trust the Lord!' Now, ole Adam Oberholzer in his business dealin's and speculatin' was always darned particular who he trusted, still, so he looked up at Reverend, and he says, 'Is he a reliable party?' Well, by gum, I bu'st right out laughin'! I hadn't ought to— seein' it was Adam's deathbed—and Reverend him just sweatin' with tryin' to work in his job to get him conwerted till he passed away a'ready. But I'm swanged if I could keep in! I just *hollered!*"

The doctor threw back his head and shouted with fresh appreciation of his story, and Fairchilds joined in sympathetically.

"Well, did he die unconverted?" he asked the doctor.

"You bet! Reverend he sayed afterwards, that in all his practice of his sacred calling he never had knew such a carnal deathbed. Now you see," concluded the doctor, "I tended ole Adam fur near two months, and that's where I have a hold on his son the school-director."

He laughed as he rose and stretched himself.

"It will be no end of sport foiling Jake Getz!" Fairchilds said, with but a vague idea of what the doctor's scheme involved. "Well, doctor, you are our mascot— Tillie's and mine!" he added, as he, too, rose.

"What's *that?*"

"Our good luck." He held out an objectionably clean hand with its shining fingernails. "Good night, Doc, and thank you!"

The doctor awkwardly shook it in his own grimy fist. "Good night to you, then, Teacher."

Out in the barroom, as the doctor took his nightly glass of beer at the counter, he confided to Abe Wackernagel that somehow he did, now, "like to see Teacher use them manners of hisn. I'm 'most as stuck on 'em as missus is!" he declared.

CHAPTER TWENTY-THREE

SUNSHINE AND SHADOW

TILLIE'S UNHAPPINESS, IN HER CERTAINTY THAT ON Saturday night the Board would vote for the eviction of the teacher, was so great that she felt almost indifferent to her own fate, as she and the doctor started on their six-mile ride to East Donegal. But when he presently confided to her his scheme to foil her father and Absalom, she became almost hysterical with joy.

"You see, Tillie, it's this here way. Two of these here directers owes me bills. Now in drivin' you over to East Donegal I'm passin' near to the farms of both of them directers, and I'll make it suit to stop off and press 'em fur my money. They're both of 'em near as close as Jake Getz! They don't like it fur me to press 'em to pay right aways. So after while I'll say that if they wote ag'in' Jake and Nathaniel, and each of 'em gets one of the other two directers to wote with him to leave Teacher keep his job, I'll throw 'em the doctor's bill off! Adam Oberholzer he owes me about twelve dollars, and Joseph Kettering he owes me ten. I guess it ain't worth twelve dollars to Adam and ten to Joseph to run Teacher off William Penn!"

"And do you suppose that they will be able to influence the other two—John Coppenhaver and Pete Underwocht?"

"When all them dollars depends on it, I don't suppose nothin'—I know. I'll put it this here way: 'If Teacher ain't chased off, I'll throw you my doctor's bill off. If he is, you'll pay me up, and pretty damned quick, too!'"

"But, Doc," faltered Tillie, "won't it be bribery?"

"Och, Tillie, a body mustn't feel so conscientious about such little things like them. That's bein' too serious."

"Did you tell the teacher you were going to do this?" she uneasily asked.

"Well, I guess I ain't such a blamed fool! I guess I know that much, that he wouldn't of saw it the way *I* see it. I tole him I was goin' to bully them direcers to keep him in his job—but he don't know how I'm doin' it."

"I'm glad he doesn't know," sighed Tillie.

"Yes, he darsent know till it's all over oncet."

The joy and relief she felt at the doctor's scheme, which she was quite sure would work out successfully, gave her a self-confidence in the ordeal before her that sharpened her wits almost to brilliancy. She sailed through this examination, which otherwise she would have dreaded unspeakably, with an aplomb that made her a stranger to herself. Even that bugbear of the examination labeled by the superintendent, "General

Information," and regarded with suspicion by the applicants as a snare and a delusion, did not confound Tillie
in her sudden and newfound courage; though the questions under this head brought forth from the applicants
such astonishing statements as that Henry VIII was
chiefly noted for being "a great widower"; and that the
Mother of the Gracchi was "probably Mrs. Gracchi."

In her unwonted elation, Tillie even waxed a bit
witty, and in the quiz on "Methods of Discipline," she
gave an answer which no doubt led the superintendent
to mark her high.

"What method would you pursue with a boy in your
school who was addicted to swearing?" she was asked.

"I suppose I should make him swear off!" said Tillie,
with actual flippancy.

A neat young woman of the class, sitting directly in
front of the superintendent, and wearing spectacles and
very straight, tight hair, cast a shocked and reproachful
look upon Tillie, and turning to the examiner, said
primly, "*I* would organize an anti-swearing society in the
school, and reward the boys who were not profane by
making them members of it, expelling those who used
any profane language."

"And make every normal boy turn blasphemer
in derision, I'm afraid," was the superintendent's
ironical comment.

When, at four o'clock that afternoon, she drove
back with the doctor through the winter twilight, bearing her precious certificate in her bosom, the brightness
of her face seemed to reflect the brilliancy of the red

sunset glow on snow-covered fields, frozen creek, and farmhouse windows.

"Bully fur you, Matilda!" the doctor kept repeating at intervals. "Now won't Miss Margaret be tickled, though! I tell you what, wirtue like hern gits its rewards even in this here life. She'll certainly be set up to think she's made a teacher out of you unbeknownst! And mebbe it won't tickle her wonderful to think how she's beat Jake Getz!" he chuckled.

"Of course you're writin' to her tonight, Tillie, ain't you?" he asked. "I'd write her off a letter myself if writin' come handier to me."

"Of course I shall let her know at once," Tillie replied; and in her voice, for the first time in the doctor's acquaintance with her, there was a touch of gentle complacency.

"I'll get your letter out the tree-holler tomorrow morning, then, when I go a-past—and I can stamp it and mail it fur you till noon. Then she'll get it till Monday morning yet! By gum, won't she, now, be tickled!"

"Isn't it all beautiful!" Tillie breathed ecstatically. "I've got my certificate and the teacher won't be put out! What did Adam Oberholzer and Joseph Kettering say, Doc?"

"I've got them fixed all right! Just you wait, Tillie!" he said mysteriously. "Mebbe us we ain't goin' to have the laugh on your pop and old Nathaniel Puntz! You'll see! Wait till your pop comes home and says what's happened at Board meetin' tonight! Golly! Won't he be hoppin' mad!"

"What is going to happen, Doc?"

"You wait and see! I ain't tellin' even you, Tillie. I'm savin' it fur a surprise party fur all of yous!"

"Father won't speak to me about it, you know. He won't mention Teacher's name to me."

"Then won't you find out off of him about the Board meetin'?" the doctor asked in disappointment. "Must you wait till you see me again oncet?"

"He will tell mother. I can get her to tell me," Tillie said.

"All right. Somepin's going to happen too good to wait! Now look-ahere, Tillie, is your pop to be tole about your certificate?"

"I won't tell him until I must. I don't know how he'd take it. He might not let me get a school to teach. Of course, when once I've got a school, he will have to be told. And then," she quietly added, "I shall teach, whether he forbids it or not."

"To be sure!" heartily assented the doctor. "And leave him go roll hisself, ain't! I'll keep a lookout fur you and tell you the first wacancy I hear of."

"What would I do—what should I have done in all these years, Doc—if it hadn't been for you!" smiled Tillie, with an affectionate pressure of his rough hand; and the doctor's face shone with pleasure to hear her. "You have been a good friend to me, Doc."

"Och, that's all right, Tillie. As I sayed, wirtue has its reward even in this here life. My wirtuous acts in standin' by you has gave me as much satisfaction as I've ever had out of anything! But now, Tillie, about tellin' your pop. I don't suspicion he'd take it anyways ugly. A body'd think he'd be proud! And he hadn't none of the expense of givin' you your nice education!"

"I can't be sure how he *would* take it, Doc, so I would rather not tell him until I must."

"All right. Just what you say. But I dare tell missus, ain't?"

"If she won't tell the girls, Doc. It would get back to father, I'm afraid, if so many knew it."

"I'll tell her not to tell. She'll be as pleased and proud as if it was Manda or Rebecca!"

"Poor Aunty Em! She is so good to me, and I'm afraid I've disappointed her!" Tillie humbly said; but somehow the sadness that should have expressed itself in the voice of one under suspension from meeting, when speaking of her sin, was quite lacking.

When, at length, they reached the Getz farm, Mr. Getz met them at the gate, his face harsh with displeasure at Tillie's long and unpermitted absence from home.

"Hello, Jake!" said the doctor, pleasantly, as her father lifted her down from the high buggy. "I guess missus tole you how I heard Tillie fainted away in a swoond day before yesterday, so this morning I come over to see her oncet—Aunty Em she was some oneasy. And I seen she would mebbe have another such a swoond if she didn't get a long day out in the air. It's done her wonderful much good—wonderful!"

"She hadn't no need to stay all day!" growled Mr. Getz. "Mom had all Tillie's work to do, and her own too, and she didn't get it through all."

"Well, better *let* the work than have Tillie havin' any more of them dangerous swoonds. Them's dangerous, I tell you, Jake! Sometimes folks never comes to, yet!"

Mr. Getz looked at Tillie apprehensively. "You better go in and get your hot supper, Tillie," he said, not ungently.

Before this forbearance of her father, Tillie had a feeling of shame in the doctor's subterfuges, as she bade her loyal friend good night and turned to go indoors.

"You'll be over to Board meetin' tonight, ain't?" the doctor said to Mr. Getz as he picked up the reins.

"To be sure! Me and Nathaniel Puntz has a statement to make to the Board that'll chase that tony dude teacher off his job so quick he won't have time to pack his trunk!"

"Is that so?" the doctor said in feigned surprise. "Well, he certainly is some tony—that I must give him, Jake. Well, good night to yous! Be careful of Tillie's health!"

Getz went into the house and the doctor, chuckling to himself, drove away.

Tillie was in bed, but sleep was far from her eyes, when, late that night, she heard her father return from the Board meeting. Long she lay in her bed, listening with tense nerves to his suppressed tones as he talked to his wife in the room across the hall, but she could not hear what he said. Not even his tone of voice was sufficiently enlightening as to how affairs had gone.

In her wakefulness the night was agonizingly long; for though she was hopeful of the success of the doctor's plot, she knew that possibly there might have been some fatal hitch.

At the breakfast table, next morning, her father looked almost sick, and Tillie's heart throbbed with unfilial joy in the significance of this. His manner to her was curt and his face betrayed sullen anger; he talked but little, and did not once refer to the Board meeting in her presence.

It was not until ten o'clock, when he had gone with some of the children to the Evangelical church, that she found her longed-for opportunity to question her stepmother.

"Well," she began, with assumed indifference, as she and her mother worked together in the kitchen preparing the big Sunday dinner, "did they put the teacher out?"

"If they put him out?" exclaimed Mrs. Getz, slightly roused from her customary apathy. "Well, I think they didn't! What do you think they done yet?"

"I'm sure," said Tillie, evidently greatly interested in the turnips she was paring, "I don't know."

"They raised his salary five a month!"

The turnips dropped into the pan, and Tillie raised her eyes to gaze incredulously into the face of her stepmother, who, with hands on her hips, stood looking down upon her.

"Yes," went on Mrs. Getz, "that's what they done! A dumm thing like that! And after pop and Nathaniel Puntz they had spoke their speeches where they had ready, how Teacher he wasn't fit fur William Penn!

And after they tole how he had up and sassed pop, and him a directer yet! And Nathaniel he tole how Absalom had heard off the Doc how Teacher he was a' *unbeliever* and says musin' is the same to him as prayin'! Now think! Such conwictions as them! And then, when the wote was took, here it come out that only pop and Nathaniel Puntz woted ag'in' Teacher, and the other four they woted *fur!* And they woted to raise his salary five a month yet!"

Tillie's eyes dropped from her mother's face, her chin quivered, she bit her lip, and suddenly, unable to control herself, she broke into wild, helpless laughter.

Mrs. Getz stared at her almost in consternation. Never before in her life had she seen Tillie laugh with such abandon.

"What ails you?" she asked wonderingly.

Tillie could find no voice to answer, her slight frame shaking convulsively.

"What you laughin' at, anyhow?" Mrs. Getz repeated, now quite frightened.

"That—that Wyandotte hen jumped up on the sill!" Tillie murmured—then went off into a perfect peal of mirth. It seemed as though all the pent-up joy and gaiety of her childhood had burst forth in that moment.

"I don't see nothin' in that that's anyways comical—a Wyandotte hen on the windowsill!" said Mrs. Getz, in stupid wonder.

"She looked so—so—oh!" Tillie gasped, and wiped her eyes with a corner of her apron.

"You don't take no int'rust in what I tole you all!" Mrs. Getz complained, sitting down near her step-daughter to pick the chickens for dinner. "I'd think it would make you ashamed fur the way you stood up fur Teacher ag'in' your own pop here last Thursday— fur them four directers to go ag'in' pop like this here!"

"What reasons did they give for voting for the teacher?" Tillie asked, her hysterics subsiding.

"They didn't give no reasons till they had him elected a'ready. Then Adam Oberholzer he got up and he spoke how Teacher learned the scholars so good and got along without lickin' 'em any (pop he had brung that up *ag'in'* Teacher, but Adam he sayed it was *fur*), and that they better mebbe give him five extry a month to make sure to keep such a kind man to their childern, and one that learnt 'em so good."

Tillie showed signs, for an instant, of going off into another fit of laughter.

"What's ailin' you?" her mother asked in mystifica-tion. "I never seen you act so funny! You better go take a drink."

Tillie repressed herself and went on with her work.

During the remainder of that day, and, indeed, through all the week that followed, she struggled to con-ceal from her father the exultation of her spirits. She feared he would interpret it as a rejoicing over his defeat, and there was really no such feeling in the girl's gentle heart. She was even moved to some faint— it must be confessed, very faint—pangs of pity for him as she saw, from day to day, how hard he took his defeat.

Apparently, it was to him a sickening blow to have his "authority" as school director defied by a penniless young man who was partly dependent upon his vote for daily bread. He suffered keenly in his conviction that the teacher was as deeply exultant in his victory as Getz had expected to be.

In these days, Tillie walked on air, and to Mrs. Getz and the children she seemed almost another girl, with that happy vibration in her usually sad voice, and that light of gladness in her soft pensive eyes. The glorious consciousness was ever with her that the teacher was always near—though she saw him but seldom. This, and the possession of the precious certificate, her talisman to freedom, hidden always in her bosom, made her daily drudgery easy to her and her hours full of hope and happiness.

Deep as was Tillie's impression of the steadiness of purpose in Absalom's character, she was nevertheless rather taken aback when, on the Sunday night after that horrible experience in the woods, her suitor stolidly presented himself at the farmhouse, attired in his best clothes, his whole aspect and bearing eloquent of the fact that recent defeat had but made him more doggedly determined to win in the end.

Tillie wondered if she might not be safe now in dismissing him emphatically and finally; but she decided there was still danger lest Absalom might wreak his vengeance in some dreadful way upon the teacher.

Her heart was so full of happiness that she could tolerate even Absalom.

Only two short weeks of this brightness and glory, and then the blow fell—the blow which blackened the sun in the heavens. The teacher suddenly, and most mysteriously, resigned and went away.

No one knew why. Whether it was to take a better position, or for what other possible reason, not a soul in the township could tell—not even the Doc.

Strange to say, Fairchilds' going, instead of pleasing Mr. Getz, was only an added offense to both him and Absalom. They had thirsted for vengeance; they had longed to humiliate this "high-minded dude"; and now not only was the opportunity lost to them, but the "job" they had determined to wrest from him was indifferently hurled back in their faces—he *didn't want it!* Absalom and Getz writhed in their helpless spleen.

Tillie's undiscerning family did not for an instant attribute to its true cause her sudden change from radiant happiness to the weakness and lassitude that tell of mental anguish. They were not given to seeing anything that was not entirely on the surface and perfectly obvious.

Three days had passed since Fairchilds' departure— three days of utter blackness to Tillie; and on the third day she went to pay her weekly visit to the tree-hollow in the woods where she was wont to place Miss Margaret's letters.

On this day she found, to her amazement, two letters. Her knees shook as she recognized the teacher's handwriting on one of them.

There was no stamp and no postmark on the envelope. He had evidently written the letter before leaving, and had left it with the doctor to be delivered to her.

Tillie had always been obliged to manœuver skilfully in order to get away from the house long enough to pay these weekly visits to the tree-hollow; and she nearly always read her letter from Miss Margaret at night by a candle, when the household was asleep.

But now, heedless of consequences, she sat down on a snow-covered log and opened Fairchilds' letter, her teeth chattering with more than cold.

It was only a note, written in great haste and evidently under some excitement. It told her of his immediate departure for Cambridge to accept a rather profitable private tutorship to a rich man's son. He would write to Tillie, later, when he could. Meanwhile, God bless her—and he was always her friend. That was all. He gave her no address and did not speak of her writing to him.

Tillie walked home in a dream. All that evening, she was so "dopplig" as finally to call forth a sharp rebuke from her father, to which she paid not the slightest heed.

Would she ever see him again, her heart kept asking? Would he really write to her again? Where was he at this moment, and what was he doing? Did he send one thought to her, so far away, so desolate? Did he have in any least degree the desire, the yearning, for her that she had for him?

"She sat down on a snow-covered log and opened Fairchilds' letter"

Tillie felt a pang of remorse for her disloyalty to Miss Margaret when she realized that she had almost forgotten that always precious letter. When, a little past midnight, she took it from her dress pocket she noticed what had before escaped her—some erratic writing in lead on the back of the envelope. It was in the doctor's strenuous hand.

"Willyam Pens as good as yoorn ive got them all promist but your pop to wote for you at the bored meating saterdy its to be a surprize party for your pop."

CHAPTER TWENTY-FOUR

THE REVOLT OF TILLIE

AT HALF-PAST SEVEN O'CLOCK ON SATURDAY EVENING, the School Board once more convened in the hotel parlor, for the purpose of electing Fairchilds' successor.

"Up till now," Mr. Getz had remarked at the supper table, "I ain't been tole of no candidate applyin' fur William Penn, and here tonight we meet to elect him—or her if she's a female."

Tillie's heart had jumped to her throat as she heard him, wondering how he would take it when they announced to him that the applicant was none other than his own daughter—whether he would be angry at her long deception, or gratified at the prospect of her earning so much money—for, of course, it would never occur to him that she would dare refuse to give him every cent she received.

There was unwonted animation in the usually stolid faces of the School Board tonight; for the members were roused to a lively appreciation of the situation as it related to Jake Getz. The doctor had taken each and every one of them into his confidence, and had graphically related to them the story of how Tillie had "come by" her certificate, and the tale had elicited their partisanship for Tillie, as for the heroine of a drama. Even Nathaniel Puntz was enjoying the fact that he was tonight on the side of the majority. With Tillie, they were in doubt as to how Jake Getz would receive the news.

"Is they a' applicant?" he inquired on his arrival.

"Why, to be sure," said Nathaniel Puntz. "What fur would it be worthwhile to waste time meetin' to elect her if they ain't none?"

"Then she's a female, is she?"

"Well, she ain't no male, anyways, nor no Harvard gradyate, neither. If she was, *I* wouldn't wote fur her!"

"What might her name be?"

"It's some such a French name," answered the doctor, who had carried in the lamp and was lingering a minute. "It would, now, surprise you, Jake, if you heard it oncet."

"Is she such a foreigner yet?" Getz asked suspiciously. "I mistrust 'em when they're foreigners."

"Well," spoke Adam Oberholzer, as the doctor reluctantly went out, "it ain't ten mile from here she was raised."

"Is she a gradyate? We hadn't ought to take none but a Normal. We had *enough* trouble!"

"No, she ain't a Normal, but she's got her certificate off the superintendent."

"Has any of yous saw her?"

"Och, yes, she's familiar with us," replied Joseph Kettering, the Amishman, who was president of the Board.

"Why ain't she familiar with me, then?" Getz inquired, looking bewildered, as the president opened the ink-bottle that stood on the table about which they sat, and distributed slips of paper.

"Well, that's some different again, too," facetiously answered Joseph Kettering.

"Won't she be here tonight to leave us see her oncet?"

"She won't, but her pop will," answered Nathaniel Puntz; and Mr. Getz vaguely realized in the expressions about him that something unusual was in the air.

"What do we want with her *pop?*" he asked.

"We want his *wote!*" answered Adam Oberholzer— which sally brought forth hilarious laughter.

"What you mean?" demanded Getz, impatient of all this mystery.

"It's the daughter of one of this here Board that we're wotin' fur!"

Mr. Getz's eyes moved about the table. "Why, none of yous ain't got a growed-up daughter that's been to school long enough to get a certificate."

"It seems there's ways of gettin' a certificate without goin' to school. Some girls can learn theirselves at home without even a teacher, and workin' all the time at farm-work, still, and even livin' out!" said Mr. Puntz. "I say a girl with *industry* like that would make any feller a good wife."

Getz stared at him in bewilderment.

"The members of this Board," said Mr. Kettering, solemnly, "and the risin' generation of the future, can point this here applicant out to their childern as a shinin' example of what can be did by *industry*, without money and without price—and it'll be fur a spur to 'em to go thou and do likewise."

"Are you so dumm, Jake, you don't know *yet* who we mean?" Nathaniel asked.

"Why, to be sure, don't I! None of yous has got such a daughter where lived out."

"Except yourself, Jake!"

The eyes of the Board were fixed upon Mr. Getz in excited expectation. But he was still heavily uncomprehending. Then the president, rising, made his formal announcement, impressively and with dignity.

"Members of Canaan Township School Board: We will now proceed to wote fur the applicant fur William Penn. She is not unknownst to this here Board. She is a worthy and wirtuous female, and has a good moral character. We think she's been well learnt how to manage childern, fur she's been raised in a family where childern was never scarce. The applicant," continued the speaker, "is—as I stated a couple minutes back—a shining example of *industry* to the rising generations of the future, fur she's got her certificate to teach—and wery high marks on it—and done it all by her own unaided efforts and *industry*. Members of Canaan Township School Board, we are now ready to wote fur Matilda Maria Getz."

Before his dazed wits could recover from the shock of this announcement, Jake Getz's daughter had become the unanimously elected teacher of William Penn.

THE ruling passion of the soul of Jacob Getz manifested itself conspicuously in his reception of the revelation that his daughter, through deliberate and systematic disobedience, carried on through all the years of her girlhood, had succeeded in obtaining a certificate from the county superintendent, and was now the teacher-elect at William Penn. The father's satisfaction in the possession of a child capable of earning forty dollars a month, his greedy joy in the prospect of this addition to his income, entirely overshadowed and dissipated the rage he would otherwise have felt. The pathos of his child's courageous persistency in the face of his dreaded severity, of her pitiful struggle with all the adverse conditions of her life—this did not enter at all into his consideration of the case. It was obvious to Tillie, as it had been to the School Board on Saturday night, that he felt an added satisfaction in the fact that this wonder had been accomplished without any loss to him either of money or of his child's labor.

Somehow, her father's reception of her triumph filled her heart with more bitterness than she had ever felt toward him in all the years of her hard endeavor. It was on the eve of her first day of teaching that his unusually affectionate attitude to her at the supper table suddenly roused in her a passion of hot resentment such as her gentle heart had not often experienced.

"I owe *you* no thanks, father, for what education I have!" she burst forth. "You always did everything in your power to hinder me!"

If a bomb had exploded in the midst of them, Mr. and Mrs. Getz could not have been more confounded. Mrs. Getz looked to see her husband order Tillie from the table, or rise from his place to shake her and box her ears. But he did neither. In amazement he stared at her for a moment—then answered with a mildness that amazed his wife even more than Tillie's "sassiness" had done.

"I'd of *left* you study if I'd knowed you could come to anything like this by it. But I always thought you'd have to go to the Normal to be fit fur a teacher yet. And you can't say you don't owe me no thanks—ain't I always kep' you?"

"Kept me!" answered Tillie, with a scorn that widened her father's stare and made her stepmother drop her knife on her plate; "I never worked half so hard at Aunty Em's as I have done here every day of my life since I was nine years old—and *she* thought my work worth not only my 'keep,' but two dollars a week besides. When do you ever spend two dollars on me? You never gave me a dollar that I hadn't earned ten times over! You owe me back wages!"

Jake Getz laid down his knife, with a look on his face that made his other children quail. His countenance was livid with anger.

"*Owe you back wages!*" he choked. "Ain't you my child, then, where I begat and raised? Don't I own

you? What's a child *fur*? To grow up to be no use to
them that raised it? You talk like that to me!" he
roared. "You tell me I *owe* you back money! Now listen here! I was a-goin' to leave you keep five dollars
every month out of your forty. Yes, I conceited I'd
leave you have all that—five a month! Now fur sassin'
me like what you done, I ain't leavin' you have *none*
the first month!"

"And what," Tillie wondered, a strange calm suddenly following her outburst, as she sat back in her
chair, white and silent, "what will he do and say when I
refuse to give him more than the price of my board?"

Her schoolwork, which began next day, diverted her
mind somewhat from its deep yearning for him who
had become to her the very breath of her life.

It was on the Sunday night after her first week of
teaching that she told Absalom, with all the firmness she
could command, that he must not come to see her anymore, for she was resolved not to marry him.

"Who are you goin' to marry, then?" he inquired,
unconvinced.

"No one."

"Do you mean it fur really, that you'd rather be a'
ole maid?"

"I'd rather be *six* old maids than the wife of a
Dutchman!"

"What fur kind of a man do you *want*, then?"

"Not the kind that grows in this township."

"Would you, mebbe," Absalom sarcastically inquired,
"like such a dude like what—"

"Absalom!" Tillie flashed her beautiful eyes upon him. "You are unworthy to mention his name to me! Don't dare to speak to me of him—or I shall leave you and go upstairs *right away!*"

Absalom sullenly subsided.

When, later, he left her, she saw that her firm refusal to marry him had in no wise baffled him.

This impression was confirmed when on the next Sunday night, in spite of her prohibition, he again presented himself.

Tillie was mortally weary that night. Her letter had not come, and her nervous waiting, together with the strain of her unwonted work of teaching, had told on her endurance. So poor Absalom's reception at her hands was even colder than her father's greeting at the kitchen door; for since Tillie's election to William Penn, Mr. Getz was more opposed than ever to her marriage, and he did not at all relish the young man's persistency in coming to see her in the face of his own repeated warning.

"Tillie," Absalom began when they were alone together after the family had gone to bed, "I thought it over oncet, and I come to say I'd ruther have you 'round, even if you didn't do nothin' but set and knit mottos and play the organ, than any other woman where could do all my housework fur me. I'll *hire* fur you, Tillie—and you can just set and enjoy yourself musin', like what Doc says book-learnt people likes to do."

Tillie's eyes rested on him with a softer and a kindlier light in them than she had ever shown him before;

for such a magnanimous offer as this, she thought, could spring only from the fact that Absalom was really deeply in love, and she was not a little touched.

She contemplated him earnestly as he sat before her, looking so utterly unnatural in his Sunday clothes. A feeling of compassion for him began to steal into her heart.

"If I am not careful," she thought in consternation, "I shall be saying, 'Yes,' out of pity."

But a doubt quickly crept into her heart. Was it really that he loved her so very much, or was it that his obstinacy was stronger than his prudence, and that if he could not get her as he wanted her—as his housekeeper and the mother of numberless children—he would take her on her own conditions? Only so he *got* her—that was the point. He had made up his mind to have her—it must be accomplished.

"Absalom," she said, "I am not going to let you waste any more of your time. You must never come to see me again after tonight. I won't ever marry you, and I won't let you go on like this, with your false hope. If you come again, I won't see you. I'll go upstairs!"

One would have thought that this had no uncertain ring. But again Tillie knew, when Absalom left her, that his resolution not only was not shaken—it was not even jarred.

The weeks moved on, and the longed-for letter did not come. Tillie tried to gather courage to question the doctor as to whether Fairchilds had made any arrangement with him for the delivery of a letter to her. But an instinct of maidenly reserve and pride which she could not conquer kept her lips closed on the subject.

Had it not been for this all-consuming desire for a letter, she would more keenly have felt her enforced alienation from her aunt, of whom she was so fond; and at the same time have taken really great pleasure in her new work and in having reached at last her long-anticipated goal.

In the meantime, while her secret sorrow—like Sir Hudibras' rusting sword that had nothing else to feed upon and so hacked upon itself—seemed eating out her very heart, the letter which would have been to her as manna in the wilderness had fallen into her father's hands, and after being laboriously conned by him, to his utter confusion as to its meaning, had been consigned to the kitchen fire.

Mr. Getz's reasons for withholding the letter from his daughter and burning it were several. In the first place, Fairchilds was "an *unbeliever*," and therefore his influence was baneful; he was Jacob Getz's enemy, and therefore no fit person to be writing friendly letters to his daughter; he asked Tillie, in his letter, to write to him, and this would involve the buying of stationery and wasting of time that might be better spent; and finally, he and Tillie, as he painfully gathered from the letter, were "making up" to a degree that might end in her wanting to marry the fellow.

Mr. Getz meant to tell Tillie that he had received this letter; but somehow, every time he opened his lips to speak the words, the memory of her wildcat behavior in defense of the teacher that afternoon in the woods, and her horribly deathlike appearance when she had lain unconscious in the teacher's arms, recurred to him with a vividness that effectually checked him, and eventually led him to decide that it were best not to risk another such outbreak. So she remained in ignorance of the fact that Fairchilds had again written to her.

Carlyle's *Gospel of Work* was indeed Tillie's salvation in these days; for in spite of her restless yearning and loneliness, she was deeply interested and even fascinated with her teaching, and greatly pleased and encouraged with her success in it.

At last, with the end of her first month at William Penn, came the rather dreaded "pay day"; for she knew that it would mean the hardest battle of her life.

The forty dollars was handed to her in her schoolroom on Friday afternoon, at the close of the session. It seemed untold wealth to Tillie, who never before in her life had owned a dollar.

She did not risk carrying it all home with her. The larger part of the sum she intrusted to the doctor to deposit for her in a Lancaster bank.

When, at five o'clock, she reached home and walked into the kitchen, her father's eagerness for her return, that he might lay his itching palms on her earnings, was perfectly manifest to her in his unduly affectionate, "Well, Tillie!"

She was pale, but outwardly composed. It was to be one of those supreme crises in life which one is apt to meet with a courage and a serenity that are not forthcoming in the smaller irritations and trials of daily experience.

"You don't look so hearty," her father said, as she quietly hung up her shawl and hood in the kitchen cupboard. "A body'd think you'd pick up and get fat, now you don't have to work nothin', except mornings and evenings."

"There is no harder work in the world, father, than teaching—even when you like it."

"It ain't no work," he impatiently retorted, "to set and hear off lessons."

Tillie did not dispute the point, as she tied a gingham apron over her dress.

Her father was sitting in a corner of the room, shelling corn, with Sammy and Sally at his side helping him. He stopped short in his work and glanced at Tillie in surprise, as she immediately set about assisting her mother in setting the supper table.

"You was paid today, wasn't you?"

"Yes."

"Well, why don't you gimme the money, then? Where have you got it?"

Tillie drew a roll of bills from her pocket and came up to him.

He held out his hand. "You know, Tillie, I tole you I ain't givin' you none of your wages this month, fur sassin' me like what you done. But next month, if you're good-behaved till then, I'll give you mebbe five dollars. Gimme here," he said, reaching for the money across the heads of the children in front of him.

But she did not obey. She looked at him steadily as she stood before him, and spoke deliberately, though every nerve in her body was jumping.

"Aunty Em charged the teacher fifteen dollars a month for board. That included his washing and ironing. I really earn my board by the work I do here Saturdays and Sundays, and in the mornings and evenings before and after school. But I will pay you twelve dollars a month for my board."

She laid on his palm two five-dollar bills and two ones, and calmly walked back to the table.

Getz sat as one suddenly turned to stone. Sammy and Sally dropped their corn-cobs into their laps and stared in frightened wonder. Mrs. Getz stopped cutting the bread and gazed stupidly from her husband to her stepdaughter. Tillie alone went on with her work, no sign in her white, still face of the passion of terror in her heart at her own unspeakable boldness.

Suddenly two resounding slaps on the ears of Sammy and Sally, followed by their sharp screams of pain and fright, broke the tense stillness.

"Who tole you to stop workin', heh?" demanded their father, fiercely. "Leave me see you at it, do you hear? You stop another time to gape around and I'll lick you good! Stop your bawlin' now, this minute!"

He rose from his chair and strode over to the table. Seizing Tillie by the shoulder, he drew her in front of him.

"Gimme every dollar of them forty!"

"I have given you all I have."

"Where are you got the others hid?"

"I have deposited my money in a Lancaster bank."

Jacob Getz's face turned apoplectic with rage.

"Who took it to Lancaster fur you?"

"I sent it."

"What fur bank?"

"I prefer not to tell you that."

"You *perfer!* I'll learn you *perfer!* Who took it in fur you—and what fur bank? Answer to me!"

"Father, the money is mine."

"It's no such thing! You ain't but seventeen. And I don't care if you're eighteen or even twenty-one! You're my child and you'll obey to me and do what I tell you!"

"Father, I will not submit to your robbing me. You can't force me to give you my earnings. If you could, I wouldn't teach at all!"

"You won't submit! And I darsent rob you!" he spluttered. "Don't you know I can collect your wages off the secretary of the Board myself?"

"Before next pay day I shall be eighteen. Then you can't legally do that. If you could, I would resign. Then you wouldn't even get your twelve dollars a month for my board. That's four dollars more than I can earn living out at Aunty Em's."

Beside himself with his fury, Getz drew her a few steps to the closet where his strap hung, and jerking it from its nail, he swung out his arm.

But Tillie, with a strength born of a sudden fury almost matching his own, and feeling in her awakened womanhood a new sense of outrage and ignominy in such treatment, wrenched herself free, sprang to the middle of the room, and faced him with blazing eyes.

"Dare to touch me—ever again so long as you live! And I'll kill you, I'll *kill* you!"

Such madness of speech, to ears accustomed to the carefully tempered converse of Mennonites, Amish, and Dunkards, was in itself a wickedness almost as great as the deed threatened. The family, from the father down to six-year-old Zephaniah, trembled to hear the awful words.

"Ever dare to touch me again so long as we both live—and I'll stab you dead!"

Mrs. Getz shrieked. Sally and Sammy clung to each other whimpering in terror, and the younger children about the room took up the chorus.

"Tillie!" gasped her father.

The girl tottered, her eyes suddenly rolled back in her head, she stretched out her hands, and fell over on the floor. Once more Tillie had fainted.

CHAPTER TWENTY-FIVE

GETZ "LEARNS" TILLIE

As a drowning man clings to whatever comes in his way, Tillie, in these weary days of heartache and yearning, turned with new intensity of feeling to Miss Margaret, who had never failed her, and their interchange of letters became more frequent.

Her father did not easily give up the struggle with her for the possession of her salary. Finding that he could not legally collect it himself from the treasurer of the Board, he accused his brother-in-law, Abe Wackernagel, of having taken it to town for her; and when Abe denied the charge, with the assurance, however, that he "*would* do that much for Tillie any day he got the chancet," Mr. Getz next taxed the doctor, who, of course, without the least scruple, denied all knowledge of Tillie's monetary affairs.

On market day, he had to go to Lancaster city, and when his efforts to force Tillie to sign a check payable to him had proved vain, his baffled greed again roused him to uncontrollable fury, and lifting his hand, he struck her across the cheek.

Tillie reeled and would have fallen had he not caught her, his anger instantly cooling in his fear lest she faint again. But Tillie had no idea of fainting. "Let me go," she said quietly, drawing her arm out of his clasp. Turning quickly away, she walked straight out of the room and upstairs to her chamber.

Her one change of clothing she quickly tied into a bundle, and putting on her bonnet and shawl, she walked downstairs and out of the house.

"Where you goin'?" her father demanded roughly as he followed her out on the porch.

She did not answer, but walked on to the gate. In an instant he had overtaken her and stood squarely in her path.

"Where you goin' to?" he repeated.

"To town, to board at the store."

He dragged her, almost by main force, back into the house, and all that evening kept a watch upon her until he knew that she was in bed.

Next morning, Tillie carried her bundle of clothing to school with her, and at the noon recess she went to the family who kept the village store and engaged board with them, saying she could not stand the daily walks to and from school.

When, at six o'clock that evening, she had not returned home, her father drove in to the village store to get her. But she locked herself in her bedroom and would not come out.

In the next few weeks he tried every means of force at his command, but in vain; and at last he humbled himself to propose a compromise.

"I'll leave you have some of your money every month, Tillie—as much as ten dollars—if you'll give me the rest, still."

"Why should I give it to you, father? How would that benefit *me?*" she said, with a rather wicked relish in turning the tables on him and applying his life principle of selfishness to her own case.

Her father did not know how to meet it. Never before in her life, to his knowledge, had Tillie considered her own benefit before his and that of his wife and children. That she should dare to do so now seemed to knock the foundations from under him.

"When I'm dead, won't you and the others inherit off of me all I've saved?" he feebly inquired.

"But that will be when I'm too old to enjoy or profit by it."

"How much do you want I should give you out of your wages every month, then?"

"You can't give me what is not yours to give."

"Now don't you be sassin' me, or I'll learn you!"

They were alone in her schoolroom on a late February afternoon, after school had been dismissed. Tillie quickly rose and reached for her shawl and bonnet. She usually tried to avoid giving him an opportunity like this for bullying her, with no one by to protect her.

"Just stay settin'," he growled sullenly, and she knew from his tone that he had surrendered.

"If you'll come home to board, I won't bother you no more, then," he further humbled himself to add. The loss even of the twelve dollars' board was more than he could bear.

"It would not be safe," answered Tillie, grimly.

"Och, it'll be safe enough. I'll leave you be."

"It would not be safe for *you*."

"Fur me? What you talkin'?"

"If you lost your temper and struck me, I might kill you. That's why I came away."

The father stared in furtive horror at the white, impassive face of his daughter.

Could this be Tillie—his meek, long-suffering Tillie?

"Another thing," she continued resolutely, for she had lost all fear of speaking her mind to him, "why should I pay you twelve dollars a month board, when I get my board at the store for six, because I wait on customers between times?"

Mr. Getz looked very downcast. There was a long silence between them.

"I must go now, father. This is the hour that I always spend in the store."

"I'll board you fur six, then," he growled.

"And make me work from four in the morning until eight or nine at night? It is easier standing in the store. I can read when there are no customers."

"To think I brung up a child to talk to me like this here!" He stared at her incredulously.

"'The rest will turn out even worse," Tillie prophesied with conviction, "unless you are less harsh with them. Your harshness will drive every child you have to defy you."

"I'll take good care none of the others turns out like you!" he threateningly exclaimed. "And *you'll* see oncet! You'll find out! You just wait! I tried everything—now I know what I'm doin'. It'll *learn* you!"

In the next few weeks, as nothing turned up to make good these threats, Tillie often wondered what her father had meant by them. It was not like him to waste time in empty words.

But she was soon to learn. One evening the doctor came over to the store to repeat to her some rumors he had heard and which he thought she ought to know.

"Tillie! Your pop's workin' the directers to have you chased off William Penn till the April election a'ready!"

"Oh, Doc!" Tillie gasped, "how do you know?"

"That's what the talk is. He's goin' about to all of 'em whenever he can handy leave off from his work, and he's tellin' 'em they had ought to set that example to onruly children; and most of 'em's agreein' with him. Nathaniel Puntz he agrees with him. Absalom he talks down on you since you won't leave him come no more Sundays, still. Your pop he says when your teachin' is a *loss* to him instead of a help, he ain't leavin' you keep on. He says when you don't have no more money, you'll *have* to come home and help him and your mom with the work. Nathaniel Puntz he says this is a warnin' to parents not to leave their children have too much education—that they get high-minded that way and won't even get married."

"But, Doc," Tillie pleaded with him in an agony of mind, "you won't let them take my school from me, will you? You'll make them let me keep it?"

The doctor gave a little laugh. "By golly, Tillie, I ain't the President of America! You think because I got you through oncet or twicet, I kin do *anything* with them directers, still! Well, a body can't *always* get ahead of a set of stubborn-headed Dutchmen—and with Nathaniel Puntz so wonderful thick in with your pop to work ag'in' you, because you won't have that dumm Absalom of hisn!"

"What shall I do?" Tillie cried. "I can never, never go back to my old life again—that hopeless, dreary drudgery on the farm! I can't, indeed I can't! I *won't* go back. What shall I do?"

"Look-ahere, Tillie!" the doctor spoke soothingly, "I'll do what I otherwise kin to help you. I'll do some back-talkin' myself to them directers. But you see," he said in a troubled tone, "none of them directers happens to owe me no doctor-bill just now, and that makes it a little harder to persuade 'em to see my view of the case. Now if only some of their wives would up and get sick for 'em and I could run 'em up a bill! But," he concluded, shaking his head in discouragement, "it's a wonderful healthy season—wonderful healthy!"

In the two months that followed, the doctor worked hard to counteract Mr. Getz's influence with the Board. Tillie, too, missed no least opportunity to plead her cause with them, not only by direct argument, but by the indirect means of doing her best possible work in her school.

But both she and the doctor realized, as the weeks moved on, that they were working in vain; for Mr. Getz, in his statements to the directors, had appealed to some of their most deep-rooted prejudices. Tillie's filial insubordination, her "high-mindedness," her distaste for domestic work, so strong that she refused even to live under her father's roof—all these things made her unfit to be an instructor and guide to their young children. She would imbue the "rising generation" with her worldly and wrong-headed ideas.

Had Tillie remained "plain," she would no doubt have had the championship of the two New Mennonite members of the Board. But her apostasy had lost her even that defense, for she no longer wore her nun-like garb. After her suspension from meeting and her election to William Penn, she had gradually drifted into the conviction that colors other than gray, black, or brown were probably pleasing to the Creator, and that what really mattered was not what she wore, but what she was. It was without any violent struggles or throes of anguish that, in this revolution of her faith, she quite naturally fell away from the creed which once had held her such a devotee. When she presently appeared in the vain and ungodly habiliments of "the world's people," the brethren gave her up in despair and excommunicated her.

"No use, Tillie," the doctor would report in discouragement, week after week; "we're up against it

"She no longer wore her nun-like garb"

sure this time! You're losin' William Penn till next month, or I'll eat my hat! A body might as well *try* to eat his hat as move them pig-headed Dutch once they get sot. And they're sot on puttin' you out, all right! You see, your pop and Nathaniel Puntz they just fixed 'em! Me and you ain't got no show at all."

Tillie could think of no way of escape from her desperate position. What was there before her but a return to the farm, or perhaps, at best, marriage with Absalom?

"To be sure, I should have to be reduced to utter indifference to my fate if I ever consented to marry Absalom," she bitterly told herself. "But when it is a question between doing that and living at home, I don't know but I might be driven to it!"

At times, the realization that there was no possible appeal from her situation did almost drive her to a frenzy. After so many years of struggle, just as she was tasting success, to lose all the fruits of her labor—how could she endure it? With the work she loved taken away from her, how could she bear the gnawing hunger at her heart for the presence of him unto whom was every thought of her brain and every throbbing pulse of her soul? The future seemed to stretch before her, a terrible, an unendurable blank.

The first week of April was the time fixed for the meeting of the Board at which she was to be "chased off her job"; and as the fatal day drew near, a sort of lethargy settled upon her, and she ceased to struggle, even in spirit, against the inevitable.

"Well, Tillie," the doctor said, with a long sigh, as he came into the store at six o'clock on the eventful evening, and leaned over the counter to talk to the girl, "they're all conwened by now, over there in the hotel parlor. Your pop and Nathaniel Puntz they're lookin' wonderful important. Your pop," he vindictively added, "is just chucklin' at the idea of gettin' you home under his thumb ag'in!"

Tillie did not speak. She sat behind the counter, her cheeks resting on the backs of her hands, her wistful eyes gazing past the doctor toward the red light in the hotel windows across the way.

"Golly! But I'd of liked to beat 'em out on this here game! But they've got us, Tillie! They'll be wotin' you out of your job any minute now. And then your pop'll be comin' over here to fetch you along home! Oh! If he wasn't your pop I c'd say somethin' real perfane about him."

Tillie drew a long breath; but she did not speak. She could not. It seemed to her that she had come to the end of everything.

"Look-ahere, Tillie," the doctor spoke suddenly, "you just up and get ahead of 'em all—you just take yourself over to the Millersville Normal! You've got some money saved, ain't you?"

"Yes!" A ray of hope kindled in her eyes. "I have saved one hundred and twenty-five dollars! I should have more than that if I had not returned to the world's dress."

"'Well, Tillie—' the doctor said, with a long sigh"

"A hundred and twenty-five's plenty enough for a good starter at the Millersville Normal," said the doctor.

"But," Tillie hesitated, "this is April, and the spring term closes in three months. What should I do and where could I go after that? If I made such a break with father, he might refuse to take me home even if I had nowhere else to go. Could I risk that?"

The doctor leaned his head on his hand and heavily considered the situation.

"I'm blamed if I dare adwise you, Tillie. It's some serious adwisin' a young unprotected female to leave her pop's rooft to go out into the unbeknownst world," he said sentimentally. "To be sure, Miss Margaret would see after you while you was at the Normal. But when wacation is here in June she might mebbe be goin' away for such a trip like, and then if you couldn't come back home, you'd be throwed out on the cold wide world, where there's many a pitfall for the onwary."

"It seems too great a risk to run, doesn't it? There seems to be nothing—nothing—that I can do but go back to the farm," she said, the hope dying out of her eyes.

"Just till I kin get you another school, Tillie," he consoled her. "I'll be lookin' out for a wacancy in the county for you, you bet!"

"Thank you, Doc," she answered wearily; "but you know another school couldn't possibly be open to me until next fall—five months from now."

She threw her head back upon the palm of her hand. "I'm so tired—so very tired of it all. What's the use of struggling? What am I struggling *for?*"

"What are you struggling *fur?*" the doctor repeated. "Why, to get shed of your pop and all them kids out at the Getz farm that wears out your young life workin' for 'em! That's what! And to have some freedom and money of your own—to have a little pleasure now and ag'in! I tell you, Tillie, I don't want to see you goin' out there to that farm ag'in!"

"Do you think I should dare to run away to the Normal?" she asked fearfully.

The doctor tilted back his hat and scratched his head.

"Leave me to think it over oncet, Tillie, and till tomorrow mornin' a'ready I'll give you my answer. My conscience won't give me the dare to adwise you offhand in a matter that's so serious like what this is."

"Father will want to make me go out to the farm with him this evening, I am sure," she said; "and when once I am out there, I shall not have either the spirit or the chance to get away, I'm afraid."

The doctor shook his head despondently. "We certainly are up ag'in' it! *I* can't see no way out."

"There *is* no way out," Tillie said in a strangely quiet voice. "Doc," she added after an instant, laying her hand on his rough one and pressing it, "although I have failed in all that you have tried to help me to be and to do, I shall never forget to be grateful to you—my best and kindest friend!"

The doctor looked down almost reverently at the little white hand resting against his dark one.

Suddenly Tillie's eyes fixed themselves upon the open doorway, where the smiling presence of Walter Fairchilds presented itself to her startled gaze.

"Tillie! *And* the Doc! Well, it's good to see you. May I break in on your conference—I can see it's important." He spoke lightly, but his voice was vibrant with some restrained emotion. At the first sight of him, Tillie's hand instinctively crept up to feel if those precious curls were in their proper place. The care and devotion she had spent upon them during all these weary, desolate months! And all because a man—the one, only man—had once said they were pretty! Alas, Tillie, for your Mennonite principles!

And now, at sight of the dear, familiar face and form, the girl trembled and was speechless.

Not so the doctor. With a yell, he turned upon the visitor, grasped both his hands, and nearly wrung them off.

"Hang me, of I was ever so glad to see a feller like wot I am you. Teacher," he cried in huge delight, "the country's saved! Providence fetched you here in the nick of time! You always was a friend to Tillie, and you kin help her out now!"

Walter Fairchilds did not reply at first. He stood, gazing over the doctor's shoulder at the new Tillie, transformed in countenance by the deep waters through which she had passed in the five months that had slipped round since he had gone out of her life; and so transformed in appearance by the dropping of her

Mennonite garb that he could hardly believe the testi-
mony of his eyes.

"Is it—is it really you, Tillie?" he said, holding out
his hand. "And aren't you even a little bit glad to
see me?"

The familiar voice brought the life-blood back to
her face. She took a step toward him, both hands
outstretched—then, suddenly, she stopped and her
cheeks crimsoned. "Of course we're glad to see you—
very!" she said softly but constrainedly.

"Lemme tell you the news," shouted the doctor.
"You'll mebbe save Tillie from goin' out there to her
pop's farm ag'in! She's teacher at William Penn,
and her pop's over there at the Board meetin' now,
havin' her throwed off, and then he'll want to take her
home to work herself to death for him and all them
baker's dozen of children he's got out there! And Tillie
she don't want to go—and waste all her nice education
that there way!"

Fairchilds took her hand and looked down into her
shining eyes.

"I hardly know you, Tillie, in your new way of
dressing!"

"What—what brings you here?" she asked, drawing away her hand.

"I've come from the Millersville Normal School
with a letter for you from Mrs. Lansing," he explained,
"and I've promised to bring you back with me by way
of answer.

"I am an instructor in English there now, you know, and so, of course, I have come to know your 'Miss Margaret,'" he added, in answer to Tillie's unspoken question.

The girl opened the envelope with trembling fingers and read:

My dear little Mennonite Maid: We have rather suddenly decided to go abroad in July—my husband needs the rest and change, as do we all; and I want you to go with me as companion and friend, and to help me in the care of the children. In the meantime there is much to be done by way of preparation for such a trip; so can't you arrange to come to me at once and you can have the benefit of the spring term at the Normal. I needn't tell you, dear child, how glad I shall be to have you with me. And what such a trip ought to mean to you, who have struggled so bravely to live the life the Almighty meant that you should live, you only can fully realize. You're of age now and can act for yourself. Break with your present environment now, or, I'm afraid, Tillie, it will be never.

Come to me at once, and with the bearer of this note. With love, I am, as always, your affectionate

Miss Margaret

When she had finished Tillie looked up with brimming eyes.

"Doc," she said, "listen!" and she read the letter aloud, speaking slowly and distinctly that he might fully grasp the glory of it all. At the end the sweet voice faltered and broke.

"Oh, Doc!" sobbed Tillie, "isn't it wonderful!"

The shaggy old fellow blinked his eyes rapidly, then suddenly relieved his feelings with an outrageous burst of profanity. With a rapidity bewildering to his hearers, his tone instantly changed again to one of lachrymose solemnity:

Gawd moves in a mysterious way
His wonders to perform!

he piously repeated. "*Ain't*, now, he does, Tillie! Och!" he exclaimed, "I got a thought! You go right straight over there to that there Board meetin' and circumwent 'em! Before they're got *time* to wote you off your job, you up and throw their old William Penn in their Dutch faces, and tell 'em be blowed to 'em! Tell 'em you don't *want* their blamed old school—and you're goin' to *Europe*, you are! To *Europe*, yet!"

He seized her hand as he spoke and almost pulled her to the store door.

"Do it, Tillie!" cried Fairchilds, stepping after them across the store. "Present your resignation before they have a chance to vote you out! Do it!" he said eagerly.

Tillie looked from one to the other of the two men before her, excitement sparkling in her eyes, her breath coming short and fast.

"I will!"

Turning away, she ran down the steps, sped across the street, and disappeared in the hotel.

The doctor expressed his overflowing feelings by giving Fairchilds a resounding slap on the shoulders. "By gum, I'd like to be behind the skeens and witness Jake Getz gettin' fooled ag'in! This is the most fun I had since I got 'em to wote you five dollars a month extry, Teacher!" he chuckled. "Golly! I'm glad you got here in time! It was certainly, now," he added piously, "the hand of Providence that led you!"

CHAPTER TWENTY-SIX

TILLIE'S LAST FIGHT

"WE ARE NOW READY TO WOTE FER THE TEACHER FER William Penn fer the spring term," announced the president of the Board, when all the preliminary business of the meeting had been disposed of; "and before we perceed to that dooty, we will be glad to hear any remarks."

The members looked at Mr. Getz, and he promptly rose to his feet to make the speech which all were expecting from him—the speech which was to sum up the reasons why his daughter should not be reëlected for another term to William Penn. As all these reasons had been expounded many times over in the past few months, to each individual school director, Mr. Getz's statements tonight were to be merely a more forcible repetition of his previous arguments.

But scarcely had he cleared his throat to begin, when there was a knock on the door; it opened, and, to their amazement, Tillie walked into the room. Her eyes sparkling, her face flushed, her head erect, she came

315

straight across the room to the table about which the six educational potentates were gathered.

That she had come to plead her own cause, to beg to be retained at her post, was obviously the object of this intrusion upon the sacred privacy of their weighty proceedings.

Had that, in very truth, been her purpose in coming to them, she would have found little encouragement in the countenances before her. Every one of them seemed to stiffen into grim disapproval of her unfilial act in thus publicly opposing her parent.

But there was something in the girl's presence as she stood before them, some potent spell in her fresh girlish beauty, and in the dauntless spirit which shone in her eyes, that checked the words of stern reproof as they sprang to the lips of her judges.

"John Kettering"—her clear, soft voice addressed the Amish president of the Board, adhering, in her use of his first name, to the mode of address of all the "plain" sects of the county—"have I your permission to speak to the Board?"

"It wouldn't be no use." The president frowned and shook his head. "The wotes of this here Board can't be influenced. There's no use your wastin' any talk on us. We're here to do our dooty by the risin' generation." Mr. Kettering, in his character of educator, was very fond of talking about "the rising generation." "And," he added, "what's right's *right.*"

"As your teacher at William Penn, I have a statement to make to the Board," Tillie quietly persisted. "It will take me but a minute. I am not here to try to influence the vote you are about to take."

"If you ain't here to influence our wotes, what are you here fer?"

"That's what I ask your permission to tell the Board."

"Well," John Kettering reluctantly conceded, "I'll give you two minutes, then. Go on. But you needn't try to get us to wote any way but the way our conscience leads us to."

Tillie's eyes swept the faces before her, from the stern, set features of her father on her left, to the mild-faced, long-haired, hooks-and-eyes Amishman on her right. The room grew perfectly still as they stared at her in expectant curiosity; for her air and manner did not suggest the humble suppliant for their continued favor—rather a self-confidence that instinctively excited their stubborn opposition. "She'll see oncet if she kin do with us what she wants," was the thought in the minds of most of them.

"I am here," Tillie spoke deliberately and distinctly, "to tender my resignation."

There was dead silence.

"I regret that I could not give you a month's notice, according to the terms of my agreement with you. But I could not foresee the great good fortune that was about to befall me."

Not a man stirred, but an ugly look of malicious chagrin appeared upon the face of Nathaniel Puntz. Was he foiled in his anticipated revenge upon the girl who had "turned down" his Absalom? Mr. Getz sat stiff and motionless, his eyes fixed upon Tillie.

"I resign my position at William Penn," Tillie repeated, *"to go to Europe for four months' travel* with Miss Margaret." Again she swept them with her eyes. Her father's face was apoplectic; he was leaning forward, trying to speak, but he was too choked for utterance. Nathaniel Puntz looked as though a wet sponge had been dashed upon his sleek countenance. The other directors stared, dumfounded. This case had no precedent in their experience. They were at a loss how to take it.

"My resignation," Tillie continued, "must take effect immediately—tonight. I trust you will have no difficulty in getting a substitute."

She paused—there was not a movement or a sound in the room.

"I thank you for your attention." Tillie bowed, turned, and walked across the room. Not until she reached the door was the spell broken. With her hand on the knob, she saw her father rise and start toward her.

She had no wish for an encounter with him; quickly she went out into the hall, and, in order to escape him, she opened the street door, stepped out, and closed it very audibly behind her. Then hurrying in at the adjoining door of the barroom, she ran out to the hotel kitchen, where she knew she would find her aunt.

Mrs. Wackernagel was alone, washing dishes at the sink. She looked up with a start at Tillie's hurried entrance, and her kindly face showed distress as she saw who it was; for, faithful to the Rules, she would not speak to this backslider and excommunicant from the faith.

But Tillie went straight up to her, threw her arms about her neck, and pressed her lips to her aunt's cheek.

"Aunty Em! I can't go away without saying good-by to you. I am going to Europe! *To Europe,* Aunty Em!" she cried. The words sounded unreal and strange to her, and she repeated them to make their meaning clear to herself. "Miss Margaret has sent for me to take me with her *to Europe!*"

She rapidly told her aunt all that had happened, and Mrs. Wackernagel's bright, eager face of delight expressed all the sympathy and affection which Tillie craved from her, but which the Mennonite dared not utter.

"Aunty Em, no matter where I go or what may befall me, I shall never forget your love and kindness. I shall remember it always, *always.*"

Aunty Em's emotions were stronger, for the moment, than her allegiance to the Rules, and her motherly arms drew the girl to her bosom and held her there in a long, silent embrace.

She refrained, however, from kissing her; and presently Tillie drew herself away and, dashing the tears from her eyes, went out of the house by the back kitchen door. From here she made her way, in a round-about fashion, to the rear entrance of the storekeeper's house across the road, for she was quite sure that her father had gone into the store in search of her.

Cautiously stepping into the kitchen, she found Fairchilds restlessly pacing the floor, and he greeted her return with a look of mingled pleasure and apprehension.

"Your father is out front, in the store, Tillie," he whispered, coming close to her. "He's looking for you. He doesn't know I'm in town, of course. Come outside and I'll tell you our plan."

He led the way out of doors, and they sought the seclusion of a grape-arbor far down the garden.

"We'll leave it to the Doc to entertain your father," Fairchilds went on; "you will have to leave here with me tonight, Tillie, and as soon as possible, for your father will make trouble for us. We may as well avoid a conflict with him—especially for your sake. For myself, I shouldn't mind it!" He smiled grimly.

He was conscious, as his eyes rested on Tillie's fair face under the evening light, of a reserve in her attitude toward him that was new to her. It checked his warm impulse to take her hands in his and tell her how glad he was to see her again.

"How can we possibly get away tonight?" she asked him. "There are no stages until the morning."

"We shall have to let the Doc's fertile brain solve it for us, Tillie. He has a plan, I believe. Of course, if we have to wait until morning and fight it out with your father, then we'll *have* to, that's all. But I hope that may be avoided and that we may get away quietly."

They sat in silence for a moment. Suddenly Fairchilds leaned toward her and spoke to her earnestly.

"Tillie, I want to ask you something. Please tell me— why did you never answer my letters?"

She lifted her startled eyes to his. "Your letters?"

"Yes. Why didn't you write to me!"

"You wrote to me?" she asked incredulously.

"I wrote you three times. You don't mean to tell me you never got my letters?"

"I never heard from you. I would—I would have been so glad to!"

"But how could you have missed getting them?"

Her eyes fell upon her hands clasped in her lap, and her cheeks grew pale.

"My father," she half whispered.

"He kept them from you?"

"It must have been so."

Fairchilds looked very grave. He did not speak at once.

"How can you forgive such things?" he presently asked. "One tenth of the things you have had to bear would have made an incarnate fiend of me!"

She kept her eyes downcast and did not answer.

"I can't tell you," he went on, "how bitterly disappointed I was when I didn't hear from you. I couldn't understand why you didn't write. And it gave me a sense of disappointment in *you*. I thought I must have overestimated the worth of our friendship in your eyes. I see now—and indeed in my heart I always knew—that I did you injustice."

She did not look up, but her bosom rose and fell in long breaths.

"There has not been a day," he said, "that I have not thought of you, and wished I knew all about you and could see you and speak with you—Tillie, what a haunting little personality you are!"

She raised her eyes then—a soft fire in them that set his pulse to bounding. But before she could answer him they were interrupted by the sound of quick steps coming down the boardwalk toward the arbor. Tillie started like a deer ready to flee, but Fairchilds laid a reassuring hand upon hers.

"It's the Doc," he said.

The faithful old fellow joined them, his finger on his lips to warn them to silence.

"Don't leave no one hear us out here! Jake Getz he's went over to the hotel to look fer Tillie, but he'll be back here in a jiffy, and we've got to hurry on. Tillie, you go on up and pack your clo'es in a walise or whatever, and hurry down here back. I'm hitchin' my buggy fer yous as quick as I kin. I'll leave yous borry the loan of it off of me till tomorrow—then, Teacher, you kin fetch it over ag'in. Ain't?"

"All right, Doc; you're a brick!"

Tillie sped into the house to obey the doctor's bidding, and Fairchilds went with him across the street to the hotel stables.

In the course of ten minutes the three conspirators were together again in the stable-yard behind the store, the doctor's horse and buggy ready before them.

"Father's in the store—I heard his voice," panted Tillie, as Fairchilds took her satchel from her and stowed it in the back of the buggy.

"Hurry on, then," whispered the doctor, hoarsely, pushing them both, with scant ceremony, into the carriage. "*Good*-by to yous—and good luck! Och, that's all right; no thanks necessary! I'm tickled to the end of my hair at gettin' ahead of Jake Getz! Say, Fairchilds," he said, with a wink, "this here mare's wonderful safe—you don't *have* to hold the reins with both hands! See?"

And he shook in silent laughter at his own delicate and delicious humor, as he watched them start out of the yard and down the road toward Millersville.

For a space there was no sound but the rhythmic beat of hoofs and the rattle of the buggy wheels; but in the heart of the Mennonite maid, who had fought her last battle for freedom and won, there was ineffable peace and content; and her happiness smiled from quivering lips and shone in her steadfast eyes.

MR. ABE WACKERNAGEL, of the New Canaan hotel, was very fond, in the years that followed, of bragging to his transient guests of his niece who was the wife of "such a Millersville Normal perfessor—Perfessor Fairchilds." And Mr. Jake Getz was scarcely less given to referring to his daughter "where is married to such a perfessor at the Normal."

"But what do *I* get out of it?" he was wont ruefully to add. "Where do I come in, yet? I where raised her since she was born, a'ready?"